I0742548

EQUILLIAN'S KEY

EQUILLIAN'S KEY

K. L. HARRIS

MAKE-BELIEVE
—PRESS—

www.make-believepress.com

This book is fiction. Names, characters, businesses, organizations, places, events, and incidents either are the product of the author's imagination or are used fictitiously. Any resemblance to actual persons, living or dead, events, or locales is entirely coincidental.

Copyright © 2019 K. L. Harris
All rights reserved. This book or any portion thereof may not be reproduced or used in any manner whatsoever without express written permission except for the use of brief quotations in a critical article or book review.

Library of Congress Control Number: 2019904305

ISBN: 978-1-7323686-0-6
First Edition, May 2019

Cover Illustration © Carlos Quevedo

*For the wind in my sails,
the anchor of my heart,
and the light that guides me home:
Ben, Kyler, and Arya*

Twinkling lights, Silent observers, Watchers of the night.
To you, past, present, and future
are not isolated totems but a single tapestry.
There is no time in your house to fade what has been
or to differentiate what is from what will be.
To your watchful gaze,
the map of our fates is forever present.
You miss nothing, recording every destiny,
in the files of that which was,
and that which will become,
history.

-The Words of the Watchers: Article 14

CONTENTS

SHATTERED GLASS
PROLOGUE

The wind howled outside Number 4 Wyndelwhere Place and the rain drummed against the cobblestones. The stone cottage stood on the corner, slightly apart from the other dwellings that crowded the street. There was a metal plaque on the door that read Finley Optical Solutions in fine gold lettering, and above it hung a painted sign depicting a pair of ornate glasses, which swung wildly in the wind.

Inside, a fire roared in the hearth. Casio sat in its warm glow on the floor pushing his toy train around its track for the hundredth time. His uncle, Rupert Finley, stood on the other side of the room absorbed in his work. He was a tall and slender man who was always neatly dressed and combed his dark hair to one side. Rupert was staring intently at the array of gadgets that littered his desk. There were huge magnifying glasses, beakers of growing crystals, glass prisms, and suncatchers alongside open books that looked a hundred years old and journals filled with inky scribbled notes.

Casio was raised in this place of old books and intricate gismos. His uncle's experiments inspired whispers from their neighbors, who had begun to question his sanity. To Casio, his uncle was, and always had been, brilliant. These last couple of months, however, Casio had begun to wonder if the rumors had a glimmer of truth. His uncle had become obsessed with his work and retreated further and further into himself. Worst of all, for the first time ever, he had forgotten Casio's birthday.

"I have filtered out the Spina Spectrum, now if I can just layer a Gruire filter on top…it might just work…," his uncle muttered to himself while busying about his desk. Casio watched him for a minute with an air of concern and then returned to his toys. He picked up his enchanted globe, which housed a miniature replica of the solar system. It was his favorite possession. The celestial bodies were so lifelike, it was as if the alchemists had found a way to clone their corner of the galaxy, and then shrunk it to fit inside the glass ball. Casio held the globe in both hands and watched the seven planets rotate around their sun. He especially loved the beautiful blue surface of Equillian, his home world—it looked like a blue pearl floating in a sea of tiny stars.

Several hours later, just when the moon was visible in the high round window and Casio was sure his special day would slip away unnoticed, his uncle let out an enthusiastic whoop of joy. "I've done it, Casio, I've done it! Come here quick, my boy," he exclaimed, beckoning for his nephew to join him. Casio reluctantly pushed himself off the floor and approached. When he saw what his uncle was holding, his face lit up. It was a pair of glasses just his size. They had intricately carved wood frames with ancient words etched into their sides and the most stunning emerald green lenses.

"They look just like the ones on your sign, Uncle! Are they magic glasses like Great-Grandpapa's and Great-Granduncle Morris's?" Casio asked.

His uncle beamed down at him adoringly. "Very clever, my dear boy! Do you remember the stories I told you about your great-grandpapa and his brother?"

"Great-Grandpapa was a magnificent explorer, and Great-Granduncle was a skilled optician, just like you! They were known as the Finley brothers, and together they discovered a way to make a pair of glasses that could harness the power of the Stars," Casio recounted.

"That's right! What if I were to tell you that I've found a way to recreate those special glasses?"

Casio's eyes widened in wonder.

"Would you like to try them on?" his uncle asked, holding them out to him.

Casio nodded eagerly and took them into his hands as if they were the greatest treasure the world had ever known. "Uncle?" he asked, pausing to study the spectacles.

"Yes?"

"What ever happened to Great-Grandpapa and Great-Granduncle?"

"It's a complete mystery. Morris joined your great- grandfather on one of his explorations and they never returned."

"Did anyone ever look for them?"

"Of course, for a long time. But eventually the search had to end, and we had to accept that they were both lost forever and with them, their special glasses. But they were very clever, you know? They kept journals with accounts of everything they did. Those books have been passed down to me and will in turn be passed down to you. It was because of these accounts that I was able to recreate what was lost so long ago. But enough about your great-grandpapa and great-granduncle. Try them on!" his uncle encouraged.

Casio carefully slipped the glasses up onto his nose and instantly the world was green. He blinked a couple of times as his eyes adjusted to the emerald hue and then, a strange substance came into focus. Fine flecks of gold covered everything. Each fleck glinted in a peculiar way, as if it was drawing in the light from all around it and then sending it out again. The whole place glittered. The gold particles even saturated the air, twinkling like glass powder in the sunlight. In places it swirled upwards, billowing like smoke, and then settled around various objects, clinging to them like metal filings to a magnet. It appeared to be drawn to him and his uncle in particular. "What is it?" Casio asked, looking down at his own hands, which glittered the most brilliantly of all.

"That's a very good question, I'm sorry to say I don't have an answer for you. At least, not a complete answer. It's most commonly referred to as the Ghost Element, because without these glasses, we have no means to detect its existence. Your great-grandfather named it Equillian's Key, because of its ability to unlock natural law. However, as to what it is…that's another thing entirely and something that still remains a mystery."

"It's *Stardust!*" Casio said excitedly, turning his hands this way and that to study the way they shone in the light.

Uncle Rupert looked at him in surprise. "What makes you say that?"

"You always say that Great-Grandpapa's glasses could harness the power of the Stars, and this stuff looks like a strange sort of dust."

His uncle's face filled with a warm smile and his eyes twinkled in the firelight. "What an interesting and wonderful theory! And I dare say, one that's closer to the truth than you know."

"What does it do?" Casio asked in awe, while attempting to shake the odd stuff from his hands.

"Why, anything you like, that's the beauty of it! Here, try it out," his uncle said.

He stood behind Casio and placed his hands around his. "Imagine something that you want to happen, anything at all."

Casio nodded, and his uncle guided his hands in sweeping motions, as if they were conducting an orchestra. As their arms glided through the air, the gold dust reacted like it was suspended in water. It floated away from their arms when they moved them outward, as if by an unseen current, and then came towards them when they brought their arms in. A mass of glittering gold collected around Casio's train, and suddenly it began to move. The engine raced around the track, sounding its whistle and blowing out steam. Casio laughed and clapped his hands in delight. Feeling confident now, he eagerly raised his arms independently and conducted a small town around the train. As the gold dust piled into place, small detailed buildings with colorfully painted exteriors, glass windows, and working chimneys arose from the floor, aligning themselves around the track.

"Look, Uncle! Look what I imagined, and now it's here!" he exclaimed, pointing to his creation.

Next, with a wave of his hand Casio made his glass globe disappear, freeing the miniature solar system inside. The small planets and stars rose into the air and hung suspended in space above the newly crafted houses.

Casio and his uncle eagerly moved to inspect what he had made, and they laughed together in complete captivation and wonderment.

His uncle knelt on one knee and hugged him. "These glasses are for you Casio. They are the greatest gift I can ever give you, the key to unlocking your dreams, and the world. Happy sixth birthday, my dear son!"

Casio hugged his uncle tightly, the moment was cut short by a heavy knock on the door.

His uncle's smile faded. "Quick, in the back you go! Don't make a sound, and whatever you do, don't let anyone see the glasses," he commanded. Casio reluctantly obeyed, hiding behind the rich velvet curtain that separated their living quarters from the workspace.

Rupert walked to his desk and recovered his flintlock pistol from its hidden compartment. He put it under one of the books on his desk and then smoothed his coat before answering the door. Standing outside were three men well dressed in suits and long overcoats. The two at the back were large and burly. They were holding burlap sacks above their heads, trying to protect their bowler hats from the rain, while a short man at the front stood comfortably under the awning. He was wearing a top hat cocked to one side and was leaning on a Blackwood cane that had a white faun's head on the pommel. "Hello, Finley, it's been a while," he said with a grin.

Rupert tensed. "Mr. Erie, how did you find me?"

"It was all thanks to Lady Luck, really. I happened to be passin' through and heard a couple of locals talkin' at the tavern about the optician who's gone mad. They said that you spend your days cooped up inside performin' strange experiments. I knew it had to be you," Mr. Erie said in a strong eastern accent. "Well, aren't you goin' to invite us inside? It's miserable out here."

"Now's not a good time. Come back in the morning during regular business hours," Rupert said.

"Haha, yeah, sure. Come on, Finley, let's not make this harder than it needs to be."

Rupert clenched his jaw and stepped aside, letting the three men into the house.

Mr. Erie walked around the animated town and the floating planets from Casio's globe, "Will you look at this! You've certainly come a long way," he said and poked one of the tiny stars. "Ow!" he yelled, pulling his singed finger back in pain. "By the Watchers! Are they real?"

Rupert ignored the question. He was busy watching the two lackeys rifle through the items on his desk.

"The boss is gonna be chuffed when he sees this! Pack up the room boys," Mr. Erie ordered.

The men began stuffing Rupert's belongings into their sacks. Impossibly, an entire floor lamp disappeared into one of the bags. Dust billowed into the air from items long undisturbed, causing Casio to sneeze behind the curtain. Everyone stopped and turned towards his hiding place.

"You didn't tell me you have company," Mr. Erie said and headed towards the thick velvet drape.

Rupert dove for his desk. He grabbed the pistol and aimed it at Mr. Erie's head just as he put his hand to the curtain.

"Don't take another step," he said sternly, cocking the hammer on his gun.

Mr. Erie paused, then slowly turned around with his hands and cane in the air. "Come now, don't do anythin' you might regret, Finley."

"Get out of my house," Rupert said coolly.

Mr. Erie studied him for a beat, and then his mouth twisted into an unsettling sneer. "Come on boys, it's clear were not welcome here," he said and began making his way towards the door. The other two stopped filling their sacks and followed after him.

"Tell Marx, the Ghost Element is nothing but smoke and dust," Rupert said to their backs and lowered his gun.

Then, in one motion, Mr. Erie turned back around while drawing a long black sword from his cane and lunged at Rupert, sinking the blade deep into his belly. Rupert gasped in surprise and dropped his pistol to the floor. The attack had been so swift, he hadn't seen it coming. "Then we don't need you then, do we?" Erie hissed in his ear. "Boss will be so disappointed, he always believed in you. Never wanted to admit that you'd betrayed us. You could've had a place by his side, he would've made you richer than a noble. Now instead, the great Finley line comes to its end." He withdrew his sword and Rupert collapsed to the floor. The two thugs stared in shock as their leader casually cleaned the blood from his weapon.

"What was that for? I thought we needed him," one asked.

"He's more trouble than he's worth. The books will give us everythin' we need. Keep packin' boys, I'll deal with the rat," he said, and turned back towards the curtain.

Casio watched in horror from his hiding place as his uncle crumpled to the ground. In that moment his world dissolved and a fire ignited in his soul, a fire fueled by injustice that quickly blossomed into rage. He felt as if he was a bystander to his fury as it took control.

The miniature solar system from Casio's enchanted globe exploded apart, each celestial object floating independently. Then all at once the stars shot across the room into Mr. Erie's back. The man dropped his sword and arched backwards in pain as the stars scorched through his overcoat and burrowed into his flesh. He opened his mouth to scream and the sun flew into it, as if being sucked into a cosmic black hole. Mr. Erie's eyes bulged, he doubled over, no longer able to scream. His skin began to crack like porcelain and a brilliant light streamed forth from every fissure. His arms flung outwards and his head lashed back as a flood of light forced its way from his chest, like water bursting through a dam. There was a blinding flash, and then Mr. Erie was gone.

The only thing left of the villain was his long black sword and its cane housing, which lay idle on the floor. The sun and stars from Casio's globe were hovering above them. They glided to the planets on the other side of the room and formed back into Equillian's solar system. The room was still. The other two intruders stared blankly at the spot where their leader had been. When they finally shook free of their paralysis, they dropped their sacks and fled in terror.

Casio stepped from behind the curtain and stared in shock at the sword on the floor. Everything had happened so quickly and so impossibly, he almost questioned whether it had happened at all. Then he saw his uncle on the ground and the undeniable reality washed over him with a cold chill that condensed into a lead weight in the pit of his belly. He took off the glasses with trembling hands and they slipped between his fingers and fell to the stone floor, shattering into a billion green shards. Casio ran to his uncle and slumped over him, his grief extinguishing his inner fire to ash.

"Uncle, what have they done to you? What have I done?" he asked, frightened.

He stared at his hands in horror as if they themselves had ripped the cruel man apart. The murder he had orchestrated surprised and terrified him, and he felt that he no longer knew himself.

Rupert pulled himself up to a seated position, he held his wound with one hand to stanch the bleeding and lifted his other weakly to Casio's shoulder. His expression held no regard for his own pain, only concern for Casio's suffering. "My brave boy, you did what needed to be done. This is all my fault…It isn't fair that you were made to face this so young, I thought that we'd have more time…I'm so sorry," he gasped for air. Then he locked eyes with Casio, who saw an urgency and seriousness there he'd never seen before. "You must listen carefully. Never forget what you've seen here tonight, never forget the *stardust* that covers our world…and whatever you do, do not share this secret with anyone. These are bad people, Casio. They will stop at nothing until they uncover the Ghost Element, and if they succeed, then it could end Equillian. You are the only one who can stop them. You must be ready. Use the glasses—they are the key to protecting our world."

Casio looked at the shattered lenses, "I can't, I'm so sorry Uncle" he whimpered, tears welling in his eyes.

"Yes, you can. You're a Finley by blood. There's nothing you can't do!"

"But how? The glasses are gone."

"The glasses aren't magic, they only allow you to see it. Take the books and mend what has been broken, my notes will explain everything. Go now, you must leave this place!"

"I don't want to go anywhere without you," Casio sniffed.

"I'll always be with you. When you need me, look to the Stars and I'll guide you."

His uncle smiled and placed his hand gently on Casio's face. "I couldn't be prouder of you, I love you, my son." A cough seized him, and blood came out of his mouth. Casio moaned at the sight of it, but his attention was diverted by a lit torch that came crashing through the window pane. The drapes caught alight and fire began to spread across the room.

"Go!" his uncle commanded as he fought for his last breath.

Time slowed to a snail's pace, and Casio's mind became crystal clear with only one thought filling it: *Get Uncle's books.* He picked up the frames of the broken glasses and grabbed the woven sacks the men had left behind and finished stuffing the rest of the books inside. The room was flooding with smoke and Casio could feel the fire's heat closing in on him. He took one last glimpse of everything he had ever known and loved as it was consumed by flame, then he hugged his precious cargo and leapt through the shattered window into the night.

WESTDOCK

CHAPTER ONE

EXTRA! EXTRA! RUPERT FINLEY DEAD!!
ENCHANTED OBJECT SUSPECTED!

Rupert Finley, the last Finley from the long family line of opticians who revolutionized the eyewear and lens industry, was found dead this morning amid the ashes of his burnt-down shop and home. Remaining intact among the pile of debris was a deconstructed enchanted globe whose celestial bodies hovered idly above the scene.

Authorities are left puzzling over this odd event. No one has ever been able to alter an enchanted object before, and if the artifact is involved, then this will be the first time that a fatality has ever been connected to the alchemists' creations. It's still unclear whether the object can be linked to the tragedy, but it does raise a series of questions. At the forefront, was Rupert tampering with the object at the time of the incident or did it come apart on its own? Either way, it contradicts what we have been told by the alchemists.

We have always been led to believe that enchanted objects are protected from tampering, and that it is impossible for them to harm a living being. Due to patent law, only alchemists know how the objects work, and we the public have blindly and trustingly incorporated them into almost every aspect of our lives. But this event has stirred up long-harbored fears around objects with ability. "We know so little about enchanted objects and how they work. It has always surprised me that they've been welcomed into our homes and given to our children with next to no regulations," said Patricia Morgan, head of the Hall of Scientific Study. Arthur Brent, head physics teacher at the University of Lachlan, stated that he has never trusted anything enchanted: "Their existence doesn't correlate with natural law, making them completely unpredictable. For all we know they could be ticking time bombs."

Even after this incident, alchemists still refuse to disclose how the objects are made, claiming their right to secrecy. But they continue to insist that there's no reason to fear them. When questioned about the case of Rupert Finley, they simply said, "No comment."

As of this morning, his supreme lordship Emperor Balthazar has ordered an emergency halt to the production of anything enchanted with one exception for Everfire, the most widely used and most commonly acquired enchanted product on the market today. Its ability to warm and light our homes without scathing or spreading as organic fire does has prevented countless accidents comparable to the devastation of Finley's residence. The emperor has stated that its ongoing use is still less of a risk than reverting to the burning alternative.

Everfire's continued production will prevent the Alchemists' House of Discovery from having to shut down operations entirely during the investigation.

The emperor suggested that unless the alchemists can prove their objects are safe, an enforced recall on all objects with ability will be considered.

Rupert's nephew and adopted son, six-year-old Casio O'Reilly, has been unaccounted for in this tragedy. There is no sign that he was in the house at the time of the incident, and currently there are no leads on where the boy could be. Finley was Casio's last living relative and neighbors say that the two kept mostly to themselves. Authorities have already issued a search party and are hoping to recover the missing child as quickly as possible. They are urging anyone with knowledge of Casio's whereabouts to contact their local authority immediately.

This is a sad day for Equillian. Rupert Finley was a great man of our time who fell victim to an unfortunate event that could have happened to any one of us. Let us hope that we can learn from his passing and use it to prevent any future accidents. May he forever be remembered and be in peace among the Stars.

Bastian carefully folded the old copy of the *Equillian Times*. He was amazed that the captain had a copy of the original newspaper from Rupert Finley's death. The article described a pinnacle in Equillian's history—it was said that the incident changed everything.

The alchemists weren't willing to give up their secrets, so it left Emperor Balthazar with little choice. Objects with ability were banned less than a year later, except for Everfire. Having an exception never made any sense to Bastian. If enchanted fire was safe enough to keep in their homes, why weren't the rest of the enchanted objects? From what he'd heard, most of them were just as practical, knives that never lost their edge but couldn't cut human skin, clocks that held perfect time and never had to be wound, smudge-free glass that never had to be cleaned. It all sounded incredibly useful and perfectly harmless, but that was well before Bastian's time. He'd never used an enchanted object besides Everfire. The older generation were the only ones who knew what they were missing.

Bastian tucked the old newspaper under his arm and made his way to the upper deck of the trawler. The winter sky was blue and cloudless, contrasting starkly against the column of white steam that billowed up from the ship's smokestack. The crew were readying the sails to bring the ship ashore. Bastian pulled on his hood to ward off the chill and tracked down Jarvis, the ship's skipper. Jarvis was a large man, with arms as thick as tree trunks and a black beard as dense as wool. He owned the only steam-powered trawler in town, which allowed him to get the biggest catch. With the inexhaustible fuel source of Everfire, steam power was on the rise. The technology was still making its way to Westdock—as usual the fishing port was ten steps behind—but Jarvis had his finger on the pulse. His business was so successful, he had people begging to be on his crew. However, he was a wary soul and incredibly selective. It had taken Bastian and his Star-brother Felix a whole year to gain the captain's trust. And now they had it, they took every scrap of work he threw their way. It wasn't much, a day here or there, but along with the other various odd jobs that lined their pockets, it covered rent and kept them fed.

"Hey, Captain, when's the last time you cleaned out the cabin? I just found a paper down there that's older than I am," Bastian said.

Jarvis took the paper from him. "That's mine, thank you. Down in front, sailor. We'll be in port soon enough."

"That paper belongs in a museum."

"Aye, the day the world changed. I would 'ave 'ad me a ship with ability instead o' this steamin' teakettle if it wasn't fer the death o' Rupert Finley," Jarvis said, with eyes glazed over as if the front-page article was a portal to another time.

"The world's changing every day, Cap. It's about time you started changing with it. When're you going to empty out that dust box down there to make way for some decent cabin space?"

"When I bloody feel like it! Didn't I give you an order? I'm not payin' ya ta stand about," Jarvis said in annoyance, coming out of his daydream.

"Aye, aye, Captain!" Bastian said with a grin and headed towards the bow.

They'd made a good catch that day, their stores brimming with lobsters, blue swimmer crabs, and a slew of other varieties of fish. Bastian hoped that meant a bonus for their pockets. He found Felix already at the front of the ship. His Star-brother was leaning against the ship's railing, welcoming the wind's embrace in his short ebony hair. There wasn't a drop of the same blood between Felix and Bastian, but the Stars had fated them together as infants, and their friendship and loyalty to each other was greater than that of any kin. They were raised together by the Order of the Stars, an ancient and well-respected order whose ecclesiastics dedicate their lives to the Night-Watchers, the guardians and spirits who weave our fates and guide us to our destinies. Their sacred temples are pantheons built in honor and celebration of the Stars and can be found in every town and city across Equillian. They are known sanctuaries for lost and neglected souls, including abandoned children who find their way to their doorstep. Once taken in by the Order, a child is absolved from their past and known from that day forward as a Star Child. Bastian and Felix were Star Children, but they were both kicked out of the temple the year Bastian was twelve and Felix, thirteen. The two of them together spelled trouble, and the sisters were never successful at keeping them apart. But that year was the final straw that broke the dragon's back. They'd picked the keeper's lock and emptied the sacred wine stores, resulting in a horde of drunk children streaking naked through the temple's halls and skinny-dipping in the sacred pools of reflection. The next day the headmistress requested a transfer, a council was held, and it was decided that the Order couldn't risk Bastian and Felix's antics tarnishing the reputation of the two-thousand-year-old establishment. And that was that. Two days later they were sent out into the wide world on their own with nothing but the clothes on their backs, a small pouch of cwips, and a copy of The Words of the Watchers. But Bastian and Felix didn't mind exchanging the care and protection of the Order for their freedom. For the last four years they'd made their way on the streets of Westdock, working odd jobs, palming coins, and pulling cons. Even though it was a humble existence, it still beat living within the strict confines of the Order.

"Guess what I just found in Jarvis's cabin?" Bastian asked Felix.

"A dead rat?" Felix inquired, his mischievous spark at home in his piercing blue eyes.

"The original article from Rupert Finley's death."

Felix's eyes widened. "You're joking? I never would've guessed there was anything interesting in that mess. I have to see it!"

"I bet the captain will still have it in hand if you hurry," Bastian said, and Felix left to satisfy his curiosity.

Bastian looked up at the Guiding Star, which shone through the noon daylight. The star was so bright, it was always visible. He imagined that it would even outshine Equillian's own sun if they were side by side. The Guiding Star never moved from the top of the sky. It marked the upward Ky direction and was a beacon for sailors or wanderers trying to find their way home.

Bastian pulled out his pocket watch. At the top of the timepiece's face was a tiny crystal that represented the Guiding Star, the middle tracked the arc of the sun and moon and around them revolved the twenty-one Time Keeper constellations. It was midday, the hour of the Balancer. On his pocket watch, the illustration of the Balancer constellation depicted a woman bearing a set of scales across her shoulders, one scale hanging down along each arm. It was her job to keep the world in order. If one side was out of balance, she'd lean towards the other. He flipped up a round dark violet lens from the back of his watch and put it against his eye. The lens was a Finley Sun Filter, which enabled the user to see the stars during daylight. He pointed the lens at the sky below the real Guiding Star. His watch had been running a little slow of late, but he was pleased to see that after his last few tweaks, it was now perfectly aligned. The actual Balancer constellation was in the sky directly below the Guiding Star, just as his watch had predicted. Bastian felt a great connection to the stars. It was to be expected, having been raised by the Order, everything they did was linked to the celestial spirits that guided the fates of humankind. But to Bastian, they were so much more. It was said that when someone died, a star was born. You could look to the stars and see everyone who came before you. Being an orphan, Bastian felt as though they were the parents and grandparents he'd never had. As long as he could see the stars, he never felt alone.

⸻⊰⊱⸻

Bastian put away his timepiece and leaned on the ship's railing, drinking in the view as they approached the small harbor town of Westdock. The horseshoe cove greeted him like a mother with open arms. The busy port was heavily trafficked by merchant ships and local fishing boats. Hills covered in rich evergreen forests loomed in the background, speckled with icy rooftops that glistened in the sun's light. The air was filled with a symphony of ship bells and seagulls as well as the rich aroma of fish and spices that was signature to Westdock's shores.

As soon as the ship reached the pier, Bastian jumped off it to catch the line and pulled her in to kiss the docks. His layered chestnut hair was disheveled by the wind's embrace. He pushed it out of his hazel eyes and helped pull the ships gangplank onto the pier so the rest of the crew could disembark. A moment later Felix was beside him. "Isn't that something? An original copy of the *Equillian Times* from almost three decades ago. The captain could sell it for a small fortune, if he wasn't so sentimental about the damn thing," he said.

"Funny that, too sentimental to let it go, and yet it has probably been buried in that mess for the last twenty-odd years."

"I wonder what happened to the boy," Felix said in thought.

"Who?"

"Rupert Finley's adopted son, Casio."

"Oh right. No one ever mentions him."

"Exactly, it's always about the incident with Rupert Finley that led to the great ban. Never anything about his son. I wonder if he's still alive?"

"I suppose that we would've heard about it if they'd ever found him, dead or alive. Unless the story just wasn't that interesting." Bastian yawned. "You ready for lunch? I'm starving," he said, his growling stomach rapidly stealing his attention.

"The plaza?"

"Perfect."

Together Bastian and Felix helped the crew carry the catch onto shore to be cleaned and sold. Afterwards, they tracked down Jarvis and the captain shook their hands.

"Thanks, fer givin' us a 'and today, lads. You were both a real 'elp out there. What a catch! You know, I could really use skills like yours more often. If you want steady work, just say the word," he said, lighting his pipe.

"Thanks, Cap, that's a generous offer! We'll talk it over and let you know by the end of the week," Felix said with his signature toothy grin.

"Truly honored, Skip," Bastian said with a respectful nod.

The captain threw them each a bag of coin, which they caught eagerly before making their way through the busy port.

The docks were alive with activity. People of every shape and color were busy shopping or trading their wares among the small stalls that crowded the shoreline. Bastian palmed an apple in passing as they weaved their way through the crowd, and Felix simmered with excitement. "Get a load of that, steady work with Jarvis's fishing crew. I can't believe that we're finally in! It's only taken us a year. You know what that means, my friend? Steady work means steady pay. Just think of all the girls we could get!" he said enthusiastically.

Bastian rolled his eyes. "That's all you ever think about these days—girls. Don't you have any other aspirations? Don't you ever want to get out of this sinkhole? On the wages of a fisherman, all we'll be doing is surviving. We can make twice as much picking pockets on market day. In fact, we might actually have something saved by now if you didn't go wasting it all on gambling and your *stupid* girls," he said, taking a bite of his apple.

"Actually, most of the women I frequent are quite bright," Felix said in good humor. He put his hand on Bastian's shoulder.

"Once you lie with one, you'll understand, and you won't be so wound up either. By this time tomorrow, your whole view on life will be changed. That's right, don't think I've forgotten that tomorrow is your big day. You'll be sixteen, Bastian, you can't argue with tradition," he said.

Bastian's shoulders deflated. He half-hoped Felix had forgotten that tomorrow was his birthday. He was acutely aware that sixteen is the age of becoming a man. It is known as a boy's Illumine Day. According to tradition, he will lose his virginity on the eve of his sixteenth birthday to a woman whose duty it is to teach him how to be respectful, skilled, and successful in the bedroom, completing the rite of passage into manhood. The woman who's his first, becomes known as his *Sweet Sixteen.*

In the highest circles there are women dedicated to the ceremony called *Illumine Roses*, beautiful women who are older and experienced. The aristocrats make a big hoo-ha of the event. They host a grand banquet the night before and usher their son off to a resplendent boudoir where an Illumine Rose is waiting. The following day, there is a magnificent party to celebrate the occasion. Those with lesser titles, and the commoners who can afford it, visit one of the many brothels on Westdock's shores, where the working girls ceremoniously ring in a boy's coming of age. And those who don't have the coin for a professional simply find a woman who volunteers to be their Sweet Sixteen. Boys eagerly look forward to the event. It's even something that Bastian had gladly anticipated once, but now that his birthday was around the corner, the thought of it brought him nothing but dread.

"My Illumine Day can go Shick itself for all I care. I don't want my first time to be with some random I have to pay for," he said irritably.

"You won't have to pay a cwip. I wouldn't leave my brother high and dry on such a significant occasion. Despite what you say, I've managed to save a few coins. Lady Luck has smiled on me of late and dealt the cards in my favor. I'm going to get you the best coming-of-age celebration that coin can buy," Felix said.

"You've completely missed the point! It's not because of coin. Call me old-fashioned, but I would like to have some sort of chemistry with the girl who takes my boyhood. Is it too much to ask to be able to choose the woman who takes my virginity, instead of some strumpet who's only bedding me because it will give her the means to buy a pretty dress or her next meal?" Bastian asked.

Felix raised an eyebrow at him. "If you don't want to choose one of the fine cathouses Westdock has to offer, then pick one of the girls in town who have already freely volunteered themselves. Any one of them would be suitable. The fault lies not in the choices before you, my friend, but in your own stupid stubbornness in wanting to choose the one woman you can't have."

And there it was. As much as Bastian made up excuses, Felix always got straight to the core of it. The truth was that Bastian did have plenty of opportunities with over half a dozen local girls in town. It seemed the less he tried to get their attention, the more they were attracted to him. And Westdock had a reputation for having some of the best brothels on Equillian. He knew if he wanted to attend one, he'd not be disappointed. But the real problem was that he only had eyes for one woman, and without her, he felt put off the whole business altogether.

"Well, that's me Shicked. The only male in Westdock sixteen and still a virgin."

"Hey, hey, hey, slow down princess, you're not sixteen yet. No brother of mine will be left unbedded on his Illumine Day.

There's an abundance of beautiful birds to choose from in West-dock, there's bound to be at least one besides Gwena Stently who fits your fancy. Mark my words, Bastian Sanders, by sunrise to-morrow, we shall find you a bombshell you can't resist and we'll convince her to make you into a man. Even if I have to learn to play the lyre and throw handpicked rose petals at her feet, you picky shicking bastard!" Felix said, ruffling Bastian's hair the way he knew he detested.

Bastian ducked his head out of the way. "Why don't you get me something I'll appreciate and buy me a one-way ticket out of Westdock?" he jested.

"And leave me? Why on Equillian would I ever do that? This place would be completely boring without you!" Felix returned with a grin.

As they walked, Bastian tossed his apple core to a goat teth-ered to a dairy stall. The road took them out of the bustling har-bor and up towards the familiar plaza at the town's center. The plaza, built in the shape of a large seven-pointed star, was paved with a mixed palette of River Rock cobblestones and outlined with dazzling Jazzily trees. The Jazzily trees were a tourist attrac-tion in Westdock because their bark and flowers changed color with the seasons. Currently their trunks were blue-grey and their branches were covered with large blossoms of sapphire blue, re-flecting the chilly tones of winter. A tall clock tower stood at the heart of the star with bright turquoise clockwork turning be-hind the constellations on its face. A small crowd was gathering around the base of the tower.

"What have we here?" Felix asked as they walked towards the commotion.

In front of the crowd was a squire standing on a small foot-stool. He was holding out a piece of parchment and clearing his throat for a speech. Felix and Bastian pushed their way into the mob to be within earshot.

"Ladies and gentlemen," the squire began, "tonight is a special occasion! It's none other than the commemoration of the engagement of our duchess, Lady Lilliana Wendrian, to Lord Henry Bardviss." He paused for applause.

The crowd cheered lightly, merely out of obligation.

"In celebration, the Wendrians shall be hosting a masquerade ball at their castle. I am here today to extend a warm welcome to all the visiting lords and ladies who are gracing our port. Please join us and help us to celebrate this night of great joy!"

There were only a handful of lords and ladies in the crowd. The rest were local fishermen and commoners, and they weren't making any effort to hide their disappointment.

"Lords and ladies, what a load of poppycock! What about the rest of us?" a fisherman cried out, and the mob joined in chorus, singing the same tune.

The squire held up a finger, commanding silence, and the town's folk reluctantly quieted.

"Ahem, as I was saying, all lords and ladies are welcome to the castle. *Now*, for those who hold lesser titles, you are not forgotten. As posted last fortnight, there will be fireworks over the harbor and music provided here in the plaza. May I remind those with food and entertainment stalls, you are encouraged to contribute to the night's festivities. Thank you and may you all enjoy this merry evening in honor of this most momentous occasion!" he said with as much enthusiasm and gusto as he could muster.

Half-hearted cheers rose from the spectators. The squire, seeing that he'd lost the favor of the public, quickly concluded with a flourish and made a beeline for the carriage he came in.

Bastian and Felix waited for the crowd to clear around them.

"A celebration at the Wendrian castle, could it be more perfect?" Felix asked.

Bastian could see his Star-brother's gears turning and wasn't sure he liked where they were going, but Felix continued before he had a chance to answer.

"That's where we'll find your special lady. I can see her now, some noble's beautiful daughter swept up by the intrigue and mystery of the adventurous orphan boy. Some of those women would probably pay to be your Sweet Sixteen. I can't think of a better way to celebrate your birthday!" he said, painting a picture for Bastian with enthusiastic gesticulation.

"I can," Bastian said dryly.

"Come on, it's perfect. Besides, it will give me the chance to woo Lady Wendrian. You know that I've always had a thing for her," Felix said.

Bastian laughed. "And the truth comes out," he said, amused. He should've known that Felix would make this night about himself. "There is no pretty girl you *haven't* had a thing for. Are your ears painted on? Or did you choose to miss the part about it being her engagement celebration to Lord What's-his-face?"

"Exactly, this will be my last opportunity. I could be her final hurrah before she signs her life away to that royal douchebag."

"How do you know she isn't in favor of the marriage?"

"There's no way that Lady Lilliana Wendrian could be in favor of an arranged marriage to Lord Bardviss. Come on, he's at least thirteen years her senior and about as charming as a doornail."

"And you think that *you* are what she wants? Felix Copperweather, the cwipless orphan boy who makes his living through dishonesty?"

"For one night, certainly. You clearly have much to learn about noblewomen, my friend. For someone in her class, a night with a common rogue can be about as thrilling as cliff jumping."

"Wow, you are shameful. You really have no morals, do you?" Bastian asked.

"Of course I do. I would never take a woman unless she wanted me. The way I see it, I'm rescuing a damsel in distress from a night of misery and mourning. She may as well enjoy her last moments of freedom and gain a memory she can savor in the darkest times of her matrimony."

"You know that only lords and ladies are invited, right?" Bastian reminded him pointedly.

Felix shrugged. "A minor detail. The theme is masquerade. There couldn't be an easier disguise."

Bastian smiled at Felix's confidence—his Star-brother had a habit of challenging the impossible—but he had to admit that his knack with women *was* impressive. Felix had a way with words that seemed to weave a spell around them. When he added his charming grin, there were few hearts that he couldn't capture. But the duchess of Westdock was a prized noble who couldn't be farther out of his league, unless she'd been a princess. Besides being far above his station, she was also renowned for her beauty and betrothed to the richest lord in Westdock. Even if Felix had half a chance of getting in her presence, nobles rarely mixed with commoners, and never in the open. Bastian shook his head. "You aim too high, my friend."

"If you don't shoot for the stars, then you're guaranteed to never reach them," Felix said.

Bastian smirked. "Well, at least standing in that crowd wasn't a complete waste of time," he said, holding up a handful of newly adopted pocket watches.

Felix grinned. "And you question me about morals?"

———◦◆◦———

Bastian and Felix joined a group of locals at the communal pit of Everfire. The town's hotspot was on a point of the star-shaped plaza which jutted out over the cliffside above the ocean. The enchanted, burning sphere of fire hovered in the air above the stone pit, warming those around it. Most people took the eternal flame for granted, but Bastian had always marveled at it. Since he was a child, he'd had an obsessive need to figure out how things worked, and Everfire completely confounded him.

"Come now, listen to reason," Felix began, as they found a place on the log bench that surrounded the fire. "The Wendrians' ball will be filled with pretty girls with deep pockets. If none of their charms suit your fancy, then at least let their coin fund you an unparalleled Illumine celebration. With a little borrowed wealth, we can return to the celebration here in the plaza and spend the night as princes. It will be a coming-of-age celebration fit for legend!" he said.

Bastian sighed. He had to admit to himself that he didn't have anything better to do.

"Alright, I'm in. But only if you manage to miraculously come up with a disguise that turns us both into lords by nightfall."

"Yes!" Felix hooted, raising both arms in triumph. "You will not regret this, my brother. Prepare for the night of a lifetime!" he proclaimed.

Bastian rose from the bench, unenthused. "Let's go home. If we're going to this thing tonight, I want to get some rest," he said. They had been awake since dawn bringing in the catch with Jarvis's crew, and by the sound of things, they weren't going to get to bed before that time tomorrow.

Felix's shoulders and enthusiasm deflated. "I'm offering you a wet dream born into reality and you want to sleep? I think your old age has dried up all your fun."

"Ha!" Bastian laughed. "Fun is only a matter of perspective. For you, chatting up girls is fun. For me, it's about as fun as peeling potatoes."

"Trust me, tonight will be fun. All you have to do is follow my lead and enjoy the ride."

"Well, if you won't let me sleep, then we better hurry up and eat something. I think my stomach finished itself off half an hour ago."

"Stay there, I know just the thing."

Felix jumped up and headed to a group of food carts that lined the plaza behind them. Several minutes later he returned with two baked meat pies and a hot spiced ale for each of them, "A meal to warm your belly and your spirit," he said, handing over his offering.

Bastian took it gratefully. The winter was setting in and the days were getting shorter and colder. As the hot meat and drink settled into his stomach, he started to feel himself again and the world became a brighter and happier place. He looked out at the vast ocean and became lost in introspection. "Would you really be satisfied being a fisherman?" he asked.

Felix turned over the question while he put his feet up on a stump and rolled some spice leaf in thyme tree paper. He handed one of the rollups to Bastian and they both lit their puff-sticks from the Everfire. "Yes," Felix said after taking a long drag. "I'm a simple man, you know that. Give me a good meal, a spiced ale, and a warm beauty to sleep next to and I'm satisfied. I don't have this urge like you do to see other places. Everywhere in the world might look great from afar, but I bet once you get up close it will all have the same stink. It's all the same, just different people with different scenery," he said.

"Like you would know," Bastian scoffed, knowing full well that Felix had never placed a foot outside of Westdock.

Felix shrugged. "I like it here. I like the people, I like our home even as the hovel it is, and I like fishing. As much as I like picking pockets with you at the market and outwitting the highborn for a taste of their privilege, we can't do that forever. If we ever want to settle down, we're going to need stable work at some point, and being one of Jarvis's men would be a respectable position. He has the best fishing operation in Westdock—people would kill to have a place on his crew. We've worked for this, earned it. Is seeing the world really worth throwing that away?" he asked as he knocked the ash from his puffer.

Bastian studied the horizon, feeling drawn by its mystery. "I know that Jarvis's offer is a great opportunity. You're right. If we stayed in Westdock, then it would be a fine and respectable profession. I wish I could be satisfied with it, I really do. But I want so much more. I'm itching to get out of this place. I want to see different scenery, meet different people. I want to be completely surrounded by strangers so that I can redefine myself. I'm tired of being Bastian the orphan boy, I want to be somebody. I want to be in real danger so I feel the worth of being alive. I want to wake up without being able to predict what's going to happen next, I want to learn new trades, I want real adventure!" Bastian exclaimed.

Felix laughed at Bastian's enthusiasm. "Wow, when you put it that way it does sound intriguing, but do you know what sounds more tempting? Having a real bed to sleep in every night, always having the coin to buy my next meal, never having to go without a hot bath. Having half-decent clothes that don't have holes in them," he said, sticking his finger through a tear in Bastian's shirt to emphasize his point. Then his smile faded and was replaced by a serious expression. "I want to be able to one day have a family," he said earnestly, turning to meet Bastian's eye. "That's what really excites me. I have dreamt of those things my whole life, and I don't care if I never see anywhere else. If I can have those few comforts and provide a real home for a family of my own like we never had, then I'll die a happy man."

Bastian saw a deep longing in his friend's gaze that he never even knew was there, and for an instant he felt like he was seeing him for the very first time. Then Felix's mischievous spark returned, and the moment was gone.

"But we must look to the present, and at least tonight, my friend, the Stars favor you, for we shall have ourselves an adventure!" he proclaimed enthusiastically, jumping to his feet. He flicked the butt of his puff-stick into the fire, then smirked at Bastian. "First matter of business, we need something to wear. Good thing we know the best tailor in town."

Bastian's face flushed crimson. Felix was talking about Gwena, the tailor's daughter; Bastian had been completely infatuated with her since childhood. "Shick no! How on Equillian am I supposed to keep her out of my head if we go and see her?" he protested.

"Come on, suck it up! We need Gwena if we are going to make our transformation successful. Our current noble's garb won't do. We could never pass as lords attending such a significant occasion with an untailored suit. Besides, this could be your opportunity. Maybe she'll want to join us," Felix said, walking backwards in the direction of the tailor's. Bastian followed reluctantly.

TAILOR MADE
CHAPTER TWO

Bastian and Felix walked down Thatcher Street towards their old stomping ground. The tailor's shop was only two doors down from the Star Temple they'd been raised in. The sunny quarter was on the southside of town, nestled in the hills overlooking the harbor. It was one of the nicer parts of Westdock. The stone buildings had room to breathe, instead of crowding together like they did in other sections. The shops and cottages along the street had pretty painted trim and colorful signs marking the storefronts. Their steep thatched roofs were overgrown with rich green moss, adding an aspect of old-town charm. Star Temples were always in nice neighborhoods, because they played such an active role in making them that way. The Order never establish temples in upper-class suburbs as a matter of principle, they believe that their services are a right, not a privilege. Because of this, many of the aristocrats don't visit them, seeing the temples as being below their station.

Bastian and Felix had hardly been back to their corner since they were kicked out. It felt strange revisiting their childhood.

As they walked towards the tailor's, Bastian's mind wandered to the last time he'd seen Gwena. It had been at least two years. She'd snuck out of her house to watch the meteor shower with them. The three of them sat together on Throne Hill, passing a bottle of spiced wine, sharing idle chitchat and laughing while the stars danced across the sky. As the night passed their inhibitions were washed away, and it felt like they were the only three people on Equillian. When Felix wandered into the woods for a piss, Bastian's and Gwena's eyes met, and they kissed. Their kiss would have appeared innocent to an observer, unlike the lascivious embrace that comes with experience. But for Bastian, it was tender and perfect, and it awoke a passion inside him that shook the foundation of his world. Felix came back immediately afterwards and Gwena and Bastian pretended it hadn't happened.

That kiss had haunted Bastian for the last two years. He had kissed half a dozen girls since then, but none of them meant anything and nothing could compare to that one simple kiss with Gwena. He had always loved her. They'd met when they were six. He could still remember it clearly. She'd come to the Star Temple with her mother for a service and wandered off into the orphanage wing. She cradled her rag doll with gold string hair until Samantha, a tall eight-year-old girl, took it. Samantha got off on terrorizing the younger children, so Bastian felt no remorse when he tripped her in the mud and took what was rightfully Gwena's. When he gave the doll back to her, she was so grateful that she brought him and Felix sweet treats every Starday after that. Samantha became Bastian's official enemy for life, but he didn't care, it had been worth it. When they were a couple of years older, he and Felix would sneak out of the temple to visit Gwena at the tailor's. Her mother would make them tall glasses of spiced tea and warm sweetbread. As the three of them grew, so did their friendship. They did almost everything together. Spending whole afternoons exploring the woods, splashing in the waves of hidden coves, and loitering in the vast network of Westdock's streets. But then Gwena's mother passed away, and a year later Bastian and Felix were kicked out of the Order.

Gwena's father banned her from seeing them after that. In truth, they probably were a bad influence. They drank, they smoked, and they made the majority of their wages by picking pockets and pulling cons. Not to mention that Felix frequented a selection of brothels in town and enjoyed gambling often. The first time that Gwena ever got drunk was with them, the first puff from a puff-stick was from Bastian's. They were the gateway to a life of debauchery, and Gwena's father needed her clean, straight, and respectable to keep up appearances for his business. He had taken her out of school after her mother died and kept her too busy to have a social life. Bastian and Felix had hardly seen her in the last few years. In the early days she'd sneak out often to see them, but that ended after that night under the stars. It was like her father knew that Gwena liked Bastian. He piled on the work, giving her more and more responsibility for the family business so she couldn't have time for anything else, and Gwena didn't fight it. Her loyalty towards her father was unshakable.

The Stently Tailors shop came into view and Bastian's heart quickened. As they approached the store, they did a casual pass by the large display window to see who was working. It was Gwena. She was wearing a pale lavender dress that outlined her hourglass figure as she leaned on the counter and thumbed through the accounting books. She was even more beautiful than he remembered. He was surprised by how much older she looked. Her long white-gold hair, which used to cascade over her shoulders in natural waves, was pulled back neatly in a knot. Her perfectly symmetrical features, which used to favor a smile, were locked in an expression of concentration, giving her an air of sophistication. Her plump lips were turned down at the edges in a subtle frown as her seafoam green eyes scanned the pages in front of her. And it suddenly dawned on Bastian—in the last two years Gwena had transformed from the young, wild girl he knew into a stunning and dignified young woman whom he was no longer sure he knew at all. She would be sixteen next month. Their birthdays were less than a month apart. There was no Illumine Day for girls. When her coming of age day arrived, she would have the grandest celebration her father could afford and she would choose the man she wanted, when she was ready. Bastian had always hoped that when the time came, she would choose him. He believed they were made for each other. But now that he saw her, his hopes were dashed across the cobblestones. What chance did he have? He was nothing but a cwipless pickpocket and Gwena was now a refined and respectable woman with real prospects.

Bastian and Felix made sure Gwena's father wasn't in the store before tapping on the glass to get her attention. She looked up, and her face lit with surprise and delight. She put the ledger down and hurried to the front door to greet them. "Bastian, Felix! By Serendipity, it's good to see you two! Go around back and I'll meet you at my window," she said, and then she locked the front door and turned the *Open* sign over.

Bastian and Felix made their way to Gwena's bedroom window at the back of the shop. Her room was on the top floor, in a loft over the family's living space. There was a large circular window just below the roof that led to her bedroom. Gwena opened it and popped her head outside. "Come up!" she invited. Bastian and Felix scaled the wall and climbed in.

When Bastian stepped into Gwena's room, he was surprised at how little it'd changed. The simple space still had the same warm, inviting feel to it. There were dark hardwood floors, cream-white walls, and a sloped ceiling which was brightly illuminated by the natural light that poured through the window. It was well kept and only furnished with the basic necessities: a single short wood stool, a washing table with a blue porcelain pitcher and bowl, and a tall white wardrobe. Her bed was on the far side of the room, blocked off by an accordion screen made of dark wood and floral fabric with tiny birds on it. The familiar surroundings and the smell of the sea mixed with honeysuckle perfume brought back a flood of memories.

Gwena hugged him. "It's so good to see you!"

"Hi Gwen," Bastian said awkwardly.

He immediately noticed how curvy her figure had become, which only made it harder to ignore his feelings for her. He diverted his attention to the woodgrain in the floorboards in an attempt to distract himself from her embrace.

He was thankful that she had at least one imperfection. A prominent scar ran across her face. It started at the top right of her forehead, traced over the bridge of her nose, and ended at the left base of her prominent cheekbone. When Gwena was seven, she wandered too close to a Jackal-bird nest and got attacked by the mother. Jackal-birds' claws were nothing to contend with. In the springtime, if you got within ten feet of their fledglings it could warrant an attack. If not for the scar's decoration, men would be lining up to ask Gwena's hand in marriage. Bastian was grateful for it. It warded away all the shallow competition. When they were kids he used to tell her it was her battle scar and she should wear it with pride. They would make up stories together about how she'd acquired it: battling pirates on the seven seas, hunting the terrifying three-headed lions, taming dragons.

Gwena hugged Felix in turn, and Felix held the embrace for longer than Bastian would've liked.

"Wow, Gwena, how you've grown! Since when did you become such a striking young woman?" Felix asked, circling her to admire her figure.

Gwena laughed and Bastian gave him a hard stare, which Felix ignored.

"I'm not the only one who's grown, look at you both!! Has it been so long? I still think of us as children. But here you are before me, as two fine men," she said with a delighted laugh and the bright smile that Bastian had always known and loved. Maybe she wasn't so different after all.

"Are you both well? What are you doing these days?" she asked.

"Oh, you know. Same ol' things really. Still hopeless rogues working for the sweet indulgence of life's fine pleasures," Felix said.

"Good. I would be disappointed if you two straightened out too much. Your faults make you the most interesting people I know," she laughed.

"How're you doing, Gwen?" Bastian asked.

"I'm all right. My life is the opposite of interesting these days, just work, work, work. It seems the more I do, the more there is to be done. But never mind that. I'm so glad you guys are here!"

"We're sorry to pop in without notice. I hope that we didn't come at a bad time?" Felix asked.

"On the contrary, you two couldn't have had better timing! My father only just left to buy new fabric in town. He should be gone for at least a couple of hours."

"Brilliant, because we're in desperate need of your help," Felix confessed.

"Of course, anything! What is it?"

"Bastian and I are attending the Wendrians' ball this evening, and we have nothing to wear."

"You two are invited to the Wendrians' ball?" Gwena asked with a raised eyebrow.

"Not exactly…but tonight is Bastian's last night before manhood, and I think that he deserves the best celebration possible, don't you?"

"Without question," Gwena said beaming at Bastian.

"The only problem is, we will never make it inside without a fitting suit that can transform us into convincing lords."

Gwena laughed, "By Kismet! Well, Bastian, I hope you don't mind getting your birthday present a little early."

"Birthday present?"

"What, did you think I forgot? It is your Illumine Day after all!" she said, and then she disappeared behind her screen. When she came out, she was holding a rich green suit fit for a lord.

"It hasn't been taken in to your measurements yet, which is why it's actually brilliant you're here. I was going to have to guess your size, and I'm sure I would've gotten it all wrong, you've grown so much! Here, try it on," she said, handing the suit to Bastian.

Then she turned to Felix. "You can choose something off the custom rack. It's behind the counter downstairs. Nothing there is getting picked up until next week. But I'm warning you, it better come back in mint condition!"

"Of course. You're an absolute star, my dear!" Felix said and disappeared down the stairs.

Gwena turned to Bastian. "You can get changed behind my screen."

Bastian started towards the privacy of her bed space. He hesitated halfway and turned back.

"Why don't you come with us tonight, for old times' sake?" he asked.

The smile in Gwena's eyes faded. "I wish I could. But there's no way that my father will let me."

"So, don't tell him. What he doesn't know won't hurt him."

Gwena sighed, "I can't. Unlike you two I still have a parent to answer to, and my father needs me here. The shop would fall apart without me! Not to mention that I've already started to get rush orders with this last-minute invitation to the ball for the visiting lords and ladies."

"Sure," Bastian said with a disappointed smile and went behind the screen to change. He was crestfallen. Gwena was the only woman in the world he wanted to spend his birthday celebration with. Without her, he found himself losing interest in the night altogether.

When Bastian stepped back into the room, Gwena stifled a giggle. The suit was about three sizes too big for him, making him look like a boy in his father's clothing.

"Don't worry. When I'm done, it will fit you perfectly," she promised.

Bastian knew that it would. She'd become the best tailor in town, far out-skilling even her own father. Though her old man never seemed to mind taking all the credit.

Gwena strapped her leather tailor's gauntlet onto her forearm. It stored every tool needed for her trade: scissors, measuring tape, pins and needles, and an array of different colored thread. She guided him in front of the tall antique mirror that hung on her wall and proceeded to pin the suit where it needed to be taken in. Bastian stood still as a statue as he watched her work. She was so graceful and precise in her movements. It was such a contrast to the wild girl he'd known.

"Do you enjoy it?" he asked.

"Enjoy what?"

"Being a tailor."

"I don't mind it. There is something satisfying about the work."

"Well, you're certainly good at it at any rate."

"Thanks," Gwena blushed. "That's only because I've had way too much practice," she added modestly.

"Do you ever get any time off?" he asked.

"We are closed Stardays, but there's always so much to catch up on. So, in short…not really, no," she said with an empty laugh.

Bastian searched for something to say that might convince her to come out with them, but words escaped him. As the silence crept on he began to feel overly self-conscious and didn't know where to put his arms. It didn't help that Gwena was now pinning the fabric on the inside of his trouser legs. He was terrified that at any moment his body might betray him. To his relief, Felix returned. He was wearing a handsome blue wool suit that fit him perfectly, complete with a blue and purple checkered vest and a rich purple tie.

"What do you think?" Felix asked, holding out his arms in presentation.

Gwena was struck with an expression of horror. "I should've known that you'd pick that one."

"What? You said to choose any one I wanted," Felix said, looking down at the suit.

"You can choose any one, but that one. That suit is for Lord Bardviss!"

Felix looked stricken. Only Bastian could tell that it was solely for fear of losing the attire.

"Come on, it's perfect!" Felix protested.

"No! If my father finds it missing, he will have my head!"

"But you said that it's not being picked up until next week."

"That's beside the point."

"You have nothing to fear, I'll look after it like it was my only child and return it tomorrow as good as new," he promised.

Gwena snorted, "I find that hardly comforting, Felix Copperweather. If you had a child, you wouldn't know the first thing to do with it!"

Bastian laughed and Felix pouted.

"My lady, your craftmanship on this piece is flawless," he said, coming up beside her and putting his arm around her shoulder. "Do you really want such a masterpiece to be wasted on the likes of Lord Bardviss? If I borrow it tonight, then you can let it go knowing it had one night of splendor with someone deserving."

Gwena sighed. "You better have it back here tomorrow, unharmed," she warned sternly. Felix kissed her on the cheek.

"You're the best, my dear, I owe you one."

"Yes, you do. And don't you forget it!" she said pointedly.

"Why don't you come out with us tonight?" Felix asked.

"Already tried," Bastian cut in.

"I can't. I have far too much work to do. Unlike you two, I have responsibilities," Gwena said.

"Unlucky you," Felix said. "Well, you can't blame us for trying. I guess all this work is what you get for being the best tailor in town, eh? Maybe you should consider cutting back from perfection?" he suggested.

Gwena beamed, "I miss you guys! Oh, I almost forgot, Bastian! I made some special alterations to your suit."

She came up behind him and reached around his waist to stick her hand in his coat pocket. Bastian froze at her touch. She pulled his pocket inside out.

"It looks like an ordinary empty pocket, right?" she asked.

"Yeah…"

"Now watch this!" She replaced the pocket and dropped a spool of thread into it, and then she reached inside his jacket and tugged on something.

"Now check your pocket," she said while stepping back from him.

Bastian patted down the outside of his jacket, but he couldn't feel the spool of thread. He reached inside and found the pocket empty. "It's not there," he said.

"Ta-da!" Gwena said in triumph.

Bastian pulled his pocket inside out, and he and Felix stared at its emptiness in disbelief.

"I didn't get a magic suit on my birthday," Felix muttered.

"That's bloody brilliant! How did you do it?" Bastian asked.

"They're magician's false pockets! Madam Pomphrey commissioned me to make her a bag like this when she came through Westdock with the travelling curiosities. It's simple really, all you're doing is pulling a false pocket over the first one. The real pocket is deeper, so that even if they feel the false one, they won't discover what you're hiding behind it. If you want the object back again, you just pull this little tab across here." She showed

Bastian a small tag on the inside of his jacket. Bastian pulled it and found the spool of thread sitting in his pocket.

"I'm not condoning those bad habits of yours. But if you're going to do it, I would rather that you didn't get caught," she said.

"You are aware that you taught us those bad habits?" Felix asked in good humor.

"I taught you sleight of hand for magic tricks. That's hardly the same thing! If I'd known how you two would be using it, then I never would've shown it to you in the first place," Gwena said defensively.

"Come on, you should be proud. Bastian and I are the best magicians you know, besides yourself, of course. We make things disappear from people's pockets all the time. Admittedly, our act is a little flawed. We aren't very good at the whole reappearing thing. But hey, no one's perfect," Felix said with a roguish grin.

Gwena crossed her arms and Bastian laughed. Gwena had been into magic for as long as he'd known her. She had an aunt who was a magician in a travelling circus. Every time she came to visit, she would teach Gwena her tricks and tell her stories from her life on the road. Gwena adored her and wanted to be just like her. She used to practice the magic tricks over and over again and then would test them out on Bastian and Felix. She had the best sleight of hand that Bastian had ever seen, and that was saying a lot considering how nimble he was with his own fingers. He and Felix had tried to persuade her to help them with cons, but she refused to use her skills for anything but magic.

"Thanks, I really mean it. It's perfect," he said in earnest.

"Wait, there's more," she said excitedly.

She pulled open the flap of his jacket and the inside was lined from top to bottom with pockets of various sizes.

"Extra pockets for every item you carry. Now you can go places without your bag and keep everything on your person completely organized," she said.

Bastian felt like he was falling in love with her all over again. "That's bloody brilliant! It couldn't be any better. You're amazing, Gwen."

"I'm so happy that you like it! Happy birthday!" Gwena said with joy and she hugged him again. Then she called over to Felix, "And I did get you something for your Illumine Day, I just haven't had the chance to give it to you. You'll find it in your breast pocket."

Felix looked down at his pocket in surprise. He pulled out a medium-sized coin that he held up to the window light. It was a gold-plated Lady Luck charm, a special decorative coin that depicted the Lady Luck constellation on one side and her daughter Serendipity on the other. They were Felix's two favorite constellations. The charms are said to bring the bearer great luck, but only if received as a gift, because luck can't be bought.

Bastian could see how much Felix appreciated it. Gwena couldn't have gotten him anything more perfect.

"I don't know how you do it, my dear. Even knowing your tricks, your magic never fails to astound me. Thank you," he said with a grin and pulled her into a hug.

Gwena hugged him back and then looked nervously at the clock on her wall. "You two better go. If I'm going to have Bastian's suit ready, I'll need to make the alterations before my father returns. Come back in an hour and it should be finished."

Bastian changed out of the suit and gave it back to her. Then he and Felix left through the window.

2

An hour later Bastian returned to Gwena's bedroom window alone. Felix had gone into town to find a couple of masks to disguise them for the masquerade. The day had turned cold and dreary. Bastian rubbed his hands together to warm them, then stuck them deep inside his pockets as he waited. Several minutes later Gwena opened the window and popped her head out.

"So sorry, I lost track of time. Come in," she said and disappeared back into her room. Bastian scaled the wall and jumped inside.

She held the suit out to him. "Here, try it on."

"Thanks."

He took the suit behind the screen. As he changed, his body buzzed nervously. He knew that this was his opportunity to find out if Gwena still had feelings for him. It could be ages before they had another moment alone together. But finding the courage to act was a different thing entirely. It would be a relief to know, even if she turned him down. At least then he could choose someone else to be his Sweet Sixteen without regret—or so he told himself.

Bastian stepped out from behind the screen and Gwena smiled.

"What?" he asked.

"It suits you, you look quite handsome when you're wearing something that fits you properly."

"See, all I needed was a talented tailor," he said.

"Do you want to see it?" she asked.

"See what?"

"The suit," Gwena laughed and steered him towards her mirror.

He looked at the glass and for a moment was taken aback by his own reflection. He looked so much older and more refined. It was as if he had transformed from a poor boy to a highborn noble in an instant. He'd dressed in a suit before on countless occasions when he and Felix were poaching the pockets of aristocrats, but the suits had always been secondhand and never fit him properly. It was clear they'd been tailored for someone else, which made him feel like an imposter. He never imagined how different it would be to wear a suit that was intended for him. Or how much his appearance influenced his own feeling of self-worth. Being dressed in that fine suit made him feel for the first time that he was truly worth something.

"It's far more than I deserve, thank you," he said in earnest.

"I'm thrilled that you like it!" Gwena beamed.

"Are you sure that you can't come tonight?" he asked. In the suit, he was suddenly feeling more confident.

Gwena hesitated. "I want to. But I really can't. I'm glad that you came by today. I have missed you both so much. I miss the old days, before mum died and I became inundated with obligation. I know that our coming of age is supposed to be something to look forward to, but if I could, I would wind the clock back and live in our childhood forever."

"I miss the old days too," Bastian said with a warm smile.

Then he looked into her eyes, searching for a sign.

She met his gaze and for a moment he had hope. He took a step towards her reaching for her hand, then the sound of the shop door opening came from downstairs and Gwena's father's voice called up to her. The moment was lost.

"Quick, out you go!" Gwena commanded.

"Can I see you tomorrow? It would be great if you could join us for my birthday drinks," Bastian said as he grabbed his clothes.

"I'll see how much work I have to do. Now go!" she whispered and practically pushed him out the window.

CASTLE CRASHERS
CHAPTER THREE

Bastian and Felix stepped onto the stone path lit by firebeetle lanterns. Handsomely adorned in their fine tailored suits, they easily blended in with the stream of nobles dressed in colorful costumes on their way towards the castle. The night was cold and clear. Orchestra music floated down from the castle accompanied by the symphony of chirping crickets that rose from the hills bellow them.

Felix had managed to appropriate a couple of half-masks from a travelling merchant who was too busy flirting with another man's wife to notice his merchandise missing. The masks were made of molded leather, and beautifully painted in the northern style. Felix's was a fox's face, and Bastian's was a black panther's. The masks covered their eyes and the bridges of their noses and was secured by a satin ribbon tied behind their heads. Bastian was pleased to have a mask that reflected the shadows. Despite Felix's intentions to make this night about women, he had other plans, and his mask suited them perfectly. The Wendrians were the second richest family in Westdock, their fortune surpassed only by that of Lord Bardviss's, and tonight was the perfect opportunity for Bastian and Felix to acquire some of that wealth for themselves.

Soon they were outside the castle's front entrance in a court-yard with a well-manicured garden of shaped hedges. A white marble fountain stood in the center featuring a statue of a beautiful mermaid. She was skillfully carved with her arms raised above her head and her long hair suspended around her face as if floating in water. The arriving lords and ladies were rapidly becoming a thick crowd, and Bastian sensed that he and Felix were going to be separated. "Stay near," he began, but before he could say another word, Felix was swept in the opposite direction.

"I'll meet you inside!" Felix called back over the noise and then turned to a young woman beside him, wasting no time in striking up a conversation.

Bastian anxiously watched Felix disappear amid the mass. He cursed himself for assuming that he had some sort of plan. Then Bastian was thrust through the crowd himself towards the grand entrance to the castle. As he was pushed along he studied his surroundings to assess his situation. There were guards lined up along the walkway and a squire greeting people at the door. He was signing names in a large guestbook with an extravagant purple feathered quill. Bastian cursed under his breath. He had been relying on Felix to get them into the castle. He was the master of verbal affectation, a true spin doctor. He only needed to open his mouth and doors would open for him, while Bastian, on the other hand, only needed to open his mouth to get thrown out of places. He was the thief with quick fingers, not a quick tongue, at least not in the way that did him any favors. He had the gift of being overlooked, while Felix had the gift of being noticed. Together they made a perfect team, but alone they were impaired in their operations. Bastian realized that without Felix, the front entrance wasn't going to be an option.

Bastian scanned the courtyard looking for another way in. It didn't take him long to locate the side gate obscured in the shadows of the castle. But he needed to find a way to reach it unobserved by the guards. Then he saw his answer. A plump middle-aged woman richly adorned as a peacock was standing on the hillside an arm's length from his destination. She was waving a handkerchief and calling out, "Axil! Oh, Axil! Where are you, my darling?!" Bastian could only presume that she had lost her partner in the throng, as he had. Taking advantage of the opportunity, he assumed the stature and stance of the lords around him and pretended that he knew her. "My darling, I'm coming!" he called out from across the courtyard.

As he'd hoped, the crowd parted to let him through and the guards ignored him. He came up to the woman assuming familiarity and embraced her, so that he could whisper in her ear, "Axil is waiting for you inside, at the banquet table."

Judging by her stature, Bastian hoped that she would be happy there whether Axil, whoever he was, was present or not. The plump woman blushed behind her half mask, "Th... thank you, sir. And what name do I have the pleasure of speaking to?" she asked flirtatiously.

Bastian was uninterested and wanted to get rid of her as soon as possible. "I'm just the messenger, no need to thank me. Hurry now, before you catch a chill," he encouraged.

The woman's rosy cheeks blushed even deeper. "Oh, what a gentleman! Well, toodle-oo for now, mysterious messenger. I hope the Stars bring us together again for a proper introduction," she squeaked and then waved her handkerchief at him as she stepped back into the crowd.

Bastian rolled his eyes and slipped into the shadows. Women baffled him. Give them a bit of mystery while showing indifference and they melted like butter. And then, when a man gave them real attention, they ignored him.

He slid through the bars of the metal gate and followed the castle wall until he found what he was looking for: the cooks' entrance. It was a single wooden door that gave the cooks access to the vegetable and herb gardens. He pushed on it. To no surprise, it was bolted shut. Luckily a locked door *was* in Bastian's line of expertise. He took a leather bundle out of his breast pocket and unrolled it. Inside was his own personal collection of lock-picking tools that he had designed and made himself. He had sacrificed every Thrixday for the last year working for the local blacksmith, in trade for the use of his forge. Bastian assessed the lock briefly. Finding that it would be no difficult challenge, he chose a piece from his collection of skeleton keys. It didn't take him long to hear the satisfying *click* that allowed the door to open. He slipped inside and closed it gently behind him.

There was a narrow stone staircase that spiraled upwards. It was brightly lit with Everfire torches, floating flames surrounded by long glass cylinders. He cautiously climbed the stairs, greatly aware of how exposed he was without shadows to hide in. If someone came down now, he'd be paralyzed like an Elderpuss in lantern light. The horned and spotted wildcats were nocturnal creatures who almost became extinct when poachers discovered they could immobilize them with nothing but a torch.

Bastian's palms began to sweat, and his hand went up instinctively to the seven-pointed star tattoo behind his left ear. It was the mark given to all Star Children. It branded them as orphans of the Order. The symbol, given ceremoniously, was said to protect them. Bastian wasn't entirely convinced by the dogma, but he couldn't help seeking its comfort in times of uncertainty.

He could hear voices and clanging above him, the sounds growing louder the farther he went up the stairs. Soon the cold night air subsided and the warmth of the kitchen enveloped him, mixed with the aroma of hot butter and spices, which awakened his appetite.

He finally came to the top landing where there was an entrance covered by a thick hanging curtain. He cautiously peeked around it and saw a large kitchen alive with activity. Cooks and their kitchen staff were chopping meat and vegetables, tending to steaming pots and sizzling pans, and artistically garnishing serving platters for an extravagant presentation. Large trays of lobsters, fine fruit, pickled delicacies, and cheeses were swept up by the serving staff and hurried out to the hundreds of guests circling like vultures. The commotion and the steam that hung in the air would have been sufficient to hide Bastian if he was wearing his usual commonplace attire, but he would never make the long walk across the kitchen in a green tailored suit. Since circumstances weren't in his favor, he settled on creating a distraction.

Bastian took a small slingshot from his breast pocket and pulled back a dried bean from the floor. He always carried his slingshot. At the Order, he used it to knock Star Fruit from the tree bellow the Reflection Room window. The Reflection Room was a small chamber with nothing but a wooden bench and a high sitting window that looked out towards the Guiding Star. Children were sent there when they were miss behaving and were expected to sit and look towards the star to reflect on their actions. Bastian was sent there a lot, always without warning and often for hours at a time. His first experience with the Reflection

Room taught him to keep distractions in his pockets. He was sure that without them he would've died there from boredom. By his third visit, he discovered that if he stood on the bench, he could boost himself off the wall to the windowsill. From there, he had a good view of the Star Tree that grew along the outer wall. Its small and pointy fruit were perfect for target practice. The slingshot fit perfectly in the palm of his hand. Since his temple days it had gotten him out of several tight binds, making it worth its weight in gold. Bastian carefully aimed at a pot hanging from a rack on the ceiling in the center of the kitchen and let go. The bean rocketed through the air, hitting the pot, and then it ricocheted off into a nearby cook's eye. "Ow!" the cook yelled in pain.

"Oh, Shick," Bastian muttered.

The cook looked around to see who the culprit was. In hot anger he blamed the chef next to him and punched him square in the face. Uproar broke out and in a matter of seconds, the entire kitchen was in a brawl. Bastian raised his eyebrows in surprise. That will do, he thought. And then he quickly slipped unnoticed past the chaos and into the banquet hall.

The banquet hall was buzzing with conversation as finely clad guests picked at the beautiful spread of hors d'oeuvres atop the long series of richly adorned tables. Every one was laden with exotic fresh fruit and pickled delicacies from every region, not to mention meat from half a dozen different animals, some of which Bastian recognized and some he didn't. His mouth watered just looking at it. He gladly picked at some roast lamb and marinated olives. The meat was cooked to perfection and the olives were an explosion of flavor. He wanted to try everything on the table, but then he remembered why he was there and decided he'd return to fill his belly after he'd filled his pockets.

He turned to leave the table and collided face first with a woman standing directly behind him. "I'm so sorry," he apologized as politely as he could.

Then he realized that it was the peacock lady he'd met earlier. She was now wearing an overbearingly sweet perfume that smelt like she'd jumped into a pool of excrement mixed with sugared roses. The woman ignored the fact that they'd almost knocked each other out and backed him against the table.

"Hello mysterious messenger, what a surprise we should run into each other again! It must be in the stars, he-he." The woman giggled flirtatiously. "You know, I still haven't found my husband. Name's Lady Ellington. You haven't told me yours," she said expectantly, holding out her hand to be kissed.

Bastian took her hand and shook it, much to her disappointment.

"I'm sure your husband's looking for you, my lady. He's probably very worried. You should continue searching for him," he said.

"Pish! You clearly don't know my husband. Him, worried about me? I doubt he's looking for me. He's probably off gallivanting with some girl ten years younger! Men, they always have to have the latest model of everything," she huffed. Then she put her lips to Bastian's ear and whispered, "What I lack in youth, I make up for in experience."

Bastian blushed. "Excuse me, I have to use the toilet," he said pathetically.

"Take me with you!" she said desperately, grabbing hold of his arm.

"No!" he said indignantly, attempting to sound offended rather than horrified.

"Well, why not?" she asked dejectedly.

Bastian paused. He knew that the proper social conduct would be to lie or to avoid the question altogether, only he was too honest for that and he couldn't risk her continual pursuit. Besides, social graces were never his forte.

"Lady Ellington is it?"

"Yes."

"There are several reasons why not. First, you're married. Second, you've completely misread me, I'm not looking to take you or anyone to the toilets. But if that's your goal tonight, then a word of advice. Try being a little subtler—your advances are as inviting as the mouth of a sea croc. And consider firing your perfume-smith. The only thing you're going to attract with that scent is flies" he said bluntly.

Lady Ellington's jaw dropped and she stared at Bastian like he had just slapped her in the face. "How dare you!" she bellowed, enraged, raising a hand to strike him.

Bastian didn't stick around to see what would happen next. He slipped passed her and disappeared into the crowd, like a magician's vanishing act. By the time he stopped putting distance between them, he found himself in a luxurious ballroom. He was trying to decide where to turn next when he spotted Felix waving at him from the back. His Star-brother was surrounded by five beautiful women. Bastian didn't know how he did it. Girls flocked to him like bees to honey.

"Oi cousin, come flatter us with your company!" Felix called out to him.

Bastian accepted the invitation, relieved to be escaping his predator. When he reached the group, Felix handed him a large blue cocktail garnished with dragon fruit that he'd taken from a passing waiter. Bastian eagerly downed half of its sickly-sweet contents before facing the surrounding company.

"You couldn't have had better timing, we were just talking about you. Everyone, this is William, William this is everyone," Felix said, introducing Bastian to the group of noblewomen.

"Ladies," Bastian said, raising his glass in greeting while making a mental note of his fictitious name.

The women smiled and giggled flirtatiously towards him and then proceeded to assess him like an object.

"He's the perfect height. Not too short, nor too tall."

"And will you feel his arms!" a woman said while touching his shoulder.

"Handsome and strong, a winning combination."

"I don't believe he's still a boy, he looks every bit a man to me," they cooed.

Bastian took another long hard drink, preparing himself for whatever it was he just stepped into. Felix relished his discomfort. "I was telling these beautiful birds all about your selfless sacrifice," he told him.

"Oh?" Bastian asked, lifting an eyebrow.

"How you're having a drawing for your Sweet Sixteen. All for charity of course, so that orphans like yourself can have a better future," he explained, as if he was reminding him why they'd come.

Bastian hid his instant terror with a plastered smile. "What can I say, I've always believed in helping those less fortunate," he said, giving Felix a hard stare.

Bastian and Felix only had one rule during their escapades: They had to go along with everything and anything that the other put forward without denying any of it, especially when it related to a con. It had turned into a sort of game of theirs that never failed to make things interesting. Bastian would have to wait to reprimand Felix later. He noted that the women in the group were all exceptionally good-looking, but that didn't make up for their outwardly conceited personalities. He wasn't interested in a pretty face that had little behind it. Felix on the other hand, was obviously enjoying himself. He had a captivated female audience and was milking it for all it was worth.

"I asked William this morning if he was worried about having an ugly duckling win the drawing, and do you know what he told me?" Felix began. "He said, 'James, all women are beautiful no matter their appearance. Inside they have the spirit of a lioness and the grace of a delicate flower. They are intricate masterpieces, only waiting to be discovered. No matter the woman, it will be a privilege to bring her pleasure.' Those were his exact words. He's the most selfless man I know when it comes to women, but in all other accounts he's a complete rogue. He's lucky he's an orphan. If I behaved like him, I would surely be kicked out of my father's castle. There's certainly never a dull moment in his company," Felix told the gathering.

The women melted with every word. A slender brunette pulled out her pouch. "How much did you say it was to enter into the lottery?" she asked eagerly.

Felix smiled warmly, "There's no fixed price, my dear. You can donate as little or as much as you choose. We don't like to dictate another's act of charity. Just remember, it's all for the children," he reminded politely.

The woman emptied her pouch into Felix's hand. "Please don't take this meager amount as any kind of reflection of my feelings on the importance of the cause or the worth of Lord William's company. If I had more with me, I would give it," she said, excusing her donation of several silver fish coins, half a dozen jolly rogers, and a rose wagon.

Felix handed the woman a paper ticket. "You'll find no judgment here, my lady. We're only grateful for your support," he said with a slight bow.

The other four women couldn't empty their pouches fast enough. It took every fiber of Bastian's willpower to act nonchalant and unsurprised by the vast sum that was being offered for his virginity. Not even his virginity, just for the *chance* at his virginity. He recalled Felix's words about noblewomen finding a thrill from a night with a common rogue and was now convinced that he was right.

"I think you beauties have earned yourselves a dance with Lord William, if you should choose to take it," Felix said, volunteering Bastian.

Bastian's cocktail stuck in his throat. Felix knew full well that he didn't know any of the upper-class dances. Give him a pub lit by a fiddle and he could dance the best to the ground, but when it came to the dances of lords and ladies, he was about as useless as a bear attempting the box step.

"Certainly," Bastian said with a forced smile.

He offered his hand to the brunette while giving Felix the evils. The brunette accepted joyfully and followed Bastian onto the dance floor. The ballroom was alive with an upbeat tune a man was playing on a grand piano in the corner. Bastian watched the dancers around him and knew that he wouldn't be able to mimic them.

"Do you want to try something new? er…"

"Sophia, my name's Sophia. What do you have in mind?" she asked.

"Well, Sophia, I met with a merchant last week who taught me the latest moves from the South. Apparently, it's all the rage over there," he improvised.

"I wouldn't have a clue of what to do," Sophia admitted nervously.

"Just follow my lead and you won't miss a beat," he promised and twirled her onto the dance floor.

Sophia laughed in delight and Bastian thanked his lucky Stars that she was a good follower. He made up steps as he went, keeping in perfect time to the music. In a matter of moments there was a space cleared for them and the other guests watched on, captivated, as the two glided, spun, and kicked across the floor. As the last notes fell, Bastian twirled Sophia into his arms and dipped her for a final finish. The crowd went wild and Bastian thanked the rosy-cheeked Sophia for the dance. She practically skipped back to the other women, beaming from ear to ear. Bastian couldn't help but feel pleased with himself. The highborn spent years perfecting the steps of traditional dances for occasions like these. And he just dazzled them with a little spontaneity.

Bastian danced with each of the lottery entrants in turn and by the last one, an audience had grown around them and was cheering with enthusiasm. Despite his earlier trepidations, he had to admit to himself that he was having one Shick of a good time.

2

Bastian excused himself from the dancers for a breath of fresh air on the balcony. The stars were bright, and he could hear the faint hum of music rising from the celebration in the town's center. He almost wished that he was down there with those less privileged. The commoners knew how to party better than anyone. With no reputations to uphold or snooty social etiquette, there celebrations were wild. He pulled out his spice box and began rolling himself a puff-stick.

"Roll one for me, won't you, mate?" Felix asked, coming out to join him.

Bastian handed him the rollup he'd just made and rolled himself another.

"Ten cwips says those stiffs will be dancing your steps next week," Felix said.

"Ha! Now that would be a sight I'd pay to see," Bastian laughed.

He pulled out his compass-sized Everfire box and flipped open the lid to reveal the small floating enchanted flame, and they both used it to light their puff-sticks.

"So, are you having fun yet?" Felix asked with his signature grin.

"You're a bastard!"

"Ha-ha, I can't deny that, but you have to admit, that was pretty brilliant! Those birds were practically tripping over themselves to empty their pockets for your *maidenhood,*" Felix laughed.

"You're lucky that was so fruitful, or I wouldn't feel as forgiving. A lottery? I told you I didn't want to pay someone for my coming of age, and you thought reversing that was the solution?"

"I know, genius, right?"

Bastian shook his head. "Shameful. What happened to helping me find a girl that I have chemistry with?"

"What are you whining about? This is perfect! Now you can pick whichever woman you want, and all I need to do is draw her name. You get the girl of your choosing and we make a small fortune, everybody wins. The hard part is going to be picking just one," Felix said.

He gave a low whistle while admiring the women inside through the large glass windows. "It won't be easy. I would gladly bed each and every one of them. They are a stunning bunch, aren't they? Who's your favorite?"

"Who what?" Bastian asked absently, thinking about his last encounter with Gwena.

"Which tapestry…which woman, you nimbat!" Felix said, drawing him back to reality.

"Right, I don't know," Bastian replied, uninterested.

"You know, if you're having trouble narrowing it down, I reckon I could get you two," Felix offered.

"Ha! That's not the problem," Bastian laughed, highly amused by Felix's sincerity with the offering.

He took another drag and looked out at the view over Westdock. He recalled the way Gwena's eyes had met his earlier that day. Was it possible that she could still be interested in him? If only her father hadn't come back so soon, then he would've known for sure.

Felix read him like an open book. "You're thinking about her, aren't you, mate?" he asked.

Bastian leaned over the railing and hung his head. "She does have a bad habit of hijacking my thoughts," he admitted.

Felix leaned on the railing next to him, "Look, mate, I get it, Gwena is one of a kind. Those girls have nothing on her when it comes to personality. But tonight is your Illumine celebration. You're not looking for a good conversation, you're looking for a beautiful woman to make you into a man. What you need is someone with experience. Someone who can show you how it's done in style and ensure that you have one Shick of a time doing it. I guarantee that every one of those birds in there is a perfect candidate for that. Forget about Gwena for one night, and then tomorrow maybe you can start thinking about actually doing something to win her hand for a change," Felix advised.

"Yeah," Bastian said absently.

He knew that Felix couldn't understand. Felix had never been in love. His affections for women fluttered from one to the next, like a butterfly in a field of flowers. Bastian would rather miss his Illumine Day altogether then celebrate it without Gwena. Even if it meant denying his manhood for as long as it took. If only Felix wasn't so determined to see tradition carried out. Luckily the ball was filled with distractions…

"And what about you? Have you had a chance to woo Lady Wendrian?" he asked Felix.

"Not yet, but the night's still young."

"Well, what are you doing wasting your time with me? Hand over the tickets and I'll look after the rest," Bastian said, putting his puff-stick in his mouth and holding out his hands.

Felix eyed him suspiciously. "Why are you so eager to get rid of me?"

"Why should you lose your chance at fun just to draw a name? You're right, any one of those women would be a fine choice. I need to get out of my head and stop spoiling a perfectly good evening," Bastian proclaimed.

Felix's show of suspicion transformed into that of respect. "Well, well, taking matters into your own hands. Bastian Sanders, I'm proud of you. You really are becoming a man," Felix said, clapping him on the shoulder.

"Go on then, Raemeo," Bastian encouraged, and Felix handed over the tickets.

"Oh, and I almost forgot," Felix said, pulling a cream-colored envelope out of his coat pocket and handing it to Bastian.

"What's this?"

"Your real birthday present."

Bastian opened the envelope and pulled out two shiny cobalt-blue tickets with gold writing. "These can't be real?" he asked in disbelief.

"As real as you and me, two first-class tickets to the Heartland on the Equillian Express. I won them with a pair of aces from a pompous cashpot who didn't know when to quit. The Stars have spoken. Looks like we'll have that adventure you've always dreamed of after all, brother," Felix said with a grin.

Bastian read the tickets. "They're for Moonday. That's only a couple of days away."

"Gives us enough time to pack and recover from this evening."

"But what about Jarvis's offer?"

Felix shrugged his shoulders. "Meh, there will be more opportunities in the future. Plenty of time to settle into a career later. We have to work this travel bug out of you first. If it takes leaving home for you to appreciate it, so be it! I can't lie and pretend that I'm not looking forward to it myself. With tonight's winnings, it will be the adventure of a lifetime," Felix said with a grin.

Bastian was awestruck. "Thank you, truly. You don't know how much this means to me."

"I think I know," Felix said.

Then he shuffled his feet uncomfortably. "Well, if I'm going to have a chance at winning the affections of the lady of the hour, I better not waste another minute," he said.

"If she turns you down, I might just think about letting you have one of my runners-up," Bastian jested.

"Don't get greedy now. If you're only going to choose one winner, then it would be rude not to at least offer the others a consolation prize," Felix said in good humor as he made his way to the door. Then he threw Bastian the bag of coin from the lottery entrants. "Hold onto that, I don't trust myself with it. And if I don't see you until tomorrow, brother, make sure you have a bloody good time. If for any reason your *cherry* isn't popped by sunrise, I'm dragging you to the brothels tomorrow!" he promised, and with that he was gone.

3

Bastian drank in his gift. He was delighted by the beauty of the first-class train tickets and the glory of what they promised. His whole life he'd wanted to leave Westdock to see the world. And the Heartland? Wouldn't that be a spectacle! The Heartland was the center of the world and the capital of Equillian. The lord emperor's palace was there, and the Hall of Scientific Study. Plus, all of the major universities and the most prestigious performance halls, not to mention that the Alchemists' House of Discovery was only a stone's throw away in South View. There is so much to see that Bastian didn't even know where they would begin. With the wealth that flowed through there, it would be a prime spot for picking pockets, and if they ever wanted to get a real job, the wages would be far superior to the pay in Westdock. The abundant possibilities and the sunny outlook that now shone on their future excited Bastian and filled him with energy. What had been closed off to him for so long now felt so close he could almost taste it.

Bastian tucked the tickets and the lottery coin away in his pockets and turned his mind to his own personal goal for the evening. He would worry about women and his coming of age later. He had no intention of participating in Felix's lottery, but he would at least draw a false name to keep up appearances once he'd accomplished his own agenda. He knew that if he wanted to get a piece of the Wendrians' wealth, he had to act now. As much fun as it was educating the upper class on freeform dancing, that charade had cost him his invisibility. It would now be ten times harder to go anywhere at the event unnoticed.

He scouted the ballroom through the glass doors. He could see a couple of the women looking for him already, so he needed to move quickly. He looked to the Stars. "Wish me luck," he whispered to them before turning back inside.

Bastian held his head down, weaving between guests to the adjacent hall. Once there, he stuck near the wall as he made his way through the tangle of corridors looking for the heart of the castle. When a guard or guest paid him notice, he put on his best impression of a drunk in search of the toilet. After several random turns, he found himself in a room that was far from the celebration. It was empty except for an extravagant marble staircase with a guard stationed at its foot snoring loudly in a chair. By the smell of it, he'd been sampling the house vintage. Bastian smiled at the sleeping man, silently thanking Lady Luck for his good fortune. He slipped off the guard's silver mask, which was signature to the castle's guard, and put it on himself before ascending the stairs.

4

Bastian made his way down a hallway that had various ornate doors branching off in either direction. He followed it to a set of double doors at the very end. It was a grand mahogany entrance detailed with carvings of dragons and two large brass handles shaped as dragon's heads. These sorts of decorations clearly gave away what the doors were hiding. The highborn thought it quaint to decorate their keeping rooms with the beast that was known for guarding treasure. Bastian tried the handle. It was locked. His heart rate quickened—a locked door exhilarated him because it usually promised something of value behind it. It gave him a thrill to anticipate what might be on the other side. He pulled out his lock-picking kit and within moments the passage was open. He slipped inside and closed the door silently behind him.

Bastian's jaw dropped. Before him was a large, extravagant sitting room, and it glittered. There were golden statues and artifacts on every table. Rare books with gold-lettered bindings lined the walls. Sparkling crystal chandeliers lit with Everfire hung from the ceiling. Fine silver and crystal ware were displayed in an ornate cabinet on the far side of the room. Even the rug was embroidered with golden thread. Bastian had never seen so much splendor in all his life.

In the center was a glass table with a gold egg the size of Bastian's fist. He carefully picked it up. It was heavy, but not as heavy as he imagined it would be. He reluctantly placed it gently back on its bronze stand. As much as he was tempted to place the egg in his pocket, he knew that something that obvious would greatly increase his chances of getting caught. If he was subtle enough with what he took, he could be long gone and have the goods sold before his deeds were discovered. He made his way to a writing desk that was under a tall stained-glass window. Sitting on the desk was a gold-coated quill that he tucked smoothly into his breast pocket, as if it had always belonged there. On a side table there lay a gold and silver chessboard. One side had men of pure gold, and the other side, pure silver. The queens and kings had real sapphires, rubies, and diamonds inlaid in their crowns. He carefully took an equal number of pieces from both sides. He took the silver queen and the gold king, two horses, and four pawns, two of gold and two of silver. He was taking a risk with the royalty, but he couldn't resist the precious stones that rimmed their crowns. He made his way back towards the door, intending to make his exit, when something stopped him. He felt an odd sort of pull towards the egg in the center of the room. He turned and looked back towards it longingly. There was something alluring about it that Bastian couldn't shake. He knew that it would be stupid to take it, but a little voice inside him whispered, Come Moonday, I'll be on a train to the Heartland, far from reach.

He decided impulsively that he couldn't leave without it and doubled back, plucking it from its decorative perch and placing it in his pocket. He slipped out of the keeping room and made his way back down the hallway trying to guess which closed door belonged to Lady Lilliana. He wanted a trinket for Gwena's birthday, the duchess was only a few years older and bound to have something she'd like. The rest of the doors were unlocked. It only took a couple of tries before Bastian found the right one. He slipped inside and closed the door behind him.

Inside, there were beautiful gowns and shoes strung about the room, as if the duchess couldn't decide what to wear. Several jeweled necklaces lay out on her dressing room table in the same indecisive fashion. Bastian opened a silver and turquoise jewelry box and found the rest of her collection. He held himself back from taking the whole lot and only chose one necklace, a small one that had a single blue teardrop pearl on a white gold chain. He thought that its elegant beauty would suit Gwena perfectly. He tucked it delicately into one of the small pockets that she'd sewn inside his jacket, happily knowing that with that item alone, Gwena would have the freedom to change her stars.

A moment later Bastian heard giggling and whispers coming up the hallway. He quickly looked for a place to hide and then dove under the large four-poster bed. Could it be two stray guests? Or worse, Lady Wendrian herself with Lord Bardviss? he wondered.

Seconds later, there was scuffling on the other side of the door. "He-he, oh you scoundrel, you are too much! Quick, in the bedroom before anyone notices us missing," came Lady Lilliana's voice.

"Please, Stars no," Bastian muttered under his breath. Please don't let me get stuck in here with a newly engaged couple, he pleaded silently.

A moment later two bodies tumbled into the room, and Bastian was struck dumb. It wasn't the betrothed couple as he expected, but Lady Lilliana Wendrian and Felix.

Oh, Shick.

He never imagined that Felix would actually be successful in wooing Lady Lilliana Wendrian. She was known as the Jewel of Westdock. Every man and his brother had eyes for her, not to mention that this was her engagement party. But Felix's way with women never ceased to amaze Bastian. His Star-brother had Lady Wendrian in his embrace and was kissing her fervently.

"My lady, you smell and taste of paradise. How anyone so fine could exist as a mere mortal is a complete mystery. Tell me that you were born among the Stars, and I would believe it in a heartbeat," Felix cooed.

Bastian rolled his eyes. He couldn't believe that women lapped up such rubbish.

"Please call me Lilliana. I think we've gotten well beyond such formalities," she said prettily.

Lilliana's beauty was true to her reputation. She was wearing an emerald green ball gown that hugged her slender figure. Her dark red hair held perfect ringlets that were fixed in an elaborate knot with a jeweled barrette. She had walnut brown skin with light freckles along the ridge of her nose and blue sapphire eyes with a yellow ring around the pupils. Her skin and bone structure was flawless, and she had a spark in her nature that reflected Felix's mischievous tone. Bastian could see why he liked her. He waited for Lilliana's back to be turned and then took off his mask and waved from under the bed to get Felix's attention. Felix's eyes widened in surprise when he noticed him. He pointed to Lilliana and gave a thumbs-up, obviously feeling very proud of himself.

Bastian shook his head, unimpressed.

"You have to help me out of here," he mouthed.

Felix ignored him and brought his focus back to Lilliana. "My magnificent darling, that bed of yours looks awfully inviting," he said.

Bastian clenched his jaw. You bastard, don't you dare even think about it.

Lady Wendrian dropped her smile. "James, you know that's to be my wedding bed in two weeks' time," she said, feigning offense.

"Please excuse me, I meant no disrespect. Is there somewhere else where we can get more comfortable, my lady?" Felix asked with a grin.

"Please, disrespect away!" Lilliana giggled, pushing Felix onto the bed and jumping after him.

Bastian took this as an opportunity to cat-crawl towards the exit.

"He-he, I almost forgot about the door," Lilliana laughed, only just seeming to realize that it had been left wide open.

Bastian froze in his tracks, certain he would be discovered. To his relief, Felix diverted Lilliana's attention with a kiss. "Say, did you hear that some lord told Lady Ellington to fire her perfume-smith?" he asked her.

Lilliana laughed. "Did he? About time! I never liked that awful perfume she wears."

"I was thinking the same thing. I would give the man a damn good handshake if I could," Felix replied with a grin.

As Bastian made his way clear of the room he smiled to himself and thought, Felix, you bastard.

5

Bastian put the silver mask back on as he descended the stairs. He was halfway down when he came face to face with Lord Bardviss, who was on his way up in a hurry. He was wearing a purple suit that was a little too small for his tall figure. His short dark grey and brown hair was neatly combed back and his hooked nose gave him the semblance of a falcon. The blood ran out of Bastian's face.

"Good evening, Lord Bardviss!" he greeted loudly and enthusiastically while blocking his way. He hoped that this would be sufficient warning to the party upstairs. Now he just needed to buy them some time. "Congratulations on your engagement, sir," he said politely.

Lord Bardviss looked at him with annoyance. "Thank you," he said rigidly and tried to step past him. Bastian side-stepped in front of him, then Lord Bardviss side-stepped the other way and

Bastian was right there in front. "Ha-ha, so sorry, my lord, we seem to be dancing with each other," he apologized.

"How are you enjoying your evening?" he asked pathetically. The gift of gab was not his strong suit. But suddenly, Lord Bardviss looked interested. "Have you been drinking on duty, soldier?" he asked, turning his full attention to Bastian for the first time.

Bastian faltered, realizing suddenly that he was still wearing the guard's mask and probably smelt strongly of the three overbearingly sweet cocktails he had downed in the ballroom. Luckily, it appeared that in his haste, Lord Bardviss had overlooked the real guard at the base of the stairs.

"No, my lord, I wouldn't dream of such a thing," he said, trying his best to sound hurt by the accusation.

Lord Bardviss studied him warily. "And why, pray tell, have you left your post to explore the Wendrians' private quarters?" he asked pointedly.

"Just doing a routine check, sir, thought I heard some commotion. But not to worry, all is as it should be," he improvised.

Lord Bardviss eyed him suspiciously and then as quick as lightning he grabbed Bastian's wrist and tore off his disguise, looking him square in the face.

Bastian froze and Lord Bardviss's voice became low and mean. "I don't know who you are, boy, or where you acquired that mask, but you aren't allowed to be up here, and if I find out that—"

There was a loud crash from upstairs that sounded like a shattering window, and then a blood-curdling scream. Lord Bardviss stopped mid-sentence. The moment he turned his attention towards the noise, Bastian forced his hand through the weak part of his grip and bolted down the stairs.

Bastian leapt over the last three steps and flew back through the castle until he found himself in the ballroom. A soft waltz played as the guests glided along the floor. There was no way across except to go through the dancers, and Bastian didn't want to risk making a commotion and getting the attention of the guards. He put on his panther mask and then pushed into a dancing couple, "May I have this dance?" he asked.

The gentleman didn't even have a chance to protest before his wife had been whisked away. Bastian mimicked the dancers around him, doing his best to blend in. He didn't bother with the footwork, he just moved in the flowing pattern of the waltz and hoped that it would be sufficient to get him to the other side. His dance partner smiled at him sheepishly. "Are you William?" she asked.

For Shick's sake! Bastian thought. He gave her a curt smile and ignored her. Somehow, she took that as an invitation to continue. "My cousin was just telling me all about you. In fact, she has been looking for you everywhere. There she is now! Olivia! Hey, Olivia, over here! Look who it is!" she called out loudly.

Bastian turned her sharply to the left hoping to silence her, but instead led them straight into a collision with another couple. He started to apologize, when to his horror he saw that it was the peacock woman and a giant of a man he presumed to be Axil.

Lady Ellington stared at him with fire in her eyes. "This, my darling, is the horrible monster who tried to take advantage of me earlier this evening!" she squawked, pointing an accusing finger at Bastian.

"I was just leaving," Bastian said, eyeing the exit, which was only a stone's throw away now.

Axil towered over Bastian with arms the size of small trees, and without hesitation he took a swing at him. Bastian ducked, making the next target his poor innocent dance partner. The woman fell straight to the floor, out cold. Bastian could see her husband shouting indignantly as he made his way across the room. It wasn't long before the man was throwing punches at the giant. All the dancing stopped, and the surrounding guests either cleared the floor or joined the brawl. Bastian could see the women from Felix's lottery scrambling through the chaos towards him. He turned from it all and made a desperate dash out of the ballroom and rounded the corner to the castle's front entryway. There were two guards stationed on either side of the double doors to his escape. He could hear the angry shouts of the lottery entrants behind him as he ran towards the exit. The guards crossed their spears, blocking the entrance. "Halt! State your name and purpose. Why do you flee?!" they commanded.

Bastian didn't stop to answer. He dropped to the floor and slid through the space beneath the crossed spears. He was up on his feet running again before the guards could figure out what happened.

"Stop that boy!" Lord Bardviss's voice came from the castle behind him.

Bastian bolted through the courtyard and into the night. He could hear several foot soldiers in pursuit. He scaled the garden wall and boosted himself onto the nearest rooftop. He crouched low and ran along its length, jumping to the next roof at its end. Westdock's canopy was like a second home to Bastian. It was the one place that he could go as a child where no one bothered him—not even Felix, who was desperately afraid of heights. The other children at the temple had dubbed him Night-walker because he would often slip out the sleeping quarters window like a shadow and not return until the break of dawn. The web of rooftops was his playground, his place of freedom. Up there, there were no rules, no one to tell him what he could or couldn't do, no boundaries or boarders, and no obstacles he couldn't overcome. Leaping across the vast chasms and scaling the high walls made him feel invincible, in a life where he otherwise felt powerless.

Bastian leapt from roof to roof, skillfully maneuvering his way across Westdock until he had gotten well clear of the castle grounds and had arrived back at his and Felix's small hovel in town.

It was a loft above a butcher's shop. The butcher let them rent it for practically nothing because their only entry and exit point was a high-sitting window. Bastian checked to make sure that he'd lost the guards tailing him before scaling the building and slipping inside.

He sighed in relief now that he was home. Their small Everfire lamp cast shadows across the walls. It was a single room with a separate half bath. The space was just big enough for the two cots, small writing desk, and bedside table that occupied it. Bastian collapsed onto his mattress. He hoped that Felix had made it out. He recalled the scream that had come from the castle bedroom and prayed it wasn't inspired by something sinister. By the sounds he heard, Bastian imagined that Felix had broken the window and found something to assist his descent. Maybe Felix breaking the glass and jumping out the window had scared Lady Lilliana. He could only hope that he was right.

Bastian rolled to his side and felt a lump poking into him. He was instantly reminded of the treasure and coin that loaded his pockets. He rolled off his bed and pushed it aside. Underneath was a loose floorboard that he pulled up to reveal a small hiding space. Nestled inside was his and Felix's life savings. It wasn't much, but with the added winnings from the castle, it became a small fortune. Bastian carefully stored the loot and smiled to himself, thinking that maybe they would be able to change their Stars after all. He replaced the board and looked at his pocket watch. It was three minutes until midnight, the hour of Shick the Star Stirrer and the dawn of his Illumine Day. He was still charged on adrenaline, and his head was swimming with Dutch courage from the castle's cocktails. In that moment he felt like anything was possible. All he needed was a woman to help him kiss his childhood good-bye. He took out the pearl necklace, and Gwena's full lips and curvaceous figure flooded his thoughts. The reality of her being his Sweet Sixteen felt like such an impossibility.

"Shick it," he declared to the empty room, standing decidedly.

He knew right then that if he didn't at least try to win her that night, he would regret it for the rest of his life.

TORN

CHAPTER FOUR

It didn't take Bastian long to reach the tailor's. He crept around back to Gwena's window and threw pebbles at it. A minute later Gwena opened it and looked out.

"Who's there?" she whispered to the night.

Bastian stepped into the moonlight, his face concealed behind the panther mask, and bowed. "My lady."

Gwena recognized him at once. "Bastian! What are you doing here?" she asked in a loud whisper.

He took off his disguise and climbed up to the window. The lamplight illuminated Gwena's face, and it was clear that she'd been crying. She turned away from him, and Bastian hurried in to her side.

Her room felt cold and empty. In an instant Bastian felt sober and forgot why he'd come. "What's the matter?" he asked.

Gwena shook her head, fighting back tears, and Bastian knew instantly that something was desperately wrong. Gwena was the strongest person he knew—he'd never seen her this upset. After a moment she managed to compose herself.

"My father discovered that the suit I lent to Felix was missing," she said in a shaky whisper. Bastian's gut wrenched. He knew what her father was like.

"Lord Bardviss came here to collect it. He'd ruined his intended attire for the ball and wanted to wear the one I'd made. He offered my father three times the amount the suit was worth to have it finished. When I said that it wasn't available, Lord Bardviss accused my father of selling it to another customer. He said he would ruin my father's business! I couldn't stand to see him suffer for something that was my fault. So, I told Lord Bardviss it was my doing, that I'd made a mistake on his suit and destroyed the evidence, hoping to make him a new one before it was due to be collected. After that he left us alone, but my father was furious."

Gwena looked up at Bastian with despair in her eyes. "He left for the pub and I thought it was finished." She looked away. "But when he came back he was drunk, he was so angry. I have never seen him like that. He took off his belt and he…he beat me," she said with disbelief. "He said that I was good for nothing and that he couldn't even pay someone to marry me," she said distantly.

Bastian pulled Gwena into his arms and hugged her. "Gwena, you are the most incredible soul I know, a star in a dark world that brings light to everything it touches. How anyone could ever think ill of you is beyond me," he said, and she buried her head in his chest and let her tears flow freely. Overwhelming anger rose up inside Bastian. He wanted to go downstairs to confront Gwena's father, but even in Bastian's intoxicated state he knew that wouldn't help anything. He felt useless. The only girl he'd ever cared for was reduced to tatters, and he didn't know how to take her pain away. He squeezed her and Gwena winced. Bastian quickly let go.

"Did I hurt you?"

Gwena's face contorted in pain. "It's ok, it's just where the belt hit me."

"How bad is it? Let me see!" Bastian commanded.

She stepped back from him. "No, it's ok, really, it's nothing," she said, trying to smile through her agony.

Bastian looked her dead in the eyes. "Gwena, please?" he asked gently.

She hesitated, and he could tell that she didn't want him to know how badly her father had hurt her. But the wound would need attending to, and she couldn't do it alone. She slowly turned her back to him and lowered her shawl so he could unfasten her dress. The fabric was torn and stained with blood. Bastian's chest tightened as he undid the buttons and gently loosened the lace on her bodice undergarment, revealing several red lash marks. Her father's belt had split her skin in a couple of places, leaving two open gashes on her back. Bastian's anger grew but he held his tongue. He knew that it took a lot for Gwena to show him this, and it would take little for her to hide it away.

"Do you have bandages and salt water?" he asked, straining every fiber of his being to keep himself from going down to Gwena's father and beating him to a pulp.

Gwena pointed to her washing station. There was already a pile of torn rags and a small bag of salt on the table. "There's hot salt water in the basin," she said.

Bastian took off his jacket and pulled Gwena's stool over for her. She sat with her back to him and timidly let the top of her dress fall to her waist, then held the fabric of her bodice and shawl to her chest. Bastian blushed at the sight of her exposed skin. He soaked one of the rags in the salted water before using it to gently dab her open wounds. She gasped at the sting, then bit her lip to quiet herself.

There was a long moment of silence between them as he patched her. Bastian didn't know what to say. How could her father do such a thing? He'd always been strict with Gwena, but this was unforgivable. Once Bastian finished dressing her wounds, he helped her to stand.

"You must be exhausted," he said.

Gwena nodded.

"Let's get you into something more comfortable, where do you keep your nightclothes?"

"Second drawer down," Gwena said, nodding to her wardrobe. Bastian opened the drawer and retrieved a plain white cotton nightgown.

"Can you help me?" she asked. "I can barely lift my arms."

"Of course."

Gwena turned her back to him and dropped her dress to the floor. The sight of her perfect bare form made Bastian fumble with the fabric in his hands. He silently cursed himself, feeling like a school boy. He never had that problem with other girls, but somehow Gwena reduced him to a bumbling fool. Bastian composed himself and then helped her step out of her dress and pulled the nightgown gently over her head and onto each arm. Then he helped her to her bed and pulled the blanket gently over her. Gwena grabbed his hand. "Don't go," she whispered. "I wouldn't dream of it," Bastian said. He sat down on the floor beside her with her hand in his. A minute later Gwena was asleep.

The silhouette of her beauty was highlighted by the moonlight streaming in through the large round window. Bastian tried to take a mental picture of her like that, peaceful and perfect. The wind blew the branches of the trees outside, making their shadows dance across the floor. He watched the shadow play for a time and reflected on the evening's events. Even though the night had ended in tragedy, there was nowhere else he would have rather been. "I love you, Gwen," he whispered to her sleeping form, and then he was asleep.

2

Bastian was woken early the next morning by the sun pouring in through Gwena's window. He was still sitting on the floor leaning against her bed with her hand in his. A minute later Gwena opened her brilliant seafoam green eyes and Bastian smiled in greeting.

"How are you feeling?" he asked.

"Better," Gwena said, smiling in return. "Have you been on the floor all night?" she asked in surprise.

"Ye-ess…," Bastian answered awkwardly.

"Bastian, I…thank you," she said, and Bastian could see the depth of her sincerity.

"Don't mention it. Do you mind if I sit on the bed? My ass is killing me."

"Of course not," Gwena laughed.

Bastian climbed up beside her.

"Happy birthday, Bastian Sanders," she said.

"Ha! That's right, I almost forgot. Do I look any older?" he asked.

"Much," Gwena smirked. Then her smile faded. "I'm sorry that I put such a damper on your birthday celebration. Were you going to sneak me out to a party?" she asked. Bastian cleared his throat and looked down at his hands. "Yeah, something like that.

You have nothing to apologize for at any rate, I'm just glad that I was here."

"Me too," Gwena said, smiling gratefully. "Did you have fun at the castle at least?" she asked.

"It depends on your idea of fun. You could say it was… eventful."

"Ha-ha, I won't even ask," Gwena laughed.

"Speaking of the castle, I have something for you," Bastian said.

"Something for me on your birthday?"

"Just a little something. I was going to save it for your naming day, but I don't have that kind of patience," he said, then used sleight of hand to make the necklace from the castle appear out of thin air. The blue pearl glistened in the morning's light.

Gwena's face lit up, and she took it into her hands with delight. "Bastian, it's beautiful!" Then her smile faded. "Where did you get this?" she asked accusingly.

"You should never ask a question that you don't want the answer to," he warned.

"Bastian! Did you steal this from the castle?"

"What does it matter? It won't be missed."

"I can't accept this! You need to give it back."

"And risk getting thrown in the Wendrians' dungeon? Gwena, nobody deserves this more than you do. I'm not giving it back, so you may as well enjoy it. Unless you would rather have me trade it for coin?" he asked.

"No! I mean, if you're not going to return it, I'll keep it," she said, admiring the necklace despite her objections.

Bastian laughed. "Here, let me help you put it on," he said and clasped the white gold chain around her neck. "It suits you."

Gwena smiled. "A necklace like this would suit anyone."

Bastian admired the happiness that his gift had brought her before saying, "You know, with the coin from selling that piece alone, you could leave this place and start a new life somewhere."

"And go where, do what?" she asked with humor.

"Anything you like. You could set up in South View or the Heartland. With your skills in tailoring, you can make far better coin there than you ever will in Westdock. Or you could become a magician like you've always wanted."

"A magician? I haven't thought about being a magician since I was a child!" Gwena said.

"Come on, don't tell me that you've lost your interest in magic? I remember when we went to see Madam Pomphrey and the travelling curiosities as if it was yesterday. I'll never forget how happy it made you. Surely, you haven't forgotten?" Bastian asked.

"Of course not. I was dying to see that show, but my father wouldn't let me, and you showed up here at my window with tickets and snuck me out so I could see it," she recounted.

"I risked my neck nicking those tickets."

"You told me that you were given them!" Gwena said hitting him playfully with the pillow.

Bastian laughed while blocking the attack. "Only because I knew you wouldn't go otherwise. After the show you wanted to run away and join the act. You went to see Madam Pomphrey to ask if you could be her apprentice…and then you chickened out and offered her a discount on a tailor service instead!" he laughed.

"True, I lost my nerve like the best of cowards. Mostly because I realized that my father would've killed me."

Bastian regarded her with a serious expression. "It's not too late, you know," he said in earnest.

"Too late for what?" she asked, with laughter in her eyes.

"To become a magician! I can see it now." Bastian stood up on the bed and pretended to be an announcer. "Come one, come all, come and see Gwena the Great, Madam Mystique, Mistress of Magic!" he declared dramatically. Gwena pulled him back down to the bed. "Don't be ridiculous, that was just a silly childhood dream!" she laughed.

"Just a silly childhood dream? Who convinced you that your dreams are silly? Was it your father?"

"Oh, come on. We have to grow up sometime, Bastian. How in this world could I be a magician? People like you and I don't have the privilege of pursuing our dreams. We're lucky if we can keep fresh bread on the table. Dreams are for children and the wealthy. The closest I'll ever get to being a real magician is making their costumes and bags. And I should be grateful for that. Most have less."

Bastian was devastated to hear her speak that way—she had always been so passionate about pursuing magic. "That's the biggest load of rot I've ever heard! Since when did you become so pessimistic?"

"It's not pessimism, it's realism. What good does it do me to hope for something more, when I'll only be setting myself up for disappointment?" she asked.

"No. You're setting yourself up for disappointment right now, the greatest disappointment there is and the only one that truly matters," Bastian said ardently.

"How so?" she asked.

Bastian sat up. "When I was living with the Order, the sick and the old would come to the temple to die. And the sisters would sit and talk with them. They keep a record of the things people value the most, their happiest moments, and their greatest regrets. Do you know what the most common regret is?" he asked.

"What?"

"Living the life that was expected of them, instead of the life that was true to themselves. This is your life, Gwen, no one else's. You have to make it exactly what you want it to be, and don't you dare settle for anything less. If you want to be a magician, then by Shick, you shall be one!" he said fervently.

Gwena smiled, but her eyes said that happiness was a luxury meant for someone else. Bastian studied her. "Let me take you away from this place," he said evenly.

The humor drained from Gwena's eyes. "I can't…my father needs me here," she said, and averted her gaze.

"Your father? After what he did to you last night, you'd be a fool to stay with him! I swear if he ever touches you again, Gwen… Stars help him, because I will not be able to stay my hand a second time."

A shadow passed over Gwena's face. "I know what it looks like, and I know that it's impossible for you or anyone else to understand. But my father is a good man, and he loves me. It won't happen again," she said stubbornly.

Bastian sighed. He knew that he'd overstepped his bounds. But he couldn't just turn a blind eye—he cared about her too much. "I'm sorry, that was unfair. I know he's your dad, and it's not my place," he said and started over, this time treading more delicately. "You see the good in everyone, it's one of the things I've always admired about you. But Gwen, you have to look at the facts. Your father hurt you, he hurt you bad. Both physically and emotionally, and now that the line has been crossed, there's no guarantee it won't happen again."

Gwena frowned. Bastian could see that she knew he was right but didn't want to admit it to herself.

"I can't leave him, Bastian. Ever since my mum died he hasn't been the same. I just know that if he loses me too, it will be the end of him."

"He's a grown man. Your mother died five years ago. Your father was left with a daughter to look after, and instead you've been looking after him! If he hasn't gotten better with the gift of your love after all these years, then he never will. He has no one to blame but himself for that. We are the masters of our own destiny. Please don't let him ruin yours."

Gwena looked out the window. "If we were to leave, where would we go? What would we do?" she asked in earnest. And Bastian's heart leapt at the possibility.

"We would start in the Heartland and from there we could go anywhere, do anything! We can see the world and have the adventure that we've always imagined," he said.

"It sounds like an impossible dream."

"It doesn't have to be," Bastian said gently.

"We don't even have the means to leave Westdock. This necklace wouldn't be enough for more than one of us. How could we ever find the coin to make such things possible?" she asked, meeting his eyes.

Bastian retrieved his coat. He pulled the train tickets out of his pocket and placed them in her hands.

"What's this?"

"The tickets to changing our stars," he answered evenly.

Gwena looked at the train tickets in disbelief. "Are these real?"

Bastian smiled and said, "Felix won them in a game of cards. With our savings and what he and I acquired last night, we could easily purchase one more and have enough coin to start the three of us off."

Gwena gazed down at the tickets and he could see her eyes spark with hope, then cloud with uncertainty. "These are for Moonday."

"Is that a problem?"

"It's just so soon…"

"As I recall, just yesterday, you said that you wish you could live in our childhood forever. Well, the Stars have smiled on us. This is our chance. Just think of it, the three of us together again, taking on the Heartland. Together, we can accomplish anything!"

Gwena smiled at his enthusiasm. She studied the tickets in silence for several minutes and Bastian waited patiently.

"May the Stars have mercy on us," she said at last.

"Is that a yes?!"

"Yes," she said with resolve. "You're right, I need to stop living my life for someone else. I won't pretend that I'm not a little terrified, or that it's not going to be incredibly hard for me to walk away from my father, but after last night…," Gwena trailed off in thought. "He's an adult. Maybe he'll do a better job of looking after himself without me around to do it for him. And nothing would make me happier than to run away with you on an adventure to write our own destinies," she concluded fervently.

"Like old times, eh?" Bastian said with a grin.

Gwena laughed with joy and hugged him.

They held the embrace for several long moments and the question of Gwena's feelings towards him rose to mind. Was something there or was it just his imagination? He had to know. If they were going to the Heartland together, it would kill him to be around her all the time with that question unanswered. But then, if he asked and she didn't have feelings for him, it would make their time together that much more awkward. He was between a rock and a hard place and knew he was most likely screwed either way. Gwena pulled from his arms to ask a question.

"Just out of curiosity, why did you come here last night?"

Oh, Shick.

"Um…about that," he said, scratching his head uncomfortably.

Gwena read his discomfort and raised an eyebrow at him. Then her eyes widened with realization. "Wait, you weren't going to ask me to be your Sweet Sixteen, were you?" she asked in surprise.

"No! I mean…maybe. Gwen, I've been meaning to tell you this for a long time. I just didn't want to mess things up between us. I…I have kinda been in love with you since…well, forever," he said, looking down at his hands. There, it's done. Stars have mercy on me. He looked up to see Gwena smiling at him. Oh Stars, now she's laughing at me. You've built your pyre now, stupid, he said to himself and ran his hand nervously through his hair. "Look, I don't expect you to feel the same way…and I never expected anything…it was just that Felix was trying to set me up with these girls at the castle who just weren't my type and I had one too many cocktails and got all caught up in the Illumine Day thing…anyway it was just a stupid idea…," Bastian stammered.

He looked up sheepishly to see Gwena's smile turn into a grin, and then she kissed him. Bastian looked at her in surprise, then closed his eyes and kissed her back, tenderly wrapping her body in his arms. All of time seemed to stop, and the warmth of her embrace felt like the sun on his heart after a long winter. He couldn't believe he was kissing her. He never thought this would actually happen, and its sweetness was beyond anything he'd imagined.

The moment was broken by the sound of shattering glass. Gwena pulled away nervously. "You have to go. If my father caught us like this, he would have our heads!"

"Let him find us, I don't care!"

"Well, I do! Soon we'll be gone, but in the meantime, please don't make this harder than it already is," Gwena said pleadingly.

"Come with me, there's no need for you to face that man again after what he did. You owe him nothing."

"That man is my father! I'll never be able to live with myself if I leave without saying goodbye," she said stubbornly.

Bastian looked at her with concern, "He'll never let you go, Gwen."

"It'll be fine! I need to pack my things anyway. I'll come to your house tonight after I deal with things here," she promised.

Bastian didn't like the idea of leaving her alone in the same house with her father, but he knew that he couldn't sway her. "Meet us at the Tipsy Tav'. They have a good cheap feed on Star-days. We should be there around the Thrixing Hour," he said.

"I'll be there," Gwena smiled.

"If you can't make it for whatever reason, you remember where our place is, right?"

"Of course, the window above the butcher's on Tucker."

"Perfect." Bastian smiled, then he looked at her protectively. "If your father does anything to hurt or upset you…"

"I'll be fine, now go!" Gwena said.

Bastian nodded reluctantly. "Until tonight then," he said, grabbing his coat and making his way towards the window.

"And Bastian," Gwena called after him in a loud whisper.

He turned.

"I have loved you since forever too."

Bastian headed towards the loft. The early morning sun was creeping up the walls of the buildings, bathing them in golden light. The dull colors of the alley were suddenly vibrant, his surroundings brighter and more beautiful than he'd ever cared to notice. Bastian felt an overwhelming optimism and had a bounce in his step, as if he were walking on clouds. He couldn't believe that Gwena had kissed him, and to top it off, she was coming to the Heartland. Bastian could still taste the subtle sweetness of her lips and longed to have her back in his arms. He reveled in the confession of her love. Suddenly, everything he'd always dreamed of was coming to pass. "Thank you, Serendipity," he muttered gratefully and jumped into the air boosting himself off a wall in delight.

He reached their small hovel and slipped in through the window. There was no sign that Felix had been back. Bastian guessed he'd spent the night with a girl and wouldn't return until later. But the thought tugged at his conscience, that if Felix hadn't made it out of the castle, then he could be strung up in the Wendrians' personal jail, or worse, lying in a ditch decorated with Lord Bardviss's vengeance.

Why do you always have to play with fire, brother? Bastian thought.

He had to find him. It was market day, he and Felix picked pockets there every week without fail. He might have headed there already, hoping to find Bastian. It was a good place to start anyway. If he wasn't there or back home by noon, then Bastian would allow himself to worry. He changed out of his suit into his common garb and then decided to put his suit jacket back on. The pockets that Gwena had incorporated into it were incredibly useful, especially if he was going to be carrying stolen artifacts in a public space. He took out the train tickets and tucked them safely away beneath the floorboards before setting out to find Felix.

4

Bastian weaved through the backstreets just as Westdock was waking up and coming to life. He passed the bakery and breathed in the rich smell of freshly baked sweet bread. He made his way towards the harbor, reaching the shore just in time to see the last fishing boats heading out to sea. As Bastian walked along the boardwalk, he played with the Wendrians' trinkets in his pockets. He hoped that Guido would be at the market. Guido handled illegal merchandise for the black market, disguising himself as a finery merchant. Bastian didn't like the man, but he bought most of his and Felix's findings without asking questions, a quality that was hard to find in Westdock. The trick was locating him—he didn't always attend the Starday market and he didn't have a permanent shop front. If Bastian palmed off the stolen goods now, he'd be rid of them before the Wendrians knew they were missing. He turned the corner and walked up the stone steps to the plaza. There were already several stalls set up for the market and many more that were being erected. He climbed to the top of a large rock outcropping that overlooked the town's center. Bastian and Felix had dubbed the perch the crow's-nest. They used it as a lookout to scout the crowd every market day. It allowed them to select their targets before heading in. The market was a pickpocket's paradise, plenty of options and enough chaos that you were almost guaranteed to never be noticed. He scanned the quickly growing crowd for Felix, but he was nowhere to be seen. Bastian watched the rest of the stalls come to life before he spotted Guido's patchwork tent. Suddenly Bastian felt nervous. He'd never gone to Guido's tent alone. Felix always negotiated their sales. *Damn you, Felix, where are you?* It didn't matter now—there was no time to wait for him. Bastian needed to get rid of the stolen goods while he had the opportunity. He put his hands in his pockets and headed for the busy market.

5

Guido's tent looked small from the outside, but once you stepped into it, the place was incredibly roomy. It had rows of wooden display cabinets with frosted glass shelves that housed a variety of gaudy decorative wares. Of course, it was all just a front for what he really specialized in: enchanted objects. The alchemists' creations had been outlawed for almost three decades, making them prime merchandise for the black market. The only hint of Guido's dodgy dealings were the two large guards stationed inside the entrance. Guido stood behind the counter studying a gemstone through a monocular loupe. He was a stout man, short in stature with a hard, round sort of face with big arching brows and a large frowning mouth that resembled a toad.

"If it isn't my favorite pair of pinchers. Have anything interesting for me?" Guido asked, keeping his eyes on his gemstone.

Bastian placed one of the gold pawns on the counter in front of him. Guido picked it up and held it to the light, then pricked it with a fine pin. "It's solid, but it's not worth much without the set. How much are you asking?"

"All I want is a fair price for the gold it's made of, you can melt it down for all I care."

Guido lifted an eyebrow and looked at him for the first time since he'd come in. "Where's your brother?" he asked, finally noticing Felix's absence.

"Busy."

"He's better at this than you," Guido said bluntly.

Bastian couldn't argue with that. Felix was a million times better at this than he was. He always created stories around the merchandise to give it value. Felix would've said something like: *The piece was sculpted by an artist to symbolize how we're all pawns of the Stars no matter how high we're born. It originally belonged to the princess of the Spotted Isles and has been passed down through our family for generations. It is our dear grandma's pride and joy. We're only selling it now because we need the money for our sick cousin.* Bastian, on the other hand, had never been good at spinning lies, and he wasn't about to embarrass himself trying.

"Do you have any more pieces?" Guido asked.

Bastian fished through his pockets and pulled out the other chess pieces he'd taken and lined them up on the counter. Guido arched his eyebrows in appreciation. He began to reach for the queen when one of his guards came up beside him and whispered something in his ear. Guido paused. "Excuse me for a moment," he said and ducked through the curtain behind him.

Bastian tapped his fingers nervously on the counter beside the chess pieces. He didn't like the way this transaction was going. If there was anyone else in town whom he could pawn the items to he would have left in that moment, but there wasn't. He looked around the shop and caught the two guards watching him intently. He waited another few moments and then the feeling of unease in his gut became impossible to ignore.

Right, he thought, I'll have to wait to trade in the Heartland. This isn't bloody worth it.

He pocketed the chess pieces and made his way towards the door, but the guards barred the exit.

"Going so soon?" Guido croaked behind him.

Bastian turned. "I have things I have to do, Guido. I can't afford to be kept waiting."

"Well, that's too bad, because you're going to have to be. You see, it has come to my attention that the pieces you're carrying have been reported as stolen from the Wendrians' castle," he said abruptly.

Bastian's gut tightened. How in the nine realms of darkness did that get out so quickly? he wondered. "Since when have you ever cared about where your goods come from?"

"Since your link to the duchess's disappearance has made the prize for your capture far more valuable than your trinkets."

"My link to the duchess's disappearance?" Bastian asked in surprise.

How could he be linked to something that he knew nothing about? And then the previous night flashed back to him. Lord Bardviss had seen him flee directly after Lady Lilliana's scream. If she and Felix left together before Lord Bardviss had reached Lilliana's bedroom, then Bastian would be the only connection to her disappearance.

"No hard feelings, I hope. I'm sure you can understand that this is purely business," Guido said with a sly grin.

Bastian shrugged. "I guess that's the price I pay for dealing with honorless swine."

"Take him out back!" Guido scowled.

The guards started closing in on Bastian, forcing him into the corner of the tent. He backed up until he was between two display cases, then planted his foot firmly on one of the shelves beside him and waited for his opportunity. As soon as the guards were within reach, he boosted himself above their heads and stepped nimbly across their shoulders. The men furiously clutched at his heels, but they were too slow. Bastian jumped to the floor past them and slid to the far wall of the tent, rolling beneath the flap into the busy market.

"After him!" Guido ordered.

In a matter of seconds, Bastian vanished into the crowd. He got halfway across the plaza before stopping behind a weaver's tent to regain himself. His head was spinning, his crime just became a lot more serious, and he couldn't afford to get captured. Suddenly the sound of trumpets filled the market and the crowd began clearing a path. Bastian looked up to see the castle's personal guard pouring into the plaza with Lord Bardviss at their head.

"Shick have mercy," he muttered.

"There he is, me lord!" a squire called, pointing at Bastian.

Bastian froze, cursing himself for wearing the suit jacket from the night before. Lord Bardviss looked at him and recognition bloomed across his face.

Bastian ran.

"Catch that boy! At all costs, do not let him get away!" Lord Bardviss bellowed.

Bastian weaved his way through the market. He cursed the crowd for parting for the castle's men instead of being angry obstacles and camouflage like any useful mob. Two guards were coming up on either side of him, working together to corner him amongst the food stalls. Bastian cat-jumped over a fruit stand and dashed between them making a beeline towards the wharf. He could hear the guards cursing behind him as they muscled their way through the vendors, knocking down everything in their path. "Stop, you fiend!" Lord Bardviss roared at the head.

Bastian doubled his pace. He reached the wharf and turned down the shoreline towards the vast web of alleyways that led to the underbelly of Westdock. But he was too late. There was already a group of guards waiting for him. He turned back the other way and found himself surrounded by the castle's men on all sides. There was only one direction remaining that was free of adversaries: a dock behind him that ran out to sea. There was an ornate merchant ship just leaving its ramp, and Bastian made a desperate run for it. The guards followed in hot pursuit. He pushed himself with every last ounce of energy he had to stay ahead of them. As he reached the end of the pier, he leapt off its boards with all his might, barely managing to grab the tail of a carved wooden mermaid that decorated the ship's stern. He hung onto the back corner of the richly adorned exterior by his fingertips and thanked the Stars for his narrow escape. He turned and saw Lord Bardviss catching up with the guards at the end of the pier. He shook his fist at Bastian. "If I find out that you have laid a hand on Lilliana, I will destroy you!" he yelled in anger. Then he turned to the castle's men. "Send my best galleon after him. I want that ship at the bottom of the ocean by nightfall!" he commanded.

The guards dispersed to follow his order. Bastian tried to ignore the future problem and focused on climbing the ship's wooden embellishments of billowing waves and mermaids that was before him.

Once he reached the top, he peered over the back railing and was relieved to find the poop deck unmanned. Hoisting himself onto it, he quickly looked for a place to hide. The last thing he wanted was to get kicked off before they'd cleared the cove. There was a large pile of heavy rope and a couple of barrels in the corner, which he managed to reposition to create a small hiding place. He tucked himself between them so he was almost completely obscured from view. Then he relaxed, and the exhaustion from the events of the last twenty-four hours hit him like a ton of bricks. He was finally floating away from Westdock.

It was something he'd dreamed of doing for years, but not like this, not when he was so close to leaving with Gwena and Felix in a first-class train carriage. His mind looped over the thought of Gwena waiting for him and his spirit sunk into an ocean of anguish. And what was all that about the duchess missing? Could Felix really have run away with Lady Lilliana Wendrian? *That dog.* If he had feelings for the Jewel of Westdock, Stars help him, he would have much bigger problems than Bastian did. It would explain why Felix had never come home. At least he knew that Felix hadn't been caught. If he had, they wouldn't have been chasing Bastian. But if Felix and Lady Lilliana had run away together, then Felix wouldn't be able to help Gwena. And as long as Felix was with the duchess, he was in danger. Bastian knew that the castle would use all its resources to find her, and when they did, they'd be looking for someone to blame. He was too tired to think about it, and too tired to fight the dark cloud that consumed him. "Look after yourself, brother. And you Gwen, my love. I'll be back as soon as I can, I promise," he whispered, and then mercifully, sleep took him.

GWENA
CHAPTER FIVE

Gwena sat on the end of her bed, smiling at the memory of Bastian confessing his feelings for her. She had loved him since the moment he'd rescued her doll at the Star Temple. To know that he'd shared her affection over all these years was a dream. The past twenty-one hours had been both too horrible and too lovely to be true. But the wounds from her father's belt and the lingering presence of Bastian's musky sweet scent attested to their reality. She was torn between following the love that burned in her heart and the loyalty she felt towards her father, but she knew Bastian was right. Her father would never change unless everything else around him did first. It still tortured her to think of how destroyed he would be to lose her. She wanted to talk to him, to heal what had been broken, but she didn't know how and wasn't even sure it could be done. They never spoke to each other about their feelings. Ever since Gwena's mother had died, her father had grown distant. They never talked about what had happened to her, each of them suffering the loss silently in their own way. Her father drowned himself in drink and poured himself into his work. Gwena cried silently when she was alone, until time finally healed the hole inside of her. If they couldn't talk about her mother's passing, how could they ever talk about this?

After Bastian left, Gwena had gone downstairs to investigate the noise they'd heard. Her father was fast asleep, snoring lightly. He'd knocked a drinking glass from his bedside table and it had shattered across the floor. The scattered shards were a perfect portrait of her and her father's relationship, too broken to be put back together. She knew that he would most likely sleep into the afternoon unless she woke him. He always overslept after a night of drinking.

She decided then that she didn't want to be there when he woke. Maybe because it was for the best, or maybe simply because it was easier. Either way, she didn't care. She had sacrificed so much for her him and for what, to be mistreated and taken for granted? Bastian was right, she owed her father nothing. Why should she miss Bastian's birthday to face him after what he'd done? She wasn't going to let him waste another moment of her life. She would go to Bastian and Felix's place and never look back. And come Moonday, the three of them would be on their way to the Heartland to change their stars.

Resolute, she went back to her room and took out her mother's quiver travelling bag, a long cylindrical container made of hard brown leather that could be carried on her back like a quiver of arrows. They were the height of fashion years before Gwena was born, and though they'd gone out of style, she'd always adored it. She packed the few belongings that she owned. Her mother's old travelling cloak, a small sewing kit, a couple of dresses, and the few coins she had. She put on her mother's favorite blue dress and tied her hair back in a knot. Then she put on her tailor's gauntlet and set to work. Her father had given her the leather arm piece for her twelfth birthday. It was the year she'd left school to start working for him. She'd worn it so much that it felt like a part of her. Gwena took out a suit that she'd started as a gift for her father's birthday several months before. It was made with fine royal blue spider silk and only lacked the final touches. She located Lord Bardviss's file and adjusted the suit to his measurements. She then embellished it with gold stitching and added fine embroidery of an insignia combining the Wendrians' house sign with Lord Bardviss's on the breast pocket. Looking it over, she was satisfied. The suit was beautiful. Gwena knew that Lord Bardviss would have nothing to complain about and that smoothing things over with him would be a far greater departing gift for her father than the suit itself. She folded it neatly and placed it on the end of her bed, and then packed her gauntlet with the rest of her things. She should've known better than to have loaned the original suit to Felix. That didn't warrant the actions that followed, but she couldn't help feeling guilty. She pitied her father—even though she didn't want to stay with him, she knew his weakness and his suffering, and through all of his faults she still loved him. She pulled out a page of parchment with a pen and inkpot and wrote:

Dear Papa,
I forgive you. I hope that you can also one day forgive me for leaving.
I have always been so concerned about your happiness that I have neglected to consider my own.
Now the Stars have offered me a chance at the greatest happiness I could ever imagine, and I am taking it.
I hope with all my heart that you find yours.
Love always,
Gwena

She placed the letter on top of the suit and shouldered her travelling bag before making her way silently down the stairs, tiptoeing passed her father's bedroom. The shop was still and well lit by the Everfire lanterns in the upper corners. Everything was in its place and well organized, just as it always had been. There were racks of ready-made suits and dresses, an array of fine fabrics folded neatly on the shelves on the wall, and a mannequin wearing a jacket in progress in the corner. Bow ties and pocket squares of every color were arranged carefully on the center table, and fine cufflinks and elegant pins were laid out for show inside the glass sales counter. A hatstand laden with the latest fashion stood near the door like an old friend, leaning towards the display window as if having a conversation with the mannequin there wearing a pink and green dress. Gwena could have navigated the place with her eyes shut, it was so familiar. It had hardly changed since she was a child, and in the last few years she'd had more interaction with the inanimate objects in that room than she'd had with the outside world. It felt so safe and predictable—everything that the outside world wasn't. But the dusk of her childhood was at hand. She would be a woman next month. The time for familiar comforts was over. Every young bird had to leave the nest if they wanted to learn to fly, and Gwena most certainly did. "Good-bye, friends," she whispered to the room, saying farewell to her childhood, the only home she'd ever known and everything in it. And then she stepped out the door.

2

Gwena made her way towards Tucker Street. Once she found the butcher's, she went around back and looked up at the window that led to Bastian and Felix's loft. She cursed silently, seeing that the only way up was by a series of wooden pegs protruding from the wall. She was going to have to scale them, which would be uncomfortably cumbersome in a dress. She made sure no one was looking before she tucked her skirt into her undergarments and made the climb.

Gwena knocked on the closed window. "Bastian, Felix?" she called, but there was no reply. She tried the latch and it opened easily. Without waiting for an invitation, she climbed inside. This was her first time in their lodging. The room was small but homey. She smiled to herself—the place was a perfect illustration of Bastian and Felix. She could easily tell which side belonged to whom. Felix's bed was neatly made and his clothes hung on the rafters above it in an orderly fashion. There was a small writing desk across from his bed that was covered with fastidiously written papers, organized inkpots, and a selection of pens and quills. A pile of nonfiction books were stacked neatly on the floor next to his bed, doubling as a bedside table. A pair of dice rested on the top of the pile next to a cheap bottle of spiced wine and a short glass. Bastian's half of the room was almost the complete opposite. His bed was unmade, and clothes were piled on the floor underneath the few that were hanging. There was a box next to his bed filled with parts from disassembled locks and pocket watches, along with some handmade metal tools. The dark leather satchel that he often carried hung from the bedpost. He had a humble bedside table that had a whittling knife and a small, half-finished wood carving of a whale on it. Next to those two items he had stacked three books, *Maps of Equillian*, *The Mechanics of Things vol. 3*, and a copy of *The Words of the Watchers*. The last book was a collection of articles written in verse that pertained to wisdom from and about the Stars, some of the pieces dating back over two thousand years.

Gwena could tell that Bastian had been there recently because his green suit pants were hanging up, one of the only garments he'd bothered to put away properly. She noted that Felix's borrowed suit wasn't there, which meant that he was either still wearing it or hadn't come home. She picked up Bastian's copy of *The Words of the Watchers* and sat on the end of his bed. She considered hanging around until the boys got back, but she was eager to join them. She guessed they would be at the market, since that was their usual stomping ground on Stardays. They never missed an opportunity for easy pickings. Gwena left her stuff in the room and wrote a short note to Bastian in case he returned before she did. Then she braved the decline to the street.

3

The market was a scene of chaos. Half the stalls were upturned, their merchandise spilled across the paving stones. Angry vendors steamed as they collected their wares, swearing at opportunists with sticky fingers. Gwena stopped a passerby, "pardon, what happened here?" she asked. The old woman stared at her scar before answering, something that Gwena had grown accustomed to. Even still, it never failed to irritate her.

"Castle's guard came tearing through. Clumsy fools knocked over half the market! Bet they won't be held accountable either. You watch, they'll blame it all on the lad they were chasing down, but I tell you what, at least he took care to mind people's property. Stupid brutes, worse than children in a china shop!" the woman said angrily. She shook her head and carried on her way.

What were the castle's guard doing in the plaza? Gwena wondered. She pushed her way through the crowd to the skeleton clock tower. It loomed in the center as a single totem of order amid the sea of disruption. She scanned the crowd for any sign of Bastian or Felix, but there was no way to find anything in the commotion. She left the market and checked the nearest pubs to see if they were there, but had no luck. She finally gave up and decided that she would have to wait to meet them at the Tipsy Tav' for tea. As much as she wanted to be with Bastian, there were plenty of other ways she could spend her time. Soon they would be leaving Westdock, and it had been too long since she'd had the freedom to enjoy it. She returned to the market and was pleased to see that it had put itself back together. If she hadn't been there earlier, then she wouldn't have known there'd been a disturbance. She bought a hot spiced bun and a glass of warm cider from a vendor and then sat at a bench to enjoy her meal. As she ate, she watched the little stories unfolding around her: A quarrel over the price of a decorated pot. Two young boys sword fighting with sticks. Lovers giggling as they found dark corners to share their affection. It was such a joy to have the opportunity to just sit and watch the world go by.

The gears in the skeleton clock tower turned punctually and an hour passed before Gwena decided to visit her and her mother's favorite spot. It was something that she'd been avoiding for some time. She walked out of town along the old railway tracks where the enchanted train line had once run. It was decommissioned after the great ban and was now nothing but a distant memory overgrown with tough grass. There was a still silence in the air, and small snowflakes began to fall. Gwena laughed as she tried to catch them on her tongue and soon she found herself at her destination. It was a large area sectioned off by a wall of sheet metal plastered with No Trespassing signs. Gwena walked its length until she found the loose piece that her mother had shown her. Inside was an overgrown clearing with a domed building in the center made of blue opal marble. The building was covered with vines, but underneath them it looked brand-new. It was as if someone had been cleaning it beneath the foliage. The building was an ancient Star Temple. All of Equillian's temples belonged to the Order of the Stars, but unlike the one that Bastian and Felix were raised in, this one was enchanted. It was one of the original Seven Wonders of the world that were built by the alchemists. People used to make pilgrimages to Westdock just to see it. However, because the entire building was enchanted, the town was forced to close it to the public. Luckily, it was impossible to destroy it. That was one of its many amazing enchantments. Gwena loved it here. She and her mother would come every summer to sit and watch the butterflies. She had always felt that the place belonged to them.

When Gwena's mother passed away, she was cremated on a funeral pyre in the traditional fashion, in order to carry her soul to the stars. Gwena removed her ashes from the urn so that she could bring them here. She remembered their coarseness, like sand rather than ash. So different from the fire's ashes that she used to replace them. But her father never noticed.

Gwena brushed aside some vines and stepped inside the temple. The interior walls were covered in murals of Equillian's constellations. The pictures were so lifelike, she felt like she was walking amid the stars. The roof of the temple was made of a special glass that filtered out the sun's light so that the stars were always visible through the domed ceiling—all except for one large circular skylight that was in the very center of the ceiling. It had no glass and exposed the sky as it was. Directly below it was a dark pool of water. During the day sunlight poured through the skylight, creating a column of light that streamed into the pool. An enchantment kept the light contained as a shaft without altering the surrounding darkness. At night, the stars shone through the skylight and reflected brightly in the pool below. Gwena's mother told her that when the temple was open, people would come at night to light candles and float them in the water amid the reflected stars. They believed that it was a sort of bridge that carried their prayers to the Night-Watchers.

Gwena saw a small candle upturned on the floor in a pile of leaves. She picked it up and dusted it off. She had no fire to give it light, but she floated it in the pool all the same and said a silent prayer. She asked the Stars and her mother for guidance and good fortune for her, Bastian, and Felix on their upcoming journey. She also asked her mother to watch over her father and to help bring him peace and happiness. Her mother's faith in the Night-Watchers and this sacred place had given Gwena a deep appreciation for the Stars. It comforted her to know that her mother was among them now, helping to guide her fate.

⸺◦⬦◦⸺

Gwena sat in the monument late into the afternoon and then decided that it was time to head back. The ground was blanketed in a thin layer of snow that glistened in the fading light. The setting sun was making pillars of the shadows. Gwena made her way back into town and headed to the Tipsy Tav' early to enjoy its warmth while she waited for Bastian and Felix.

The pub was already filling up with patrons. Gwena found a small table at the back before they were all taken. She ordered herself a hot hard apple cider and a bowl of spiced clam fritters while she waited. The men and women laughed and boasted loudly around her. She enjoyed listening to scraps of conversations, imagining what the lives of those people were like. From the corner, a fiddle player and a guitarist were serenading the room with traditional sea chanteys. They struck up a well-known song and the entire pub paused to join in the singing. An older gentleman asked Gwena to dance, but she declined for fear of losing her table.

An hour and a half later the boys still hadn't arrived. She began to watch the clock nervously. She stood on her seat a couple of times to see if they were there and hadn't seen her, but they weren't. Gwena stared into her empty glass, and a knot started to form in her stomach. She had the right place, didn't she? Bastian had said the Tipsy Tav'. Maybe he said this place but was thinking of somewhere else? Why else wouldn't they be here? she wondered. Maybe they were celebrating somewhere else and got held up. Surely Bastian would have remembered their plans? It was now a quarter past the hour of Snuff, the sun extinguisher. She'd just decided that she would head back to the loft to wait for them, when her ears caught the conversation of the table next to her.

"Did ya see the chase down at the wharf this mornin'? The castle's guard had a young lad cornered at the pier and he slipped right past 'em. Managed ta jump onto a merchant ship just as it be leavin' port."

Gwena looked over to see a portly merchant talking to a middle-aged sailor.

"Aye, Lord Bardviss looked irate! I recognized the lad too. 'E occasionally works as a fisherman's 'and on Jarvis's boat. Can't remember 'is name fer the life o' me," the sailor replied.

"I wonder what he could've done ta upset the castle. Ya think it could've been related ta the duchess's disappearance?"

"No! Surely not, 'e be a good lad always in good spirit. Seemed ta 'ave been honest enough from the time I shared with 'im. Can't even imagine what 'e could 'ave done."

Gwena froze. *"Felix,"* she whispered. Could that be why he hadn't returned home? She cleared her throat and leaned towards their table. "Pardon, I couldn't help but overhear your conversation. Are you talking about Felix Copperweather?" she asked.

"Aye! That's right, Felix be the name o' the other lad always by 'is side. No, I mean 'is friend, what's the other one's name?"

"Bastian?" Gwena asked with dread.

"Bastian, that's right. Never 'ave been any good with names. 'E was wearin' a fine green jacket," the sailor said.

A lump formed in Gwena's throat. That had to be him.

"Did I hear you correctly when you said that he left on a merchant ship this morning?"

"Aye, like none that I've seen before. 'Ad carvin's o' mermaids an' waves on its back. The lad was escapin' arrest by the castle's men. Don't know what 'e got 'imself mixed up in. But 'e was lucky ta get away, by the looks o' it."

"And you're sure that he was alone, Felix wasn't with him?"

"Just 'im. Though, now that ya mention it, I think it be the first time I seen the two o' them apart," the sailor said.

"And what was that you said about the duchess?" Gwena asked the merchant.

"She went missin' from her own party last night and still hasn't turned up. Complete mystery. The castle's guard have been all over town lookin' fer any sign of her. Was a whole article about it in today's paper. I have gotten rid of mine now, but if ya can get yer hands on a copy it will tell ya all about it."

"Thanks!"

Gwena grabbed her cloak and pushed her way out of the crowded pub.

Gwena searched through the streets for a newsy. Most of them would be home by now, but there were usually one or two who lingered, hoping to make a final cwip. The snow was still coming down, and Gwena held her cloak around her tightly. Finally, she found a boy who looked about eight with a small stack of newspapers tucked under his arm. He was standing in the doorway of a pub rubbing his hands together to keep them warm.

"Are you selling those?" she asked.

The boy looked her up and down. "For a price," he said.

"I'll take one, how much?" she asked, holding out her hand for the paper.

The boy handed her one. "Two cwips."

"Two cwips, that's double its worth!" she protested.

"Give it back then."

"What are you going to do with them? Come tomorrow, your papers won't be any good!"

"Not true, with a feature on the duchess's disappearance, these papers will be worth more tomorrow."

"Aren't you a little swindler."

The boy shrugged. "Do you want the paper or not?"

"I'll take it for the two cwips. But only because I'm grateful that you're still out selling papers in this weather," she said, pulling the two cwips out of her pocket.

"I'm only out here because I'm waiting for my uncle, not for the sake of stragglers like you," he said.

Gwena handed him the coins. "And charming too. Does your mother teach you to behave like a little snot, or do you have to work exceptionally hard at it?" she asked.

The boy pocketed the coins and smiled at her, showing a row of dirty teeth. "Comes naturally, miss."

Gwena sat on Bastian's bed with the small Everfire lamp beside her and the newspaper in her hands. The front page featured the article in bold print. Gwena pored over the words:

WESTDOCK'S DUCHESS: MISSING!

VANISHED AT ENGAGEMENT CELEBRATION

In Westdock last night there was a grand celebration at the Wendrians' castle to commemorate the engagement of their duchess, Lilliana Wendrian, to Lord Henry Bardviss. In the wake of the lavish affair, moods turned somber when it was discovered that the lady of the hour was missing. Moments after a scream was heard, her fiancé found her room in a disheveled state with her three-story bedroom window smashed to smithereens. However, there was no sign that the duchess went through the window, nor was there a trace of her being anywhere else in the castle. "It was as if she simply disappeared," Lord Bardviss reported. No casualties were found, or evidence of roughhousing, which has left authorities guessing. The meaning behind her disappearance is unclear, the whole circumstance a mystery. Detective Stanley Fin reported, "There's no reason to imagine anything sinister. It's far too early to jump to conclusions. There are many possible explanations as to why Lady Wendrian is unaccounted for. Until we have further evidence, there's no reason to assume the worst." Lady Lilliana's disappearance has been hard hitting for both her fiancé, Lord Bardviss and the entire Wendrian family. The blow was clearly intensified by the lingering pain of Sir Drake's disappearance two years ago. Lady Everitt Wendrian, head of the house and mother of ladies Lilliana and Natasha and wife of Sir Drake, commented late last night with tear-soaked eyes, "I just don't understand how this could've happened. Lilliana was surrounded by friends and family in her own home. If anyone has any information regarding my daughter's disappearance, please come forward, I beg of you!" Lord Henry Bardviss has already offered up a handsome reward for any information provided on the duchess's whereabouts, commenting, "We can only hope that the duchess is safe and will be back at the castle before long."

Gwena stared at the paper, flabbergasted. Bastian didn't say anything about this! I wonder if he and Felix saw anything at the castle? And why was Lord Bardviss chasing Bastian in the first place? The chaos at the market flashed back to Gwena and she recalled the old woman's words about a boy being chased. That must have been Bastian! If he was being pursued by the Wendrians' personal guard and Lord Bardviss, then they must be connecting him to the duchess's disappearance. But surely it's a mistake. He spent the night with me…wait, where was Felix? Stars, could he have done something and gotten Bastian mixed up in all of this? By the look of things, he'd never come home. If the castle was after Bastian, then there was no doubt that Felix was involved. Maybe he was there at the market and got caught while Bastian got away. Without Bastian, Gwena would be his only hope of rescue. That was a daunting thought. Gwena's heart sank. She couldn't believe that this was happening—they were so close to leaving Westdock and changing their stars. Why couldn't those boys stay out of trouble for one day? Gwena just wished she knew what it all meant. What had happened to Lady Wendrian? Was it really possible that Bastian and Felix could've had something to do with this?

She took a deep breath. She was sure there had to be a logical explanation for everything. She just had to find it. If only Gwena knew someone at the castle who could give her some proper intel. Then she remembered her old school friend Sam who had taken a job at the castle's stables, and she became hopeful. If she could find him, maybe he would have some answers. Exhaustion washed over her. The last twenty-one hours had been emotionally taxing. She curled up on Bastian's bed, wondering where he was and what ship he'd jumped onto. "Stay safe, Bastian William Sanders, wherever you are. And find your way back to me, ideally before our train departs," she whispered to the night, and then she was asleep.

5

Gwena wrapped her travelling cloak tightly around her shoulders as she turned the corner towards the castle grounds. The snow on the cobblestone path had been trodden to a muddy mess, she lifted her dress above it as she navigated the foot traffic that was passing to replenish the nobles' stores. There were wagons filled with wine barrels, carts carrying large wood buckets brimming with winter produce and bags of freshly milled flour. It was enough food to feed a village for a week. Gwena had heard of the castle's lavish feasts held for the privileged few. That's what nobles did. They weren't any worse in Westdock, only it was unsettling when their people were starving in the streets. She imagined that with all the waste there must be, the castle's pigs probably ate better than she did.

The slender towers and beautiful stained-glass windows of the castle came into view. Gwena reached the gardens and followed them along the side wall until she reached the horse stables. The log building was well looked after. There were several draft horses eating contentedly from large sacks of oats. To Gwena's delight, she saw her old school friend Sam brushing down a grey and white spotted mare. She hadn't seen him for years. Ever since she'd left school, her work had kept her from having a social life.

Now her school days felt like a lifetime ago, and yet here Sam was, so close to her own home and looking like he'd never changed. He was a robust fellow, with sandy hair and kind brown eyes. Gwena was surprised by how excited she was to see him. Until that moment, she hadn't realized how much she missed her school friends.

"Sam!" she greeted.

He looked up in surprise. "Gwena! I wasn't sure if I'd ever see you again. What brings you to the castle?" he asked with a warm smile.

"I need your help, and we're well overdue for a catch up."

"Indeed, we are. It has been way too long!" Sam said and pulled her in for a hug.

Gwena welcomed the embrace.

"I don't knock off until four, but if you can wait ten minutes, I can take an early lunch," he said.

"Perfect." Gwena sat on a hay bale while she waited.

"I hear that your father's tailor business is now the best in Westdock. I'm sure it's no coincidence that its reputation grew after you started working for him. Do you enjoy it?" Sam asked as he finished brushing the horse and began to clean its hoof.

"Not really," Gwena said, and then she laughed at her own blatant honesty. She was surprised by how good it felt to finally admit that to herself and to say it out loud. "Actually, I'm thinking of leaving Westdock, at least for a time."

Sam raised his eyebrows. "Wow, that's great! I wish I could do that. I'll probably be brushing these beasts until retirement."

"There's nothing wrong with that, at least it's work of your choosing."

"Aye, I don't mind. They make better company than most people do."

"I believe it!" Gwena laughed.

Sam finished his work and they walked together towards town.

"Pig's Head?" Sam asked.

"I haven't been to that place in years! It will be good to see it again."

The Pig's Head was a real dive. It was frequented by adolescents due to its dark corners and cheap drinks. But it had a certain charm and was quiet enough to hold a conversation. More important, Gwena knew that she didn't have to worry about her father being there.

The Pig's Head had a raging wood fire in its hearth and was filled with the rich aroma of freshly baked spice mince pies. Gwena took a seat near the hearth, it was such a novelty to see real fire. She liked the quaintness of it. Sam ordered them a couple of hard ciders while she settled in.

"So, to what do I owe the pleasure of your company?" he asked, returning with two brimming schooners.

"I'm hoping that you can tell me what's happening at the castle. I have a couple of friends who were celebrating there last night, and now they're missing. I'm worried that they might've been involved with all the commotion."

Sam looked at her inquisitively. "Are your friends two common lads who snuck into the Wendrians' ball, by any chance?"

"Yes…"

Sam leaned in close to her and lowered his voice conspiratorially. "You mean to tell me that you're friends with the two guys who snuck into the ball, convinced half the women to pour their coin into a false lottery, stole some of the Wendrians' most prized artifacts, and then wooed Lady Lilliana at her own engagement party?" he asked.

Gwena's eyes widened. "*They did what?!*"

Sam grinned. "I can't believe that you know them! Everyone at the castle is talking about it. Word is, one of them got "friendly" with the duchess. He followed her up to her bedroom just before her disappearance. Lord Bardviss ran into his friend coming down the stairs, but the lad slipped right past him and evaded the guards. He was probably up there nicking the treasures while Lady Lilliana was distracted by the other one. But that's not even the best part of it. On his way out, he riled the entire ballroom into a fist fight. Apparently, there wasn't a single guest who didn't join the squabble. I would've loved to have seen that. Imagine, a whole room of nobles duking it out. Those two gentlemen have created quite the storm!"

"I would hardly call them gentlemen," Gwena muttered.

She knew full well the boys were capable of such things. In fact, Sam's story had Bastian and Felix written all over it. She expected them to con the guests or steal something, and if there was anyone audacious enough to woo lady Lilliana Wendrian at her own engagement party, it was Felix. But what surprised her was that Bastian hadn't mentioned *any* of it.

"Wait, who are those two to you? You're not seeing one of them, are you?" Sam asked.

Gwena blushed. "That's none of your business!" she said indignantly.

Sam raised an eyebrow at her. "You'd be wise not to. By the sounds of it, those two are nothing but trouble." He looked around to make sure no one was listening. "They might have kidnapped Lady Lilliana," he whispered.

"Not a chance! Those two might be a bit careless when it comes to other people's property, but they certainly aren't kidnappers! They wouldn't hurt a soul. Trust me, they're old friends of mine. I have known them since we were children," Gwena said reassuringly. But part of her wondered how much she still knew Bastian and Felix.

"Well, if they didn't, I don't know who did. According to Jill who was working the floor last night, Lady Lilliana and your friend went upstairs together. Now you say he's also missing? If he didn't kidnap her, then maybe they ran away together?" Sam suggested.

Gwena wrinkled her nose. That didn't make any sense. Why would Felix run away with the duchess when he and Bastian were planning to leave Westdock tomorrow? Besides, she thought, Felix is terrified of commitment. There's no way he'd ditch Bastian to run away with a girl, no matter how beautiful or prestigious she was.

"So, you're saying that the castle doesn't know what happened to the man who was with Lilliana? They don't have him locked away in their dungeon or anything? Gwena asked.

"Stars no. I would've heard about that for sure. I doubt that the nobles know anything about your friend having been with the duchess."

"Wait, you mean Jill and the other staff haven't told them?"

"Are you kidding? No one would dare suggest to Lord Bardviss or Lady Everitt that Lilliana, their own fiancée and daughter, had been unfaithful. Do you know what kind of trouble that would cause? Being a witness to that kind of thing is more of a liability than anything. Nobles will do unmentionable things just to sweep their dirt under the table."

So, that's why Lord Bardviss was chasing Bastian. He's their only lead to the duchess's disappearance, Gwena thought. It was beginning to make sense now, but it still left the question of what had happened to Felix and Lady Lilliana.

"Can you tell me about the chase that was in the market yesterday?" she asked Sam.

"Sure, Lord Bardviss got a tip that someone was attempting to sell the stolen artifacts. I think that after last night, he's waging a personal vendetta against your friend. He was adamant on accompanying the castle's men in the chase. But on the up side, I heard that your friend escaped on a ship that was leaving the harbor. He seems to have a knack for slipping past the royal guards. Lord Bardviss was so irate that everyone at the castle has been avoiding him since."

"How do you know all this?" Gwena asked.

Sam smiled slyly. "The castle has over two hundred staff members. The nobles treat us like we're invisible, but we see and hear everything. You wouldn't believe some of the things that I've heard from the gossip mill."

"I can only imagine," Gwena said with a smirk.

Sam looked at his pocket watch. "By the Time Thief, that's me done. Don't get much of a break. I hope that was helpful? If you find out what happened to your friends, let me know. I would pay ten cwips to hear that story," he said and got up from the table.

Gwena stood with him. "Thanks, Sam. It's great to see you. I'm so glad that you're doing well," she said warmly.

"Anytime. It's really good to see you too. Don't be such a stranger. Hey, some of the other staff and I are coming here for after-work drinks. It would be great if you wanted to join us. We still need to have that proper catch up," he said.

"Thanks, I'll try and make it."

"Well, hopefully until tonight then," Sam said with a smile and left to return to work.

Gwena sat staring into her mug, mulling over what Sam had told her. So that was it. Bastian was on an unknown merchant ship and Felix was officially a missing person. She had no way of knowing when, or if, Bastian would return. If he'd gotten off the ship at a nearby port, then it was still possible that he could make it back to Westdock before their train left tomorrow. But with the castle's men looking for him, it would be foolish for him to return at all. If only she could find Felix, then together they could come up with a plan. But Gwena had no idea where Felix was or how to find him. She could only hope that he would head back to the loft at some point. The question was, what was she going to do if he didn't? What was she going to do if neither of them did? If she stayed in Westdock, then her father was bound to find her sooner or later. The thought of going back home felt like a rock in her belly. Now that she had cut ties and stepped out that door, she never wanted to go back. But what else could she do? She couldn't leave Westdock on her own, even if she wanted to—Bastian had the train tickets. The only way that she could acquire the means to buy another ticket would be to sell the necklace that Bastian had given her, but if Bastian had been caught trying to sell the stolen artifacts from the castle, then most likely the necklace would be flagged too.

Gwena slumped in her chair. She regretted not going to the Wendrians' ball. If she had joined the boys that night, then none of this would've happened. Her father would've scolded her fiercely the next morning and probably would've grounded her for life, but he wouldn't have hit her. He would've had the chance to cool off and sober up. And Bastian and Felix would still be here. They got into so much mischief when she wasn't around. A lottery? Whatever could it have been for? she wondered. And wooing Lady Wendrian, at her own engagement party! How could Felix be so foolish? That was never going to end well. Leave it to them both to cause so much trouble in a single night. And why hadn't Bastian told her about any of it? Would he have if there wasn't so much else going on? She wasn't sure. She was beginning to think that there was more mystery to Bastian Sanders than she'd realized.

They had hardly spent time together these last few years, and even though their feelings for each other held true, she had no idea who Bastian had grown up to be. Of course, he didn't know that about her either. So much had changed since they were children. All she knew was that she wanted to know him more than anything. She wanted the chance to learn every secret, every hope, every aspiration, dream, and dark corner of who he had become. Please, please find your way back to me, Bastian, she whispered.

Gwena used one of the few cwips she had left to order a meat pie. She thought about leaving the Pig's Head, but she had nowhere better to go. The pub at least was warm, and now that she had ordered something, she had the luxury of holding her seat in front of the fire for as long as she liked. She pulled out a piece of embroidery that she kept with her for these moments. It was just smaller than her hand and lavished with so much color and detail that it looked like a painting. Working with her hands always eased her mind. Once she found a rhythm with her needlework, she was able to calm her nerves and focus on detangling the problem at hand.

PISTOL-WHIPPED

CHAPTER SIX

Felix leaned on the wall beside Lady Lilliana, distracting her as she closed her bedroom door. He smirked at Bastian's narrow escape, he'd only just cleared the entrance. As soon as the door was shut, Felix embraced Lilliana against it and kissed her passionately. He couldn't believe that he was seducing Lady Lilliana Wendrian, the jewel of Westdock. She was the cream of the crop, a duchess, wealthy, and drop-dead gorgeous. He slid his hand towards the small of her back to undo the tie on her dress and then froze, feeling something hard and cold against his scrotum.

"One more move, and you lose them," Lilliana hissed in his ear.

Felix looked down to discover a flintlock pistol aimed true. His passion instantly evaporated. "Why, come now my lady, that's completely unwarranted. If you wanted me to stop you should've said so. I was under the impression that this was completely mutual," he said in defense, stepping back from her.

It wasn't the first time that he'd been threatened with a gun, but considering its current target and his complete confusion over Lady Wendrian's intentions, the unpredictability of the situation made him nervous.

Lilliana's eyes darted to a small clock on her dressing room table, and then she ditched her heels for a pair of travelling boots.

Felix studied her curiously. "Is this a fetish of yours, my lady? Because if it is, I would love to play along," he said, grinning widely.

"Is your head ever anywhere but the bedroom?" she asked.

"Not if I can help it," he admitted with a shrug.

Lilliana scowled distastefully, leaving Felix utterly perplexed. Two seconds before she was as giddy and flirtatious as a school girl, and now she was threatening his manhood? He couldn't tell if this was some sort of roleplay, or if she actually had a more sinister agenda. Then Bastian's voice rose up from the stairs: "Good evening, Lord Bardviss!" Lilliana and Felix exchanged worried glances and her pistol evaporated from Felix's mind. If Lord Bardviss found them like this, then he would have a much bigger problem on his hands. A problem that even *he* couldn't talk his way out of.

He scouted the room for an escape route. The tall windows were several castle-stories high and the door no doubt would have Lord Bardviss behind it in a matter of seconds. He knew that Bastian's loud greeting was meant as a warning and that he would stall Lord Bardviss for as long as he could, but the gift of gab had never been one of Bastian's strengths. Felix frowned at the compromising position he found himself in. "I could hide in the closet while you distract him?" he suggested.

Lilliana ignored him and pulled a packed bag out of her closet, then motioned with her pistol for Felix to go to the back of the room. "Over there, now!" she commanded. Not seeing an alternative, Felix did as he was told. There was nothing there but a large, tasteless portrait above a tall looking glass. Lilliana came up behind him and pushed a golden rose in the frame of the portrait, there was a faint *click* and then the mirror swung open to reveal a hidden staircase. Felix raised his eyebrows in appreciation. "You certainly are full of surprises, my lady," he commended. She pushed her bag into his arms and nudged him into the secret passage. Felix entered the darkness cautiously and Lilliana returned to her bedroom. A moment later there was the sound of shattering glass and Lilliana's piercing scream. For an instant Felix thought that she'd thrown herself out the window, but she reappeared behind him in the secret passage, completely calm and collected as though nothing had happened. Felix couldn't see a single scratch on her. The question formed on his lips, but before he could voice it, Lilliana shut the door and they were swallowed by darkness.

The duchess pulled an Everfire lantern from her bag and took its cover off. The flickering light instantly illuminated the stone walls of the passageway. She tossed the lantern to Felix, and he caught it reflexively, taking in their surroundings. They were standing on a narrow stone spiral staircase that went to Stars knew where. He held the light while Lilliana armed something resembling a bear trap at the top of the stairs and he silently reminded himself never to mess with a woman scorned.

He couldn't help but be highly intrigued by this side of Lilliana. She had completely changed from the flirtatious young woman whom he'd followed to the bedroom. Once she'd finished her handiwork, she took the lantern from him and urged him down the stairs. He complied, happy to be escaping the threat of Lord Bardviss. But as he descended the long stairwell, he wondered what he'd gotten himself into. Lilliana had clearly been prepared for this, whatever it was. The weight of her bag suggested that it wasn't a short holiday. He waited patiently for an explanation, thinking that surely it would come at any moment. But it didn't. And by the time they reached the bottom of the stairs and began proceeding down a dank, dark stone hallway, Felix began to worry. The corridor had no distinct markings and passages branched off on either side at various intervals. He realized then that without Lilliana, he wouldn't have a chance of finding his way out.

He looked behind him to see her walking deep in thought, absently pointing her pistol at him. He cleared his throat. "So… my lady, are you going to tell me what's going on?" he asked. He was clear by this stage that it wasn't a fun roleplay for the bedroom, much to his disappointment.

"You're helping me get out of Westdock," she said matter-of-factly.

"Am I? Good to know. There's no need for hostility. If you want my help, you only have to ask for it."

To Felix's relief, Lilliana lowered her pistol.

"Fine, I need your assistance," she said curtly.

"Ok…that's a good start. Why do you want to get out of Westdock? Our charming town not interesting enough for you?"

"It's not the place that bothers me, it's my betrothed," she said.

She was looking down each corridor as they passed it. Felix prayed to the Stars that she knew where they were going.

"Well, that's understandable. Can't you just call it off?" he asked, wiping a cobweb from his brow.

"Ha! Commoner, you wouldn't understand," Lilliana scoffed.

"Commoner? Wait, what makes you so sure that I'm not a lord?" he asked, surprised that she'd seen through his disguise.

Lilliana rolled her eyes. "Please. I know every lord and lady within a hundred miles of Westdock. It would take more than fine clothes to hide your common birth."

"Fair enough. But if you didn't, would you have guessed? I mean, you have to admit I make a pretty good noble," he said, grinning playfully.

"Ha! Even if I hadn't known the surrounding families, I would've spotted you a mile away. You clearly have no understanding of the lives of lords and ladies," she said snootily.

Felix smirked at Lilliana's naïveté. Over the years he'd made it his personal business to understand the lives of lords and ladies. The upper class were his and Bastian's signature target. They only ever took from those who could afford it. And he had been successful at blending in with bluebloods on every previous occasion. He was greatly curious as to what had given him away. Even if Lilliana did know every lord and lady within a hundred miles, he could've been a lord from one of the neighboring precincts in Equillian. They'd invited every visiting noble who was in port. So, it had to have been something else. But what was it? he wondered.

"Go ahead then and try me. You might be pleasantly surprised by the things I know," he said challengingly.

"Doubt it," she muttered.

Felix grinned. He highly enjoyed a good game of cat and mouse. Even with Lilliana's conceited colors, he still found this side of her intriguing.

"Alright, let's see… Your mother arranged your marriage to Lord Bardviss for his prosperity, not his personality. With your father missing, she's looking to you to bear the burden of securing a life of financial comfort for you and your family. She cares more about that than your happiness and is giving you no say in the matter. With your family's wealth waning, if you refuse Lord Bard-viss then you will be responsible for your family's ruin. But, if you marry him, then you're condemning yourself to a life without love," he concluded. "Ringing any bells?" he asked smugly.

Lilliana frowned. "It's not that simple. But I wouldn't expect the likes of you to understand. You have no idea about public responsibility and arranged marriages. Your lot can marry any-one you please. You only have to worry about basic things, like finding shelter and your next meal. You have no idea about the complexity of upper-class life and the complication of real prob-lems!" she blurted angrily.

Felix blinked in disbelief and then burst out laughing—he couldn't help himself. Surely, she must be joking?

"Wait a minute here, *real problems*? No offense, my lady, but in comparison to our '*basic*' worries, your upper-class woes are about as much of a problem as a piece of excrement stuck to the bottom of my shoe. I mean, don't get me wrong, having to marry someone you don't love stinks. But I hardly think it could be worse than homelessness and starvation. At least with Lord Bardviss's wealth, you will have enough coin to drown your sorrows in any pleasure you please," he said unsympathetically.

Lilliana flushed angrily. She clearly wasn't used to being spo-ken to so plainly.

"You think that riches make your life easy? Foolish peasant, the only reason why you think that coin can solve everything is because you don't have any. Well, it doesn't. It only makes things more complicated!" she said passionately.

"You're right, my lady, I really can't understand your up-per-class '*problems*.' Having all that coin must be really tough. I'm so sorry, you poor unfortunate soul. I can only imagine the misery it must bring you," he said sarcastically.

Everything about Lilliana that had seemed fun a moment before, now screamed spoiled and overprivileged noble. He was beginning to wonder why he'd ever found her so attractive in the first place.

Lilliana's face turned a dark rouge. "I would stop talking if I were you," she growled threateningly.

"If you were me? My lady, you couldn't handle being me. If I were you, then I would grow a pair and suffer Lord Bardviss for the benefit of my family. Or, I would break off the engagement and tell them all to go Shick themselves, rather than run away like a little girl."

"I'm not running away!" Lilliana said in outrage.

"Could've fooled me," Felix shrugged. "I'm dying to know—what part do you expect me to play in whatever this is?" he asked, no longer interested in helping her cause.

"*You're* kidnapping me," she said triumphantly.

Felix stopped dead in his tracks.

"Wait, that's what this is about? Me kidnapping you? No, no, no, no, no. You're the one who's kidnapping me. Kidnapping you would be a very stupid thing to do! I am definitely *not* kidnapping you," he said firmly.

"Jumping into bed with Lord Bardviss's fiancée was the stupid thing to do. I was under the impression that stupid things were your forte?" Lilliana returned.

"Point well made," Felix admitted, "but adultery doesn't incriminate me, where this does in a very *big* way. I understand and sympathize with your predicament, my lady, but I have a good thing going here. I like my life. If I kidnap you, then I will never be able to return to it."

The Everfire lamp cast an eerie orange glow over Lilliana's face, and Felix could see that there was resolve in her eyes. "You're right, you won't. And I'm sorry to have to do this to you, but you sealed your fate the second you accepted my invitation to my bedroom. If you were an honest man, then this never would've happened," she said accusingly.

"Oh, come on! That's not fair. Any single man who had one iota of interest in the female sex would've accepted your invitation!" Felix protested, though he was beginning to think that if he'd known her first, he might not have been so eager.

"Lord Humphrey didn't," Lilliana countered.

"My point exactly! Wait, you asked that idiot Lord Humphrey before me?"

Lilliana blushed. "What? His family is almost in ruin, which would've given him the perfect motive. And he's slow of wit, so he would have been easy to manipulate. Unfortunately, a little too slow of wit. My invitation went right over the poor man's head. And I certainly wasn't going to spell it out for him," she admitted.

"Ha! Like that counts, he didn't even know what was being offered. But if you already had someone lined up, then why did you take me?"

"After Lord Humphrey turned me down, I panicked. And you made it so easy. I could see you gawking at me from the other side of the room. Besides, it was to my benefit that you're a commoner. I knew that no one would question your motive," she said.

"I'm only easy when I'm willing, Duchess, and you're quickly losing my interest. I'm not kidnapping you. If you want to run away, you can do so without using me as an accomplice," he said angrily, and he dropped her bag on the floor.

He was done playing nice. It was the first time that anyone had ever played him, and he didn't like it. More so, he was incredibly annoyed that Lilliana was ruining a perfectly good evening. If it wasn't for this charade of hers, he could've been helping himself to the remaining spoils of Bastian's lottery and helping his Star-brother ring in his Illumine celebration.

"I don't remember giving you a choice," Lilliana said.

Felix looked up to see her pistol pointing at him for the second time. He stared down the barrel for a beat, and then he met Lilliana's eyes. "There's always a choice, my lady," he said evenly. And then with one fluid motion, he disarmed her and stuck the pistol behind him in the belt of his pants.

Lilliana turned on him in outrage. "How dare you!"

"How dare I? You're the one who's trying to set me up! I'm truly sorry for your predicament, my lady. Lord Bardviss is a detestable man. But as pretty as you are, I'm not willing to throw my life away for you."

Lilliana glared at him coolly. "I don't have time for this nonsense," she growled.

She pulled a large dagger from her boot and spun around Felix, pulling him into an armlock and pushing her blade against his throat with expert precision. "You're coming with me, and you'll follow my command, or you will die, and I'll grab another rat off the street to replace you. End of discussion," she said venomously.

All of the innocence and girlish charm had left her, and it was then that Felix realized he had greatly underestimated the duchess of Westdock.

SEABOUND

CHAPTER SEVEN

Bastian woke to the gentle rocking of the sea. For an instant he thought he was back in his own bed. He jolted in surprise at his unfamiliar surroundings and his predicament flooded back to him. The sounds of seagulls, crashing waves, and singing men encircled him. His legs were sore and cramped and one of his arms had fallen asleep. He massaged it while he gained his bearings. He took out his pocket watch. It was already late afternoon—The hour of Karmithos, the karma keeper. The sailors on the lines high above him were singing with strong accents as they adjusted the sails for the changing wind.

> *"Haul on the ropes boys, raisin' all the sails boys,*
> *Haul on the ropes boys, the ropes now haul!*
> *Haul on the ropes men, out ta sea and back again*
> *Haul on the ropes men, the ropes now haul!*
> *Haul on the ropes lads, there's treasure waitin' ta be had*
> *Haul on the ropes lads, the ropes now haul!"*

Bastian braved a peek around the barrels obscuring him. There were three large masts littered with open sails. Each mast's surface was covered with detailed carvings of giant sea creatures, mermaids, selkies, and legends of Davy Jones. The craft was heavily gunned with cannons lining either side of the deck. One thing was certain, whoever owned this ship had a very successful business and cargo worth protecting. Bastian couldn't recall having seen the vessel before. He recognized most of the traffic that came and went from Westdock's port and knew he would have remembered this one.

The men he could see were dressed in eclectic garb. Most of them wore baggy fisherman pants tucked into knee-high leather boots with colorful scarves around their waists or thick belts over loose cotton shirts. Some wore vests and were adorned with fine jewelry. Suddenly the hairs on the back of Bastian's neck stood on end and he could feel eyes on him.

"What 'ave we 'ere?" a gruff voice asked.

Bastian looked up into a large round face with a thick black beard. The man was grinning down at him. Bastian put up his hands in a gesture of surrender. "I mean no harm, I am seeking refuge," he declared.

The sailor stared at him for a moment as if he thought he might be joking. When Bastian's serious expression didn't falter, he erupted into hearty laughter. "Yer seekin' refuge ya say? Seekin' refuge, on the Black Mary?"

The Black Mary, why did that name sound familiar? Bastian wondered. "Yes, if I could just speak to the captain, then I can explain everything."

"Oh, ye'll speak ta the cap'n alright, don't ya worry about that! Ha-ha-ha-ha, wait till the lads get a load o' this!" the sailor said, laughing heartily. He bent down and grabbed Bastian by the scruff of his jacket and lifted him over the barrels.

"I'm perfectly capable of walking on my own!" he protested.

He had a bad feeling about this and began to wonder what he'd gotten himself into this time. Could they be slavers? he speculated with growing dread. Soon they reached the quarterdeck where a small crowd of curious sailors formed around them. "Oi Rhino, what 'ave ya got there?"

"Can we eat 'im?"

"Nah, look at 'im, wouldn't be any good. The lad doesn't 'ave an inch o' fat on 'im."

"That don't matter, Doc can boil 'is bones ta make us a nice broth," the men jeered.

Bastian started to feel sick to his stomach. His immediate instinct was to jump ship and escape like he always had, but there was nowhere to go. Even if the water wasn't freezing, there was no land in sight and every sailor around him was armed to the teeth. Any sense of security or control that he'd felt over the situation was long gone. Just as his fear was beginning to escalate, a gunshot split the air and everyone's voices fell.

Outside the captain's quarters on the balcony above them stood a tall, slender man with brown skin, wild black hair beneath a black brimmed hat, and a well-groomed boxed beard. He was dressed in a dark, full-length naval jacket adorned with brass buttons and golden trim. Two crisscrossing leather belts hung low on his hips, housing a cutlass with a revolver tucked neatly by its side. Another revolver was smoking in his hand from the shot just fired. "Why aren't ya scallywags doin' yer duties?" he demanded.

The crew quickly parted to reveal Bastian.

"I found a stowaway, Cap'n, said he be lookin' fer refuge," Rhino said with a deep chuckle.

The men surrounding them burst into laughter and one half of the captain's mouth curled into a smile. "That be so?" he asked. He looked Bastian over with curiosity. "We be the ones ye should be runnin' from!" he declared.

Then he made his way down the stairs and towered over Bastian. He didn't look particularly old. Bastian placed him to be in his mid-thirties, but when he caught sight of the man's eyes, a shudder ran down his spine. The left one was blue black and the right one was a dark green. They were both deep pools that spoke of a dark and tempest-tossed soul that had weathered a thousand years. Bastian felt great intrigue and complete terror all at once. He had never encountered a person with such a presence, and suddenly he remembered where he knew the ship's name. *The Black Mary*, a ship of legend, a famous pirate ship led by the great and feared Captain Muerte Tormenta. He was known for rising to power very quickly by his ruthless and unsympathetic command. The rumors told of powers that no mortal could possess. He took everything and anything he wanted, and no one had ever been able to stop him. Bastian knew better than to believe those stories were anything more than a fictitious exaggeration, but even tall tales held a reflection of truth. His spirit sank. Give me slavers, give me Lord Bardviss, but please Stars, don't give me this, he pleaded silently to the Night-Watchers, wondering what he had ever done to deserve such bad luck. What the Shick were pirates doing at Westdock anyway? he wondered angrily.

The captain took him from Rhino with an iron grasp and addressed the crew. "What should we do with 'im, lads?"

Immediately there was a song of suggestions, one on top of the other. "Make 'im walk the plank."

"Feed 'im ta the sharks."

"Set 'im ta dance on hot coals."

Bastian was starting to feel lightheaded when the captain motioned for silence, and like an anvil it fell. Next, he addressed

Bastian with a voice that boomed over the crowd. "What do ya say lad, any last requests?" he asked.

The men gave their full attention to him. Bastian's head raced. *How in the Stars can I get myself out of this one?* He thought of what Felix would do. He could've used his brother's silver tongue in that moment. And suddenly Felix's words came to him.

"You have to sell yourself, mate, make them believe that they need you, that they want you. In the right light, even an old rusty tin can will look like gold."

That was Felix's advice for picking up girls. Bastian never cared much for his suggestions on the subject, but in that moment, he thought it might actually prove useful. He certainly didn't have anything else to draw from. He cleared his throat and pulled together every bit of confidence he could muster. "If you let me live, I'll offer you my assistance," he suggested casually.

The captain raised an eyebrow, amused. "That be so? And what on Equillian could a callow landlubber like yerself possibly 'ave ta offer us?"

"I am a thief," Bastian replied matter-of-factly, as if a thief was the greatest asset they could ever hope for.

The captain laughed, "What makes ya think that I want a dodgy pickpocket lurkin' the boards o' me ship?"

"I'm not a pickpocket, I'm a thief, and a good one at that," Bastian corrected.

He pulled out the gold egg from his coat pocket and held it up to the crew. Sounds of approval passed through the crowd. Gaining confidence, Bastian continued, "I took this from the Wendrians' castle last night. There's no lock that I can't pick, and no hiding place that I can't find. You might have brute strength with your men, but you can only get so far using force."

"Brute force 'as never failed us before!" a large pirate declared, hitting his fist against his chest.

The captain raised a hand to silence him and Bastian continued with renewed hope. "The most valuable treasures are kept behind the strongest locks, some of which can't be broken. So why try, when I can simply open them for you?" he suggested.

The men fell quiet, waiting for the captain's reply with bated breath.

"The lad 'as balls, ya got ta give 'im that. Stupid, but 'e's got balls," one sailor grunted to another.

The captain eyed Bastian with renewed interest, his dark eyes piercing to his core.

"Prove it," he said.

A lump swelled in Bastian's throat as the captain motioned to one of his men. "Bring me the chest."

The sailor disappeared below deck, returning a moment afterwards with a large rusted and barnacle-infested box that he dropped at the captain's feet. The captain pushed it towards Bastian with his boot.

"If ye can unlock this chest, I might spare yer miserable life an' give ya the refuge ye be lookin' fer. If ya can't, then ta Davy Jones's locker ya go," he declared.

The men cheered in excitement. Bastian could see the crew calling bets around him. The captain pulled an hourglass from his coat pocket and placed it on a crate beside him. "Ye 'ave five minutes, thief," he declared, and the sand began to fall.

Bastian's head swam, and his nose started to itch terribly. It was something that happened to him on rare occasions when he was under pressure, and in that moment, it was far from welcome. He took a deep breath, pulling his attention to the chest's lock.

It was a heavyset warded lock. The front of the Keyway had a different design from any he'd seen before. Instead of being a common fish shape, it was a complicated geometric form which provided a much smaller opening to work with. Warded locks had two crucial parts, wards and a lever. The wards were solid obstacles inside the keyway that blocked the wrong key from turning, and the lever was a small switch at the back of the key-way that had to be pushed for the lock to open. Bastian reached into his breast pocket and took out his lock-picking tools. His self-made kit had never failed him, but then, he had never tackled a lock like this one. To make matters worse, Bastian could see that the lock had already been tampered with. It looked like someone had shoved a cutlass straight into its guts and gone to town. It even had blast marks where they had clearly tried to blow it open.

Already a minute had passed on the hourglass. Bastian cleared his mind, set out his notebook with a piece of charcoal and picked up two L-shaped feelers. He stuck them gently into the lock and felt his way through every nook and cranny trying to decipher what kind of wards were inside. Every bump or ob-trusion that he felt he drew onto his notepad to create a blue-print. Within five seconds he realized that something was wrong. This lock wasn't a lock at all. It was a misdirection, a disguise, a fake. He pulled out his feelers, furious and desperate. He had heard of these chests. They were made by master blacksmiths on the Spotted Isles. Impenetrable safes with several defenses for transporting precious cargo. No one could replicate their crafts-manship, and without the proper key they were virtually impos-sible to open. As far as Bastian knew, these chests had a hidden lock somewhere that turned a complicated locking mechanism on the inside of the chest. Sometimes there were even two or three hidden locks that all had to be turned simultaneously, in which case, even if Bastian had the keys, he could never open it on his own. He had three minutes left. He took a moment to wipe the sweat off his brow, then set to trying to find some other way into the vault.

The men were watching, enthralled. The captain stood over him with crossed arms and an expression of skepticism. Talk about pressure, Bastian thought. As if the looming death sentence wasn't enough. He touched every detail of the chest, looking for something that might be hiding a keyway. An instant later five locks sprung into view behind various pieces of the chest's design. Bastian wasn't even sure what he'd touched. Oh great, as if two weren't trouble enough, Shick, he thought to the Star Stirrer. He was desperately aware that his failure and death were quickly racing towards him.

There was one minute left in the hourglass. He started to pull out his best skeleton key in a last attempt of desperation when his nose began to itch uncontrollably. Bastian stopped what he was doing and rubbed it for a moment of relief. Than he saw it. A faint gold glow was coming from underneath the chest. He rubbed his eyes to chase away any visions straying from reality, but the glow remained. There was thirty seconds of sand left. Bastian turned the chest on its side. On the bottom was a clear outline of a key and a keyway in glowing gold light. If it wasn't for the light, it would have been impossible to see. The five locks must have been purely misdirection. Bastian instinctively pushed the circle in the top of the key, there was a faint *click, click, click,* and then the key popped up out of the wood. Bastian picked it up and pushed it into the outline of the keyway, which had no opening. The wood fell away in front of the key as if it was butter, and as the last grains of sand fell, Bastian turned the key and the chest flew open. He sat back in relief. The men surrounding him stood in silence. Than a cheer went up like a crashing wave, and Bastian couldn't help but grin. He leaned forward to look into the chest, but the captain kicked the lid shut and grabbed the box before he could glimpse its contents.

"Well, landlubber, looks like ye 'ave earned yerself another day," he said, and then he addressed his crew. "Now fer ye sorry lot, shake a leg and turn to before I skin yer ugly backsides!"

"Aye, aye, Cap'n!" the crew returned in unison, quickly dispersing to their duties.

The captain turned to Bastian. "Yer life is now mine, maggot, with a small price o' yer gold," he said expectantly. Bastian reluctantly surrendered his egg and the captain threw him a mop in exchange. "Make yerself useful until I call," he ordered and headed for his cabin.

Bastian's heart was racing a million miles an hour while his mind tried to catch up to what had just happened. He couldn't believe that he was on the infamous *Black Mary*. And that somehow, he'd managed to convince the most notorious pirate, Muerte Tormenta himself, not to throw him overboard. He felt like soiling his pants and whooping in a cheer of joy all at the same time. Only, now that he'd convinced the captain to keep him on the ship, he had to find a way off it. Bastian recalled Lord Bardviss's command as the ship was leaving port and his feeling of dread returned. If he didn't get off the Black Mary soon, the entire crew could end up paying a visit to Davy Jones. Pirate ship or not, Bastian didn't think it could survive an attack from Lord Bardviss's galleon.

"Oi, Captain!" Bastian called, chasing after him.

Muerte Tormenta stopped and looked back over his shoulder, lending Bastian his attention.

"The man I'm seeking refuge from has sent a pursuer after me. I heard him order to have your ship sunk by nightfall. You were right—how much use can a thief be on a pirate ship? If you drop me off at the next port, then my pursuers and I will be out of your hair. For all it's worth, I never intended to burden anyone else with my predicament. I'm truly sorry for the inconvenience," he said earnestly.

The captain's mouth curled into a half smile and his eyes twinkled with amusement. He nodded and then continued on his way, leaving Bastian alone.

Bastian could only hope that his confession would inspire trust, not punishment. He'd found that being honest ultimately worked in his favor, even when the truth was difficult. Either way, it wouldn't do Bastian any good to withhold the information. If the ship went down, then he'd go down with it. If he was left at port before day's end, then maybe he'd have half a chance at finding his way back to Westdock to meet Gwena and Felix for their train.

Bastian took in his surroundings with a new measure. The sailors were already back at their duties, disinterested in him, and the ship was encircled by nothing but the open sea. He counted fifteen sailors on deck. The men were a mix of races and statures, some of which he had never seen before.

"Oi, Dodger, nice jacket."

Bastian turned to see a sailor walking towards him who didn't look much older than he was. The lad was slim but toned with short sandy hair and a kind face. Not the sort of person Bastian would expect to be a pirate.

"I'll trade ya fer it," the pirate offered, standing beside him.

"Sorry, what?"

"Yer jacket, I like it and ya look ta be about me size. So, I'll trade ya fer it. I 'ave plenty ta offer fer exchange," the pirate said, holding his arm beside Bastian's to measure the length.

"Sorry, it's not for sale or trade," Bastian said, stepping away from him.

"Shame, it'd look better on me. If ya die, can I 'ave it?" the pirate asked.

Bastian didn't know how to take that. Luckily the pirate didn't wait for him to answer.

"Name's Cricket. I've been assigned ta show ya about. Ye will be shadowin' me fer the next few days. Don't be a smart arse an' we should get along fine," he said cheerfully, holding out a hand.

Bastian shook it warily. "Thanks, but I don't think that I'll be here that long. I'm—" Bastian started to introduce himself, but Cricket cut him off.

"Save yer birth name fer softer places, mate, ye be Dodger now."

"Why Dodger?" Bastian asked.

He wasn't planning on giving Cricket his birth name regardless, and Dodger was just as good as any fictitious alternative, but he was still curious as to why it was chosen.

"Cause ya just dodged death, matey," Cricket said, clapping him on the back. Then the pirate picked up a bucket of sudsy water and dropped it between them.

"Dodger it is," Bastian agreed.

Dodger had a nice ring to it, and somehow it felt more appropriate for his current surroundings. He was grateful for Cricket's company. The pirate wasn't gruesome like the rest of the crew Bastian had seen and being with someone close to his age made the place feel a little less intimidating. He dipped his mop in the bucket and began making use of it.

Cricket wet his own mop and began working beside him. "So, tell me then Dodger, how did ya do it?" he asked him.

"Do what?"

"Open that cursed box. That chest be a suicide task, mate. Ye 'ave no idear how many sorry souls 'ave tried ta open that thin' before ya. Fer the last seven years the cap'n 'as been tryin' ta open its jaws. We found it at the bottom o' Davy Jones's piss hole, an' not a thin' er one could make it budge. So tell me true, how did ya do it?"

Bastian was confused by the question. He thought the answer was obvious.

"Didn't you see it?" he asked.

"See what?"

"The light and key beneath the chest?"

It had clearly been enchanted. He presumed that everyone had seen it.

Cricket stared at Bastian like he was mad.

"If yer seein' thin's, mate, then ya might want ta think about gettin' yer 'ead looked at. There be nothin' but solid wood beneath that chest, I 'ave seen it dozens o' times."

Bastian hesitated. Surely the pirate was having him on? He laughed uneasily and Cricket narrowed his eyes at him. "By Shick, ya really are mad!"

"You really didn't see it?" Bastian asked again in earnest.

"Ye 'ave clearly been through a lot today. I wouldn't worry. Once ya rest up ye'll be as right as rain," Cricket consoled, slapping him on the shoulder.

Bastian scratched his head. He knew what he saw. Didn't he? Maybe part of the enchantment was that the person who activated it was the only one who could see it. Surely something he'd touched on the chest had triggered the glowing key? Either way, if he was the only one who saw it, then his feat would've looked that much more impressive. He wasn't sure if that would prove to be a benefit or a disservice. He needed just enough skill to keep himself alive, but not enough that he was too useful to be let go.

"What's the next port?" he asked, changing the subject. It was the real question burning in his mind. He needed to figure out how he was going to get back to Westdock.

Cricket paused his work to wipe his brow.

"Our next port on the mainland be Port Trinity, but we 'ave one stop ta make before then. Why ye be askin'?"

"Port Trinity? That's perfect! I need to get back to Westdock as soon as possible. Do you know how frequently the train runs on Sundays?" Bastian asked.

Port Trinity wasn't far from Westdock. By train, it would only take a few hours to get back. The fee would most likely eat into every treasure that still occupied his pockets, but it was well worth it and it would be easier to find a buyer in Port Trinity. It was the capital of entertainment, known for its high-caliber shows and its extravagant night clubs and gambling dens. Some called it the Port of Pleasures. Selling stolen merchandise there probably wasn't even considered dodgy dealings. But, before he could do anything, he would need to construct a disguise to avoid the castle's men...

Bastian realized that Cricket was looking at him with an amused smirk.

"What?" he asked.

"Ye 'ave no idear what ye 'ave gotten yerself inta, do ya?"

"What do you mean?"

Cricket ignored the question. "I thought ye be runnin' from that place, seekin' refuge an' all?"

"I was…but only to lose my tail. It's crucial that I get back as soon as possible."

"Then ya jumped on the wrong ship, mate. Once ya join the Black Mary, there ain't no turnin' back."

"I have no intention of joining the Black Mary," Bastian said pointedly.

"Too late fer that," Cricket laughed.

"Pardon? I only jumped on this ship for a quick escape from Lord Bardviss. Not to become a bloody pirate!" Bastian blurted.

A couple of sailors paused in their duties and turned their attention towards them.

"Back ta work, swabbies!" a rough-looking man with an eye patch ordered.

"Aye, aye, Snibs," Cricket answered cheerfully.

The man scowled. Cricket grabbed Bastian's arm and pulled him aside. "Ya better keep yer voice down when ye be mentionin' treason. Especially when we be in earshot o' the quartermaster," he said in a low voice.

"Treason?" Bastian asked in surprise.

Cricket motioned for him to follow him towards the back of the ship. Once there was distance between them and the other men, he spoke again. "Listen mate, yer part o' the crew now whether ye like it er not. Which means that any mention o' abandonin' 'er be treason. I get the impression that ye don't quite understand the weight o' what that means? Well, I'll tell ya. The only reason yer still alive be the captain 'as some sort o' use fer ya. Once ye leave the ship, yer of no more use now, are ya? But what ye will be, be a loose end an' liability. The cap'n won't rest 'til the crew 'as 'unted ya down. If fer nothin' else, then ta make an example out o' ya. An' trust me, mate, when yer bein' made an example o', it won't be a pretty and quick death," Cricket warned.

"You're telling me that now that I'm here, I'm part of the crew and there's no way for me to leave?" he asked evenly.

Cricket nodded. "Not with yer life, unless ye 'ave given a lifetime o' service, that is." Then he narrowed his eyes at Bastian. "What did ye leave behind in Westdock that be so precious anyway?" he asked.

Bastian hesitated. "Something irreplaceable," he muttered, having no interest in elaborating.

Cricket studied him for a beat, and then he lowered his voice to a whisper. "That golden egg wasn't all ya stole, was it? Ye left the greatest part o' yer prize hidden behind in Westdock, didn't ya?"

Bastian started to correct the misassumption, and then stopped himself, thinking better of it.

Cricket's eyes widened, mistaking his silence as confirmation. "I knew it! I knew there be no way ye made it inta a castle without takin' more than a golden egg. What be it? A statue o' pure gold? A chest full o' diamonds an' rubies? Er, perhaps some enchanted artifact from old times, eh?" he pressed.

Bastian couldn't help but smile at Cricket's enthusiasm. It appeared that the mention of treasure really did make a pirate's eyes sparkle. He lowered his voice to mirror Cricket's. "What if I told you that if you were to help me escape this ship, I would give you the greatest part of the Wendrians' treasure?"

"Ha! I would tell ya ta go Shick yerself," Cricket laughed.

Bastian frowned. It wasn't the reaction he was hoping for.

"First o' all mate, me mum taught me ta never trust a thief, no offense. Secondly, I be more loyal ta this ship than me own mother. An' thirdly, even if I did want ta 'elp ya, it not be possible ta escape the Black Mary and live ta tell the tale," Cricket said matter-of-factly.

Bastian stared at him in disbelief. "You can't trust a thief? What about me trusting you? You're a bloody pirate!"

"Ye would be wise not ta. Fer one thin', we only just met, an' fer another, as stated, I am a pirate. I 'ave a mad thirst fer anythin' shiny that I be willin' ta do dark thin's just ta quench," he grinned.

"But not mad enough to help me off this ship?"

"I said that I 'ad a mad thirst fer treasure, not that I be mad in the 'ead, mate," Cricket corrected. He put a comforting hand on Bastian's shoulder. "If ye treasure yer life, than ferget about yer past and the prize ye left behind."

Cricket's words hit Bastian like a bullet through the chest. He couldn't just forget Gwena and Felix and leave them behind. Especially when they were both in the midst of trouble. Bastian had never failed at escaping impossible situations before. The Black Mary would be no exception. There was always a way—he just had to find it.

"Keep yer chin up, mate. If ye keep yer 'ands clean an' do what ye promised, then per'aps one day we will find the right moment ta uncover yer gold, but that moment ain't now. On the upside, I 'ave never known a soul in the crew that 'as wanted ta escape this ship. Just think, ye get the opportunity ta see the world, girls at every port, experience adventure in every sense o' the word. An' we be known ta 'ave a bit o' fun every now an' again," Cricket said cheerily.

Bastian returned his smile, but it didn't meet his eyes. And then the clang of a loud bell split the air.

"Ah, just in time. Nothin' like supper an' a drop o' grog ta lift yer spirits, eh? " Cricket said and led Bastian inside the ship.

TAKING FLIGHT
CHAPTER EIGHT

Lilliana was aiming her pistol at Felix's chest. He'd surrendered her gun after she held him at knifepoint. The way she'd handled the blade left him without doubt that she knew how to use it. He was feeling incredibly bitter about his circumstances. But he knew that if he wanted to win the game, he needed to fold this round and wait until he had a better hand.

"I'm not carrying your bag. If you want it, you can carry it yourself," he said stubbornly, and stepped over it before proceeding down the corridor in front of the duchess. Lilliana huffed in annoyance, but she picked up her bag and followed him.

They traversed the passage with an iron curtain of silence between them for a time, and then Lilliana finally spoke. "Just so we're clear, I'm not running away. Nor do I have wedding jitters, or some romantic notion about love. My life doesn't allow such luxuries."

Felix no longer cared. "Are you going to tell me what you *are* doing, then?" he asked, uninterested. His predicament and current company had drained him of his usual optimism and put him in a foul mood.

"I'm saving everyone from having to suffer Lord Bardviss as the next duke of Westdock."

"How very noble of you," Felix replied dryly.

He couldn't care less about having Lord Bardviss as the next duke of Westdock. He made a habit of ignoring the laws no matter who was making them. Lilliana was clearly peeved by his lack of care and understanding,

"Don't you realize what that would mean? Lord Bardviss is a monster with delusions of grandeur. He's only marrying me for my family's position. I overheard him talking about wanting to be the next emperor of Equillian. Being duke is only the first step in this crazy scheme of his to take over the world! My mother can't see it, but I know that as soon as we're wed, he'll cast my family and me aside and do whatever he pleases," she said passionately.

Felix held up his hand and rubbed his thumb and pointer together to mimic playing a tiny violin.

"You are infuriating!" she said in exasperation. "Don't you care about anything but yourself?"

"Honestly, Duchess, I don't give a cwip about Lord Bardviss or your predicament. Of course, he is marrying you for your position, and you are marrying him for his wealth. I thought that you were supposed to be the one educating *me* on arranged marriages? Will Lord Bardviss be a terrible duke just because he has delusions of grandeur? I don't know. Politics aren't any of my concern, remember? I have less important things to worry about, like starving to death and ensuring there's a roof over my head. What I don't understand is how faking your kidnapping is going to solve anything."

"If I'm kidnapped, then Lord Bardviss will have to look after my family and show good behavior in order to maintain our betrothal for as long as I'm missing. It should buy me enough time to find my father, the real duke of Westdock."

"Your father? As in Drake Wendrian, who's been missing for the last two years?"

"That is my father."

"Wow, you really have gone off your rocker," Felix remarked dryly.

Lilliana kicked him in the back, sending him flying several steps forward. He let the rage he felt boil down to a simmer before he spoke again. "Face it, Duchess, your father is missing for one of two reasons. Either he's dead or he doesn't want to be found. You would be wise to marry Lord Bardviss. Someone with skin as soft as yours wouldn't fare well without a castle to sleep in. You think that marrying a man you detest is the worst of it? I tell you now, that it's far from it. Wait until you've gone over a week without food or had to do darker things with your body to earn your keep than shicking an unwanted husband. Then you will know the definition of a real problem, my lady," he said coolly.

Right after his words fell he knew that they'd stabbed deeply. He could see a faint blush on Lilliana's cheeks and a glimmer of uncertainty in her eyes. For a moment he almost felt pity for her. He had to admit that it took courage to do what she was doing. It was bloody stupid, and her plan was full of holes, but it was still brave, at least for a highborn.

As Felix walked silently down the stone labyrinth with Lilliana, his mind turned to Bastian. He wondered how long it would take for him to discover that Felix was missing and what he would do once he had. He recalled hearing him speak to Lord Bardviss on the stairs right before they departed, and his heart sank. That encounter would link Bastian to this whole mess. If he could at least stay hidden until Moonday, then he could use the train tickets to escape and Felix could meet him in the Heartland. Felix knew then that he needed to find a way to contact him and ensure that he got on that train. If he didn't, his brother would have to forget about seeing the world, let alone anything but the inside of the Wendrians' dungeon.

Felix decided that if Lilliana was going to force this fate on him and Bastian, then she sure as Shick better compensate them generously for it.

"I have a proposition for you," he announced.

Lilliana gave him her attention more easily than he imagined she would. "I'm listening," she said skeptically.

"You and I are both in a bind. You need a kidnapper, and I need coin. So, here's what I propose. Hire me."

"Ha! How about you help me, or you forfeit your life?" Lilliana suggested, waving her pistol to remind him that it was there.

Felix shrugged. "Ok, kill me then," he said indifferently. He stopped and turned around to face her and her weapon, holding his arms out welcomingly.

Lilliana's face paled. "Do you have a death wish?" she asked angrily.

"Shoot me. I'm not going to help you for nothing, so you may as well get it over with. I'm sure you can easily find another—what was it? *Rat off the street* to replace me? I mean, with me being *common* and all, you shouldn't have too much trouble."

Lilliana looked livid, which only encouraged him.

"See, the problem with your chosen subject here is that I have nothing to lose. I don't have family, or riches, or a lover. Which leaves you with a weak hand. On the flip side, I do happen to have a wealth of knowledge and experience on subject matters that you would find incredibly useful in your current circumstance. Which, of course, would make it counterproductive for you to kill me. And threatening me around-the-clock will get tiresome for us both very quickly, trust me. However, give me a pile of coin that I can cherish after this fiasco is over, and you can have the benefit of my services and save yourself a world of trouble."

"What skills and knowledge could you possibly have that would benefit me?" Lilliana scoffed.

"Let's see…, star navigation, advanced forgery, blackmailing, impersonations and linguistic expertise, and bullshit artistry, for a start," he said with a grin and a humble bow.

"Charming," Lilliana said sarcastically. "I never knew bullshit was an art form."

"I could teach you a lot that you don't know," Felix said with a condescending smile.

Lilliana ignored him. "Fine. I will hire you. As payment for being my kidnapper you can keep whatever ransom you inspire from Lord Bardviss. But you have to run every letter you send past me, you're not to promise him my immediate release, and you must stay under my service until I dismiss you," she said.

"Plus, one hundred gold duckets from your own purse. A written guarantee of your protection. Safe passage after the job is done, with a personal guard. And my name cleared in Westdock," Felix countered.

"I will give you no more than sixty gold duckets, guaranteed protection while you're under my employment, and I will give you our house's official seal of protection to take with you after, but I'm not giving you any personal guard. I will clear your name in Westdock if, and only if, we are successful. And if you even think of betraying me, then your life and gold are forfeit."

"Done," Felix said, holding out his hand.

Lilliana shook it. "You can start your service now," she said, and dropped her bag in his arms.

Felix shouldered the bag grudgingly, but he smiled to himself as they continued down the corridor. The deal was even sweeter than he'd hoped for. Sixty duckets was a small fortune in itself, but Lord Bardviss had far more riches than the Wendrians. Drawing out this little scheme meant the potential for a grossly generous sum.

"Does this Star-forsaken labyrinth have an end?" he asked.

Lilliana walked ahead several paces and then stopped at the fork in front of them.

"Only if you know the way out," she replied and hit the ceiling with the butt of her pistol. A shower of dirt rained down revealing a trapdoor. "A little help?"

2

Felix climbed through the trapdoor behind Lady Lilliana into a huge underground hangar. The extensive space was empty and well lit with Everfire torches. Felix did a double take—in the center was a large airship that was almost invisible. His jaw dropped. It was the design of a sloop with masts and sails on its deck, except that it was floating, suspended off the ground by a giant oval-shaped balloon above the sails. The sails, the balloon, and the body of the ship were reflective like a mirror, camouflaging it with the surroundings. He'd always known of airships, of course, everyone did. But to be standing in the presence of one was something different entirely. The vessel was so magnificent it took Felix's breath away.

"Where did you say it was that we're going?" he asked, without peeling his eyes from the ship.

"I didn't. We're going to the Windswept Isles. My cousin is one of the largest dragon breeders in Sky View," Lilliana said.

"Of course they are," Felix muttered, and he pinched his arm to make sure he wasn't dreaming.

The Windswept Isles were a network of beautiful islands that were suspended thousands of feet in the air. Sky View was the wealthiest precinct in Equillian. Due to its monopoly on dragons, it had the largest economy in the world. Never in his wildest dreams did he ever imagine that he would have the opportunity to see it. The precinct was known as a paradise populated by aristocrats that was only accessible to the privileged. Anyone of common birth could only dream of seeing its surface. And *dragons,* Felix thought, what a spectacle that would be.

A tall man smartly dressed in aviation garb came out onto the balcony of the airship and then slid down a ladder onto the ground in front of them. He was middle-aged with black hair peppered with thick lines of grey on either side of his temples and a well-groomed mustache. He walked towards the duchess with a free-spirited swagger. "Just in time, my girl, better hurry aboard. The fireworks are due to start any minute," he said.

Lilliana leapt into his arms and hugged him. "You're a breath of fresh air, Uncle Roy. Is the ship ready?"

"As far as I can tell. It's been so long since she's flown, we won't know for sure until she's skyward. Who's the new recruit?" he asked, nodding towards Felix.

"Oh right, this is James, my hired opportunist," Lilliana said.

Felix had almost forgotten about his fictitious name. Thank you, Serendipity, he thought, while rubbing the Lady Luck charm in his coat pocket.

The aviator held out his hand. "Always good to have extra support, name's Roy, I'll be piloting this bird."

Felix took his hand and shook it firmly. "Pleasure," he said.

"Ever ridden on an airship before?"

"Unfortunately, I can't say that I have."

"Good, I always like providing a maiden voyage. Besides, it gives us an excuse to celebrate," the pilot said with a wink, and he produced two spiced cigars from his coat pocket, offering one to Felix.

"A man with good taste, much obliged," Felix said appreciatively, and suddenly his whole outlook on the situation brightened.

Roy guided them aboard the airship. As Felix climbed the ladder, his stomach started doing somersaults. He figured it was a waste of breath at this point to mention that he was terrified of heights. Instead, he sucked on the unlit cigar like it was his antidote for poison.

Felix had been on over a dozen different ships working as a fisher's hand, not to mention the hundreds he'd seen coming in and out of Westdock's harbor, but he'd never seen anything like this. On top was an observation deck armored with a harpoon at the stern. There was a large telescope and a slew of circular instruments at the bow, and in the center was a huge round pillar of Everfire surrounded by a glass cylinder that directed the heat upwards towards the balloon. There were two propellers at the back of the vessel and sails interspersed amid the many lines that attached the ship to its floatation device.

Below the main deck there were five sections. At the front was a flight deck with a wraparound window above a large control station. Behind that was a luxurious common space with two expensive-looking armchairs, a mahogany table, and a small kitchenette with basic amenities. Branched off that were two bedrooms, each with their own privy. On a separate deck below the main cabin was the boiler room. The ship had two Everfire-boilers which created the steam necessary to power the back propellers. She was a beauty.

Felix sat in one of the leather armchairs and looked out the porthole as the ship began to rise. He was greatly curious as to how they were going to pass through the ceiling, but somehow, they did. In a matter of moments, he could see the night sky all around them. As they continued to rise he caught sight of the large doors they had passed through closing below them. The doors had opened outward from the ceiling of the hanger, which also happened to be the floor of an open field behind the castle. A layer of thick grass, over the doors, making them virtually invisible once they were closed. The ship started rapidly elevating and Felix focused on his hands to distract himself from the height.

A loud *bang whiz* came from outside and colorful lights reflected in the window next to him. Felix ignored his stomach to satisfy his curiosity and looked out. They were now at least a hundred feet above the castle, facing a shower of colorful fireworks erupting over the harbor. The guests had crowded onto the balconies to catch the spectacle. Felix marveled at the clever and well-timed distraction. He was enjoying the show himself. The view was incredible. Every time a firework went off, he caught a bird's-eye glimpse of Westdock. The town that speckled the hills along the shoreline quickly receded beneath them. And in that moment, he realized just how small Westdock and his life truly were.

The airship was gliding through the midnight clouds, the castle and Westdock far behind it now. Felix reclined in the armchair, looking out the window while he enjoyed his cigar and shuffled his lucky deck of cards, deep in thought. Now that the ground wasn't visible, his fear of heights had passed and he was enjoying the view of the stars. He had never been so close to the Watchers. They were magnificent.

Roy was on the top deck adjusting the sails for the changing wind and Lilliana was pouring over a map on the table behind him.

"Isn't it three days' travel to Sky View from here?" he asked her.

"So, the street rat knows his geography," Lilliana said mockingly.

"Just because I'm not highborn, doesn't mean I'm uneducated. Unlike you, I've experienced the world beyond books. Could teach you a thing or two."

"Oh really? Where have you been beyond Westdock, oh worldly one?" she asked with derision.

"Beyond Westdock? Don't get ahead of yourself, Duchess. You don't even know what's happening in your own streets. Once you have some experience of life beyond your castle, then you can question me about my travel history."

"This isn't my first time to Sky View, I'll have you know," she said proudly.

"Wait, you mean, you've seen another castle? Wow, I bet that was enlightening," Felix said sarcastically. He put out his cigar and made his way to the ladderway that led to the top deck. "As much fun as your company is, Duchess, I think I would rather face the freezing wind," he said and ascended before she had the chance to make a comeback.

3

A cold gust met Felix like a fist to the face. He held tightly onto the line and made his way to the cylinder of Everfire in the center of the deck, putting his hands against the glass tube to warm them. He was quickly regretting his decision to come outside, but his pride and stubbornness wouldn't let him turn back.

Roy was just ahead, tying a knot in one of the lines.

"Beautiful night, isn't it?" the pilot asked above the gale.

"If you're into the affections of a frost witch, I could see the appeal," Felix called back.

"Ha! It is dangerously cold up here. Did you bring any other clothes?"

Felix looked down at the fine suit Gwena had made. It wasn't exactly tailored for keeping out the elements. "No. Somehow I missed the memo that I was going to be traversing the clouds today."

"Don't worry, I'll get you sorted. You can borrow some of mine until we can get you settled in Sky View. If you open up that compartment behind you, you'll find a spare coat," Roy said.

Felix eagerly sought out the compartment and pulled out a fur-lined aviator jacket. It was a little big, but he was beyond grateful to have it. He put it on and welcomed the warm hug from the fur lining.

"Ah, that's much better. Thanks," he said.

"Give me a minute, I'm going to try and get us above the wind," Roy called over the gust. Then he moved to the base of the Everfire housing and started pulling on the levers. The Everfire shot up through the tube with fervor and the ship began to rise. They passed through a layer of clouds and almost instantly the wind was gone.

"I was talking about the stars before, when I said that it was a nice night," Roy said, coming up beside Felix and motioning to the view around them.

"That makes so much more sense," Felix said, grinning.

He took in their surroundings. Now that they were above the clouds, the night was crystal clear and there was a serene stillness. The ship was completely encircled by bright stars that flooded the sky and reflected off every surface of the ship. It was as if they were gliding on a milky ocean of starlight. "Wow," he whispered.

"Beautiful, isn't it?" Roy smiled.

"It's magnificent," Felix said in awed wonder, leaning over the railing to take in the spectacle. "Can I ask you something?" he asked after a time.

"Of course, sport."

"Why are you supporting Lilliana in this? Is Lord Bardviss really that bad?" he asked.

Roy turned the question over before he answered. "No. I can't say that I approve of the marriage, but it's not my place to stand in the way of Everitt's decision. She loves her daughters dearly and has been put in a tough position. No, I am here to find Drake and to bring him home."

"You really believe that the duke's still out there?"

"If there's a chance in the nine realms of darkness, then he's out there. I've known Drake Wendrian most of my life, and the story we've been fed just doesn't add up. He was at his family's estate when his brother passed. Then the morning after, Drake supposedly flew into the Everstorm without rhyme or reason and never returned. I didn't set out to find him then because I was assured that the best people were already on it. And to tell you the truth, I had trouble believing it. The whole business felt surreal. I always imagined that he'd show up at my door one day. Of course, every man meets his end, but I don't think that he's met his. Drake is as tough as nails and has always been a survivor. Regardless, I can't spend another day doing nothing when there's a chance he could still be out there," Roy said, looking out towards the Watchers.

"So, you and the duke aren't really brothers, then?" Felix asked.

"No. Not by birth at any rate. John, the brother who passed away was Drake's only sibling. Lilliana calls me uncle because I've known her and her sister since they first laid eyes on this world. We have always thought of each other as family."

Felix could understand that better than anyone—he and Bastian were brothers in every sense of the word but blood. Even if he had a real brother somewhere out there, Bastian would always take precedence as his family.

"The idea that blood is thicker than water is a load of bull. A person who earns their title is far more valuable than one who's merely born into it," Felix said.

Roy nodded appreciatively. Then his expression was lost in introspection.

"I know Lilliana puts on a hard front, but she is much more fragile than she seems. She's gone through a lot since her father's disappearance. She could really use a friend," he said.

"You mean she's not always this charming?" Felix jested.

Roy smirked. "Her father and I used to call her little Everspark. She can be as stubborn and as fiery as her father and mother put together, and if you knew either of them, then you would understand the weight of that statement," Roy laughed.

"I can only imagine," Felix grinned.

Roy put a hand on his shoulder. "Let's head back in. The wind's only going to get worse," he said, and then he made his way towards the cabin.

Felix waited until Roy was inside and he was alone on deck, then he looked to the Stars. "Look after Bastian, won't you? And please Stars, help me ensure that he gets on that train," he prayed to the Watchers, and then he followed after.

INITIATION
CHAPTER NINE

Inside the Black Mary's belly, the mess hall was filling up with men. Bastian and Cricket stood in the dinner queue, waiting to fill their bowls. The interior of the ship wasn't as ornate as the outside, but she was clean and well kept. Every surface was a smooth dark wood that was dimly lit by firebeetle lanterns on the walls. Chatter filled the room as the sailors mingled with one another. Bastian's stomach growled, and he realized that he hadn't eaten since the duchess's banquet table. Just thinking of the gourmet spread from the night before made his mouth water, and he found himself wishing that he'd allowed himself to indulge when he'd had the opportunity.

At the front of the line, there was a large middle-aged man with muscles like rocks and skin as black as night who dished soup into their bowls. Cricket pulled Bastian up beside him for an introduction. "Evenin', Doc. I want ya ta meet our newest recruit, this be Dodger, our resident thief. Dodger, this be Doc, best cook on the seven seas and our prized surgeon. If you could only be friends with one sailor onboard, this would be your man."

"Welcome aboard, Dodger," the cook greeted, handing Bastian a bowl brimming with the aroma of fresh spices and herbs.

"Nice to meet you, and thanks. It smells delicious," Bastian said graciously.

"Lad's got manners, I like 'im already," Doc said with a grin, then moved to serve the men behind them.

Three rows of long wooden tables stretched through the center of the mess hall. Bastian joined Cricket at the middle one and eagerly dug into his supper. The hardy stew warmed his belly, and he was pleasantly surprised by the immense flavor. "This is really good," he said with a full mouth.

"I wasn't lyin' when I said that Doc be the best cook on the seven seas," Cricket said.

The tables filled up around them and the room resounded with the sailors' boisterous voices calling over one another. Bastian counted thirty-six men when they were all together, a small crew for a ship of that size. They were a rough-looking bunch. Many had tattoo-covered arms and scars of all different sizes. Their skin was leathered from the sun and several of them were un-whole, missing a leg, a hand, or an eye. But the obvious hard conditions they had weathered didn't seem to dampen their spirits. Their faces were filled with humor and their laughter rang throughout the hall.

Cricket handed Bastian a black leather stein brimming with drink and encouraged him to drain it.

Bastian accepted it gratefully and took several large gulps before he registered the sweet taste and the subtle heat in his throat. "What's this?" he asked.

"Ye don't know what grog be? 'Ave ye been livin' under a rock, mate?" Cricket asked in surprise.

"Almost, Westdock," Bastian said with a smirk.

"Ha-ha, ye 'ave truly never been beyond its borders?"

"Nope, but not from lack of trying."

"Well, yer in fer a real treat, mate. Equillian 'as much ta offer beyond yer corner. This be grog, rum an' water. By mixin' the two together both last longer. An' the cap'n don't approve o' us bein' half-seas over while on duty. But tonight, we will be given real drinks in 'onor o' this special occasion. Thanks be ta yer fine skills, we 'ave somethin' ta celebrate!"

Cricket held up his black stein. "Ta wenches, treasure, and mates. May we both 'ave plenty fillin' our fates!"

They clashed their steins and drank.

As soon as they had finished their bowls of stew, Cricket jumped up on the table to make a speech. "Oi, scallywags, lend me yer ears!" he called loudly, and the men's voices quieted as they gave him their attention.

"Tonight, yer Black Jacks will be filled with gulpers o' Doc's finest brew, an' ye 'ave one man ta thank fer it. Fer 'e 'as single-'andedly rid our trials with that wretched, Star-fersaken box! Give a warm welcome ta the master o' locks, the dodger o' death, our thief an' the newest member o' our crew, Dodger!"

Oh *Shick*, Bastian thought.

Cricket pulled him up on the table beside him and the men erupted in cheer. After a minute, Cricket quieted them again. "Dodger 'ere 'as never been beyond Westdock's shores. I think it only be proper ta introduce the lad ta what 'e 'as been missin'. What do ya say, lads, shall we start by showin' 'im 'ow we welcome new recruits ta the Black Mary?"

The crew cheered again loudly, banging their spoons on the tables and lifting their Black Jacks high.

"Aye!" "Initiation!" men called out around him. Then they began hitting their Black Jacks on the tables in unison and chanting his name, "Dodger, Dodger, Dodger…"

Bastian had a bad feeling about what might happen next.

A tall, lanky pirate with dark red hair and a freckled face jumped up on the table beside them and used a jug to refill the Black Jack in Bastian's hand.

"This be the good stuff," he said to Bastian with a wink.

"Dodger, Stork. Stork, Dodger," Cricket introduced.

"Welcome aboard the Black Mary," Stork said, then he pulled out a metal shot glass with a flexible target attached to the top and held it up to the enthusiastic crowd. From a small pouch, he poured something into it that looked like black sand.

"What's that?" Bastian asked.

"Black Powder," Stork returned cheerfully.

"No, no, no," Bastian said, and he tried to get down from the table. But he was pulled back up by the two pirates.

"Yer not a coward, are ya, Dodger?" Stork asked.

Bastian shook his head uneasily.

"Didn't think so. Now stand real still," he instructed.

Bastian swallowed his fear and stood as still as a statue while Stork proceeded to balance the shot glass on the top of his head.

"Don't worry, it's not gonna kill ya," Cricket consoled. "Stork 'ere knows what 'e be doin', don't ya, Stork?" he asked the redhead.

"O' course, matey, ain't this a face ye can trust?" Stork asked, grinning at Bastian.

The men cheered as soon as the shot glass was balanced in place.

Cricket turned to the men behind them. "Bullseye at the ready?" he called.

Bastian carefully turned his head. There was a tall man with a tattooed target on his forehead who was holding a bottle of rum in one hand and a pistol in the other.

"Aye, at the ready," Bullseye said and cocked his pistol, pointing it at Bastian's head.

Bastian's eyes widened and Stork and Cricket turned him back around.

"The only danger be in movin'. Stand still as a statue, mate, an' ye 'ave nothin' ta fear," Cricket advised.

Bastian tensed. He could feel the pistol aimed at the back of his head. Stork jumped off the table and Cricket stepped aside.

"Aim…"

Bastian's stomach dropped. He closed his eyes. The shot glass stood balanced on his head, and the full Black Jack shook in his hands.

"Dodger, Dodger, Dodger…," the men's voices echoed around him.

Bastian prayed to the Stars.

"Fire!"

The gun made an ear-splitting roar as the lead left the barrel. The ball made its way skillfully to the flexible target on Bastian's head and brushed a circle of flint in the bull's-eye. The target bent forward, dipping the sparking flint into the metal shot glass and igniting the powder.

Sparks flew around Bastian's head as the flaming shot glass fell forward into the Black Jack in his hands. The potent spirit instantly caught fire.

Cricket came up beside him and put his Black Jack over Bastian's, extinguishing the flame.

The men cheered loudly and then began a new chant, "Skull, skull, skull…"

Bastian was stunned, he stood starring at the bullet that had lodged itself in the wood beam in front of him.

"Drink up, mate," Cricket grinned.

Bastian took a deep breath and knocked back his stein. Despite the harsh burning sensation in his throat, he welcomed the stiff drink.

The men cheered him on and once he'd finished, he turned his stein upside down and put it on his head in triumph. The room erupted in a roar of approval.

As if on cue, an upbeat sea chantey filled the air and the sailors pushed the tables aside. Cricket helped Bastian down and clapped him on the shoulder. "Welcome ta the Black Mary, mate," he said cheerfully.

Bastian's head was swimming. He noticed that the music was being played by a half man on the fiddle.

"That be Dagger. Don't let 'is stature fool ya. 'E might be small, but 'e be deadly," Cricket said.

Bastian had heard of the short men from Dragoon, an island on the Southern Sea, but he'd never actually seen one. The man played the instrument with skilled vigor and sang in tune as the sailors began to dance around him. Bastian's surroundings blurred as the liquor took hold, and the next thing he knew, he was being pulled out onto the dance floor to join them.

"Naow, when I wuz a little lad,
me kind mother told me
That if I didn't kiss the gals,
me lips would all grow moldy.
But ta me fine mother then,
I surely didn't listen,
I sailed the seas fer many a year
not knowin' what I wuz missin'.

One day I met a mermaid dear,
who touched me lips and set me clear.
I changed me course and set me sails
afore the gales ta be kissin'.
Oi I go a shilly doe da,
oi I go a dally!
Round the world fer all the girls,
findin' which I fancy!…"

2

Bastian woke in the wee hours of the morning, his head still foggy from his initiation. He found himself in the sleeping quarters lying in a hammock without the faintest memory of how he'd gotten there. He checked his pockets and was relieved to discover that everything was accounted for. The motion of the sea rocked him gently back and forth as he tried to wrap his head around the fact that he was on a pirate ship. And how, he'd already faced death on two occasions. He dreaded what the next day might bring. Then it hit him: They hadn't pulled into port. He took out his pocket watch. It was the hour of Faya, the muse for creativity. He rolled out of his hammock, being careful not to wake the sleeping men around him, and snuck out of the sleeping quarters and up to the top deck. It was snowing. The deck was already covered in a thin layer of snow that was glittering in the starlight. Bastian buttoned his jacket and stepped outside. It was freezing. He walked up to the railing and saw they were still encircled by the open sea with no land in sight. At least Lord Bardviss's men hadn't caught up to them. He found the Guiding Star and used his hand to measure its distance to the adjacent constellations. They were heading west. That was strange—Port

Trinity was in the opposite direction. There was nothing west of Westdock but the Desert Ocean. And there was nothing in the Desert Ocean. Bastian was well versed in geography, but if they were headed west, then he had no idea where they were going. And if they were going west, it meant there was no chance that Bastian would make it back to Westdock by Moonday. He slumped against the ship's railing in defeat. He'd been so close to fulfilling his dreams, and now this. It felt like a terrible nightmare. He only wished it was a nightmare, then at least he could wake from it. He was acutely aware that with each passing moment he was getting farther and farther from Gwena and Felix. He had no idea how long it would take him to find a way back to Westdock—if he even could. He needed to let them know what had happened. If he could only get in touch with them, then he could tell them to go to the Heartland without him, and he could meet them there when he was able. At least they would both be out of harm's way in the capital.

Bastian returned below deck and sat at the base of the stairs. He pulled out his notebook and began to write a letter in the half-light.

Hi Gwen,

I'm sorry that I couldn't be there to meet you at the Tipsy Tav' as promised. I hate to think of you waiting for me with no explanation. If I'd been given the choice, I wouldn't have missed it for the world. You have ruined me. Since you confessed your love, I can think of nothing else. I find myself, by strange circumstances, stuck on a pirate ship — just like one of the make-believe stories we used to play as children. In the past I would have gladly welcomed the adventure and left Westdock behind. But now that your lips have touched mine and fed the fire in my heart, I want to be nowhere else than back

Bastian didn't have any idea if Gwena would ever see his letter. But writing it eased his mind all the same, as if somehow by scribing the words, she would know his thoughts. The notion of her waiting for him and Felix at the Tipsy Tav' tormented him. But the worst thought of all was Gwena having to return to that house with her father. Bastian could still see the lash marks clearly in his mind. He hoped deeply that Felix and Gwena got on the train to the Heartland together.

Bastian returned to his hammock and suddenly realized that he'd completely forgotten that it had been his birthday. Reflecting on the last twenty-one hours, he decided that his coming of age had been both the best and the worst birthday he'd ever had. So much had happened, it felt more like a year than a single day, and he knew then that, however unconventional, his Illumine Day had truly marked the end of his childhood.

LANGUAGE OF SONGS
CHAPTER TEN

Felix woke with a stiff back. He spent the night on a fold-out cot that somehow managed to be more uncomfortable than the thin mattress he was used to. Roy had lent him a spare set of silk pajamas so that he could remain "respectable" outside of his suit. Felix was happy to accept, especially considering that it wasn't particularly warm on board the airship.

He made his way into the main cabin, where he found Roy and Lilliana seated at the table. Roy was reading a newspaper and Lilliana was enjoying jammed toast and a pot of tea.

Yawning, Felix sat down beside them.

Lilliana ran her eyes disdainfully over his disheveled hair and lack of proper dress.

He ignored her and helped himself to a piece of toast.

"Well, my dear, your disappearance has certainly been noticed," Roy said, without taking his eyes from the paper.

"Let me see," Lilliana said.

She stood behind him and peered over his shoulder. Felix stared at them quizzically and sought out the date on the back page. "How on Equillian did you manage to get this morning's paper?" he asked in astonishment.

Roy peered at him over the Equillian Times. "By Sendsong. How do you get your morning's paper?" he asked with genuine curiosity and surprise, as if there was no other way.

"From the newsy on the corner of Pine and Tucker…"

Lilliana cleared her throat. "James doesn't come from a noble house, he isn't used to our conveniences," she explained.

"Oh…is that so?" Roy asked in surprise, regarding Felix with a new measure.

"Yeah…," Felix said uncomfortably.

He wished that Lilliana hadn't outed him. As soon as a noble knew you weren't one of them, they tended to treat you like a second-class citizen. At least Roy's surprise proved that Felix hadn't lost his touch in playing a convincing blueblood.

To Felix's relief, Roy brushed past the information as if he hadn't heard it. "Sendsongs really are quite fascinating. I suppose that I take them for granted, they are so commonly used in my circles. I don't know what I'd do without mine. In truth, I'm incredibly lucky to possess one. There were only fourteen hundred made. I inherited my whistle from my father, Stars rest his soul. It's a shame the ban took them out of production. They really are a wonder. If you'd like, I can take you on deck with me next time I call mine."

"That would be brilliant," Felix replied in earnest.

He had no idea that nobles still used Sendsongs. The original birds were sacred to the Order. They had been extinct for centuries, but somehow the alchemists had found a way to recreate a mechanical version, replicating their abilities. Felix knew that enchanted objects were prized among the aristocrats. The Enchanted Objects Collection Agency, or the E.O.C.A, confiscated enchanted objects from anyone who wasn't a blueblood and then sold them to the highest bidder. It was one of the stings of being common born—the same rules didn't apply to the upper-crusters. The whole system was filled with corruption. The aristocrats bought the objects for ridiculous prices and competed with their peers to own the most impressive collections. Felix had always imagined that the enchanted objects sat in display cases, collecting dust. But if they were used so commonly, that meant that they weren't dangerous. And if they weren't dangerous, then that meant they were banned for a different reason entirely. Felix recalled the article that Bastian had discovered in Jarvis's cabin the day before. Events surrounding Rupert Finley's death suddenly took on a whole new perspective. If there hadn't been an enchanted object malfunction, then something was being covered up. But what was it? And why weren't the nobles asking these questions? But then again, why would they? They were benefiting from the ban. Undoing it wouldn't be in their best interest. Suddenly Felix felt incredibly naïve, realizing for the first time just how different his life was from those more privileged. He'd always prided himself on being able to mingle with aristocrats, but he was beginning to see now that, in reality, their lives were worlds apart.

"There's no mention in here of me being kidnapped," Lilliana said, referring to the article in front of her.

Felix came out of his thoughts and turned his attention towards her.

"What are you talking about?"

"The article says that I've gone mysteriously missing. It says nothing about me being kidnapped."

"That's no surprise. Detectives won't make conclusions without having solid evidence," Roy said.

"But there was solid evidence. I left a note."

"And you're certain that they received it?" Roy asked.

"It was impossible to miss. I left it right on the bed."

"What did it say?" Felix asked, interrupting the exchange.

"That I was being kidnapped and that the kidnapper would be in contact with demands."

"Well, you can't get much clearer than that," Felix said.

"Why wouldn't they disclose that to the public?" she asked.

"Maybe your mother wants to keep it quiet?" Roy suggested.

"Or maybe someone else does," Felix said.

Roy and Lilliana turned to him.

"There's no doubt that Lord Bardviss was the first one in that room. We could hear him on his way up when we left. Could there be a reason he'd want to hide your ransom letter?" Felix asked.

Lilliana and Roy exchanged a worried glance.

"Is that a yes? Because if he called your bluff and wants you gone, all he needs is a letter forged with your handwriting to make a convincing case that you ran away."

Roy crossed his arms uneasily. "It's true. If Lord Bardviss can make it look like you ran from your betrothal, then he'll have no obligation to get you back. He can make a show to look for you for a time, and then move on…maybe even marry your sister," he said solemnly.

Lilliana's face paled and she collapsed into her chair. "I'm so stupid. How did I not see this? I just gave Lord Bardviss exactly what he wanted," she gasped and buried her face in her hands.

Roy placed a consoling hand on her shoulder. "Come now, my dear, once we find your father all will be resolved," he said.

"That's *if* we find him. Even if we do, once Lord Bardviss marries Natasha, it will be too late," Lilliana said, keeping her face buried.

Felix bit his tongue, he knew that this could be his opportunity to get out. If Lilliana wasn't kidnapped, then she wouldn't need him anymore. But Roy's words about her were still fresh in his mind, and she expressed such genuine anguish that he couldn't help but feel sorry for her. He'd always been such a sucker for damsels in distress.

"It's not too late, my lady," he said.

Lilliana looked at him, hopeful. You're a damn fool, Felix, he thought to himself. But he'd already uttered the words.

"It will take Lord Bardviss at least a few days to organize a forged letter in your hand, if that is his intention. And the earliest that he could marry your sister would be at the ceremony intended for you. When did you say your wedding is scheduled for?" he asked.

"Starday after next," Lilliana said hopelessly.

"Right, that gives us exactly two weeks to figure things out. And keep in mind this is all hypothetical. We don't know for sure why your kidnapping wasn't reported. So, take a deep breath, my lady, your world will not fall apart today."

Lilliana took a deep and shaky breath. Felix scrounged to find the silver lining. "On the upside, if Lord Bardviss did conceal the letter, then he's given you exactly what you wanted. Reasonable cause to cancel the matrimony," he said. Lilliana sat up suddenly, her hope restored.

"You're right. I just need to write a letter to my mother and explain what happened, and she will cancel the wedding!"

"Whoa, not so fast," Felix and Roy said together.

"We still don't have any evidence that Lord Bardviss took your letter," Felix said.

"And if we turn back now, then we ruin the one chance we have to find your father," Roy added.

Lilliana's optimism deflated.

"With all due respect, my lady, this is what you hired me for and where my expertise lies. Let me take it from here and earn my keep. Lord Bardviss is no different from any of the nobles I've dealt with in the past. He's playing a stupid game that, luckily, I happen to be exceptionally good at. If we play our cards right, then we should be able to get Lord Bardviss to incriminate himself, giving us the opportunity to look for your father while we simultaneously secure his position," Felix said.

"Well, well, master opportunist. Perhaps you weren't lying about your worth after all. Alright, I'll give you a chance to prove yourself. So then, where do we begin?" she asked.

Felix grinned, glad that he could represent his class with at least one thing they had up on the aristocrats. "We need to send another ransom note to Lord Bardviss. It doesn't matter if he destroys it, we're fishing for information. Whatever action he takes will confirm or deny our suspicions and guide our next move. We also need to send a letter to your mother. It needs to be in your hand, Lilliana. Tell her that you've been kidnapped, but that you are currently unharmed. That your captors are only after a ransom from Lord Bardviss and then promise to release you. Make it convincing."

"Captors, plural?" Lilliana asked.

"An organized group is more threatening than an individual. Make it plural and leave the rest to me."

"I'm on it," Lilliana said, and she disappeared into her quarters.

Felix was surprised and pleased by her willingness to cooperate. He picked up the newspaper from the table and scanned the article for himself.

"Since you got this paper, I presume that you have a way to send a letter to the castle from here?" he asked Roy.

"Of course, we can send it via Sendsong directly to Lord Bardviss."

"And it's dependable and untraceable back to us?"

"Totally untraceable and secure. He can even return mail to the sender via our Sendsong without ever knowing whom he's talking to."

"That's brilliant. I better get to writing then," Felix said, rising from the table. He knocked back the rest of his tea and grabbed another piece of toast before heading for the private quarters.

"Sport," Roy called after him.

Felix turned.

"Thank you."

"Don't thank me yet," Felix said, then left to find some ink and parchment.

2

Lord Henry Bardviss,

Rest assured that despite your fiancée's uncooperative nature, Lady Lilliana is presently safe and unharmed. However, in order to maintain her well-being, we need assurance that we have your complete and utter cooperation.

Felix rolled his Lady Luck charm across the backs of his knuckles as he looked over his letter to Lord Bardviss. Wagons were Equillian's second highest coin—a purseful would give him and Bastian enough to travel to anywhere on Equillian, and he was hoping that he could later inspire an even larger sum. He read the letter several more times until he was satisfied. He was proud of his penmanship. He'd spent well over a thousand hours practicing his writing skills in order to pull off believable forgeries, and it was certainly paying off now. The letters' curves were as well drawn as any noble's, giving the ransom note an air of sophistication.

He'd used his skills over a dozen times previously, mostly to blackmail those who could afford it. And his experience had taught him that the more vague he was, the better. It was best to offer suggestions and let his adversaries fill in the blanks with the darkest parts of their imagination rather than accuse them of anything directly. The shadows of their fears were more menacing than anything he could conjure up. And more often than not, it inspired confessions far beyond the dirt he had on them already.

It would've helped to have known a little more about Lord Bardviss. Knowing the weaknesses in his character would've allowed Felix to tailor the letter more skillfully to him in particular. But he'd have to be satisfied with what he had to work with.

His mind turned to Bastian. If he could get a letter to Lord Bardviss, then maybe he could get a letter to him. The only problem with sending Bastian a letter via Sendsong was that if the castle's guard were looking for him, then sending him correspondence via an illegal enchanted artifact could put him in a highly compromising position. If only there was another way to reach him. And then it hit him. Gwena.

He pulled out a fresh piece of parchment and started another letter.

An hour later, Felix found Lilliana and Roy in the common area looking over a map of Equillian that was laid out on the table.

"Ready for delivery," he said, announcing his presence.

Lilliana turned towards him. She was wearing an aviator jumpsuit that hugged her curves and he couldn't help but note how attractive she looked in it.

"I want to read the letter before you send it," she said.

"I would be disappointed if you didn't," Felix replied, handing the ransom note to her. "I hope you don't mind if I do the same?" he asked, referring to the letter for her mother.

"You don't trust me?"

"Trust has nothing to do with it. Consistency is of the utmost importance, my lady. If we leave any room for error, we will not succeed."

"You have an answer for everything, don't you?" she asked.

Felix didn't answer. Instead, he regarded her with an expression of indifference, then a smug smile.

She rolled her eyes and turned her attention to his letter while he looked over hers. Lilliana's letter to her mother hit all of the points Felix had asked for and was convincing enough. He folded it up carefully and stowed it in his pocket.

"The Debt Collectors?" Lilliana asked after finishing his letter.

"You have a better name?"

Lilliana opened her mouth to reply, but she was interrupted by Roy taking the letter from her hand. "The Debt Collectors—I like it. It has a nice ring to it," he said, looking it over.

"Thank you," Felix said, smiling at Lilliana with satisfaction. She ignored him.

"What are we going to do with my letter? We can't send mine and the ransom note together."

"No, we can't," Felix agreed. "We need someone to hand-deliver your letter to your mother to ensure it's not intercepted by Lord Bardviss. If the Sendsong gave it to her at the wrong moment, then our plan would be ruined. We need someone we can trust, someone who can get it to her undetected, and someone who has no connection to you or Roy."

"How in the Stars are we going to find someone like that?" Lilliana scoffed.

Felix grinned, "You're in luck, because I know the perfect person. But I will need a breakdown of your mother's schedule."

"What for?"

"So we can ensure that your letter reaches her. Is there a time when she routinely leaves the castle?"

"She goes to the flower market with her handmaiden every Moonday morning."

"Perfect, I'll need every detail."

Lilliana nodded. "Alright then, let's do this."

3

Felix stood on the top deck with his back against the Everfire's housing. Roy stood across from him looking over the railing. The pilot was clearly more resilient to the cold than he was. The sun was directly above them, its light illuminating a blue and cloudless sky. Felix imagined that if someone had looked at a picture of their surroundings, they would swear it was a summer's day, but the reality was quite the opposite. Even with the furred jacket he wore, the cold still penetrated to his bones.

Roy took a slender gold whistle from a chain around his neck and held it to his lips. Felix watched as he blew it, but there was no sound.

"Is something wrong?" Felix asked, puzzled by the whole business.

"Not at all, Sendsongs hear a frequency that we can't register."

"That doesn't sound like much of an enchantment," Felix said while rubbing his hands together to warm them.

"The frequency is impossible to produce by natural means."

"Ah, I stand corrected."

Felix pulled out his spice leaf case and rolled himself a puff-stick.

"The whistle isn't what makes the enchantment so amazing, at any rate. It's the birds themselves. Every whistle is linked to a single Sendsong. Together they make a pair—one is useless without the other," Roy said.

"What happens to the birds if the whistle is lost?" Felix asked.

But before Roy could answer him, their conversation was interrupted by the sound of large beating wings. Felix looked up to see a magnificent white bird approaching the ship, with a wingspan half his size. Despite its stature, the bird landed gracefully on the ship's railing in front of them.

"Is that…is that it?" Felix asked in wonderment.

Roy nodded.

Felix was expecting the bird to be dark—the Order's depictions of the original Sendsongs were dark blue-black. This one couldn't have been more luminous. Its feathers were made of white glazed porcelain that shone in the sunlight. It had a white plume on its head and one long turquoise tail feather that curled up behind it. Its beak was a striking metallic gold. The bird started to casually preen its feathers and then turned its eyes on Felix. They were bright lavender with stark black pupils, and they stared straight into him as if judging his very soul. He could hear the sound of gear work whirring inside of it, and he recalled his lessons at the Order about the original Sendsongs. The ancient birds were blind. But, they had a keen sense for the vibrations, or *songs,* of the universe. All you had to do was say the name of a person or place and the very sound of the word would match the vibration of the person or place, leading the Sendsong directly to it. The birds could find anything from anywhere. "It's so lifelike," Felix said in awed wonder, his puff-stick turning to ash, forgotten in his hand.

"Even though it's without flesh and bone, I couldn't swear to you that this bird is any less alive than you or I. I have no idea how the alchemists do it, but this Sendsong has a will of its own," Roy said. He bowed his head respectfully to the bird, and Felix watched in fascination as the Sendsong politely bowed its head in return. There was a clicking noise and then a compartment opened in the bird's chest that had been invisible the moment before. It looked like the interior of a gold letterbox. Roy pushed a metal button inside that was marked with the number 2 and instantly a divider popped up through the center of the box, turning it into two separate compartments. Roy motioned for Felix to place the letters inside. Felix took the two envelopes from his breast pocket and cautiously placed one on each side of the divider.

"Now, you have to tell her where you want her to take them," Roy said.

"How do I do that?"

Roy smiled. "Just the names."

Felix cautiously stepped forward and leaned in towards the bird. The Sendsong cocked its head to the side and stared at him with those metallic lavender eyes. He felt like it could read his intentions, seeing the dishonesty in him as clearly as daylight. Felix lied often and easily in his life. As long as it was for the right reasons, he didn't see why he shouldn't. Reality was the fiction that you painted it to be. Painting it the way he liked instead of falling victim to someone else's brush just made him smarter, didn't it? Under the bird's gaze, he suddenly found that he wasn't so sure. For the first time he felt incredibly guilty about things that he'd never felt guilty about. It was almost as if the bird's eyes were reflecting Felix back to himself and he was seeing his soul clearly for the first time. Whatever it was, he didn't like it. Things were easier without a conscience.

He cleared his throat. "The ransom note needs to go to Lord Henry Bardviss, and the other envelope to Gwena Rose

Stently. If you can deliver to each of them when they are alone, I would be much obliged. That is, if you have control over those things…" He was suddenly aware that he was rambling and stopped himself. "Thanks," he said uncomfortably and then stepped back from the Sendsong. The gears whirred and the divider moved to one side, hiding Gwena's letter and leaving Lord Bardviss's exposed in the box as if it was the only one there. Then the Sendsong's chest snapped shut. The movement startled Felix, and he jumped back in surprise.

Without wasting a moment, the magnificent bird lifted its great wings and leapt into the air, flying gracefully towards the horizon.

Felix watched the bird go until it was completely out of view.

"Does it do that to everyone?" he asked.

"What?"

Felix searched for the words but couldn't find them. Roy watched him struggle for a beat, and then he smiled, his eyes twinkling.

"You mean, strip your soul with a single glance and then force you to face yourself?" he asked.

"Yeah…exactly."

"I don't know, I've never asked anyone. I suppose that in the language of songs, things are how they are instead of how we interpret them to be."

"Interesting," Felix said, still watching the horizon, and then pulled his hand back in pain from the burn of his forgotten puff-stick.

SPECIAL DELIVERY

CHAPTER ELEVEN

Gwena stood outside the Pig's Head three tall ciders and two Oyster Shots past tipsy, inhaling a puff-stick that she'd bummed off Sam.

She had stayed at the Pig's Head until Sam returned with his coworkers. Feeling like the butt of one of Shick's awful jokes, she was hoping that a couple of drinks and some familiar company might cheer her up. The hours she'd spent trying to reason with the current state of her life had accomplished nothing. She was left depressed and wishing that she'd had enough cwips to drown her sorrows in the bottom of a glass. Sam and his friends helped her with that. They bought her drinks all night and she drank way more than she should have. With her inhibitions erased, she spent the evening telling sailor's jokes and performing basic magic tricks. She had worked up an audience by the end of the night and convinced the whole pub to join her in dancing the Whisky Tumble, a choreographed number that everyone on Equillian knew by the time they were eight.

She was feeling more herself than she had in years. It was so liberating to able to make her own decisions without having to worry about the repercussions with her father. She knew that one day she would have to find steady work and carry the burden of adult responsibilities, but she was barely a woman and had been helping her father bear that burden for the last four years. It wasn't fair. She had missed so much. She found herself feeling envious of the camaraderie that Sam and his friends shared. There was a time when her friendship with Bastian and Felix felt like that. They did almost everything together. But that time had long passed.

Gwena took a long drag from her puff-stick. She hadn't smoked since she was thirteen, when she occasionally shared one with Bastian and Felix. She could still clearly remember the last one she had. She and the boys were sitting on Throne Hill watching the new train come into the station. It was a brand-new engine, painted peacock blue and powered by Everfire steam power. It was the first of its kind and could go record speeds, getting passengers from one side of the mainland to the other in only three days. Everyone in town was talking about it. They passed Bastian's last puff-stick between them in silence as they admired the great machine with smoke billowing behind it. It was a nice moment, one of those filled pauses in life where she was completely present and content. The memory was encapsulated in a bubble in Gwena's mind, perfectly preserved. It made the puff-stick that she was enjoying now all the sweeter.

"You were a real hit in there. I haven't seen that side of Gwena Stently since the seventh grade," Sam said, coming out to join her.

"Ha! That's probably the last time it saw daylight. I think my fun side has been bottled up for so long that it just exploded in there. Please apologize to your friends for me. The offended look on Jess's face with that sailor joke…I'm sure she despises me."

"Are you kidding? That look on Jess's face was priceless! The guys love you. You should come out with us more often."

"Thanks, Sam," Gwena laughed. "Well, I better get back before it gets too late."

"Can I walk you home?"

"No!" Gwena said abruptly. Her response was so sudden that Sam looked offended.

"I'm not hitting on you, Gwena. I just want to get you home safely," he said defensively.

"I know, sorry, it's just that…I'm not going home…and my whole situation is a little more complicated than I feel like explaining right now."

"Wait, you haven't run away to one of the cathouses, have you?" Sam asked with concern.

"Stars, I'm not that desperate! I would like to think I'll always have options besides the brothels," Gwena laughed.

"Ok…so how about I walk you to wherever it is you're going, and we pretend that it never happened? No questions asked."

"I suppose that's better than risking the shadows that lurk the alleyways this time of night," Gwena smiled.

"It is, believe me."

They said good-bye to Sam's friends and walked through the snow-covered streets towards Tucker Street. The Everfire lamps cast their dancing light on the cobblestones and made the snow glitter.

"I like your friends, they're nice," Gwena said.

"Yeah, thanks. Me too. They're not a bad bunch."

"It seems like the castle has been really good for you?"

"I'm happy there. The work might not be exciting, and I can't say that I love working for the nobles, but I really like the people I work with. We have a lot of fun together," Sam said.

Then he paused for a moment, a question hovering on his breath, "Are you ok?" he asked.

"Why do you ask that?"

"Let's see, you're not staying at home, you're mixed up with criminals, and you said you might be leaving Westdock. I know I said that I wouldn't pry, but I have to ask. I mean, I'd be a pretty bad friend if I wasn't concerned about you."

"Fair enough. I really do appreciate your concern, Sam, but you don't have to worry. It's not as bad as it sounds, promise. I just need some space from my father is all. I've finally realized that I've been spending my life working towards his goals and ignoring my own. I'll be a woman next month, and I feel like I've barely had the opportunity to be a child. I completely missed my window to run amuck and make mistakes like any normal person my age. I'll never get that time back and there's nothing I can do about that. But at least I can do something about now and make sure I don't waste my future."

"I get that. I think that's very wise. You've always been wise beyond your years. I'm proud of you, Gwena. And I wouldn't worry too much, you haven't missed as much as you think you have. You still have plenty of time to muck about and make mistakes. Look at my brother, he's twenty-five and still mucking about. Not to mention my Uncle Earl. He's almost forty and still acts like an adolescent," Sam said.

Gwena laughed. "Thanks, Sam. Well, this is me," she said, stopping across the street from the butcher's.

"You're kidding, you want me to leave you alone, *here?*"

"What? I'll be inside in two seconds."

"This is the worst side of town!"

"You said you wouldn't ask any questions," Gwena said accusingly, and then she added, "Besides, this isn't the worst side of town. Just a bad one." As if that made all the difference.

Sam sighed, "I better not be seeing your murder in the papers tomorrow."

"I'll be fine! Thanks Sam, for everything. I had a really good time tonight."

"Me too. I hope you come out with us again."

He took a puff-stick from behind his ear and handed it to her. "For later."

"Thanks," Gwena said and took it gratefully.

Sam started to go, hesitated and turned back.

"You can go, Sam, I'm fine!" Gwena said.

"It's not that. There's something I have to tell you."

"What is it?"

Sam shuffled his feet uncomfortably and then looked at her with concern. "I overheard the guards talking. Lord Bardviss sent two galleons after the ship your friend's on…. He commanded them to sink it."

Gwena felt like she'd been punched in the stomach.

"Why would Lord Bardviss do that? Even if Bastian had kidnapped the duchess, it doesn't make any sense to kill him when she's still unaccounted for."

"I don't know, it's crazy. The fact that Lord Bardviss would drown an entire crew just to defeat one man is completely insane! I've never liked him, but this is another level. And to think, he's going to be the next duke of Westdock. Stars help us."

Gwena's mind began racing, she didn't want to believe it. "The merchant ship had a head start and could dock at the next port before Lord Bardviss's men catch it."

Sam shook his head. "I wouldn't count on it. Even if they were headed to the closest port, it's unlikely they made it. The castle's galleons are ships of war. Two of them outmaneuvering a single merchant ship is ridiculously unfair."

Gwena started to feel light-headed. "Thank you for telling me. Good night, Sam," she said and walked briskly towards the butcher's.

Gwena climbed into the loft and her strength gave out. She couldn't breathe. She sat on Felix's bed and put her hand to her chest, gasping for air. The thought of losing Bastian was too much. "Please Stars, not Bastian," she pleaded to the Watchers. He had always been her light in the darkness. When she acquired her scar, he made her feel like it was a badge of bravery instead of something to be ashamed of. When her mother died, he was there to comfort her. And then the other night, he was there again right when she needed him most, like a guardian sent by the Watchers. She'd been able to get out of bed the next morning because of Bastian. He had breathed life into her, just as he always had. If something happened to him, she knew that the darkness would consume her.

She gasped at the pain in her heart and curled into a ball, weeping.

An hour later Gwena had exhausted her tears. She felt numb. She sat near the open window with her knees pulled up to her chest, smoking the puff-stick that Sam had given her. She looked at the empty room feeling truly alone. She knew that she couldn't stay there any longer. Being surrounded by Bastian's and Felix's things without them was too hard. She upturned her coin purse and stared at the two cwips she had left. They would barely get her through breakfast. She might be able to get work for one of the other tailors in town, but that would quickly get back to her father and cause a right mess. What was she going to do? She wanted to go to the Heartland—the possibility of starting a new life in the capital with Bastian had excited and invigorated her.

Suddenly, a giant white bird swooped over Gwena's head into the room. She ducked in surprise and the bird landed on the post of Felix's bed behind her. She gasped with recognition.

"A Sendsong!"

What on Equillian is a Sendsong doing here? she wondered. She had only seen one once before. When she was a young girl, her aunt had sent a letter to her mother via Sendsong. She occasionally worked for a highly prestigious family who allowed her to use it to send word of their ailing father. The enchanted creatures were a rarity, and no doubt worth a fortune. Gwena's father was furious that her aunt had sent an illegal artifact to their house. Her parents had a heated argument over it and Gwena took advantage of their distraction to study the bird. She still remembered the way its gaze had pierced to her core. The Sendsong that was before her now studied her intently with its metallic lavender eyes.

"Hi," Gwena said.

The Sendsong bowed its head in greeting. Gwena could hear the hum of the machinery running inside it. There were three clicks and then the compartment in the bird's chest popped open. Gwena jumped back in surprise. Seeing the envelope inside, she cautiously reached into the gold compartment and pulled it out. As soon as the mail was taken, the bird's chest snapped shut. Then the Sendsong turned its gaze on her and their eyes locked. Instantly, Gwena felt exposed. It was as if all her inner secrets and desires were laid bare, naked to the Sendsong's penetrating stare. Then the mechanical bird lazily blinked its eyes, and she felt released from its spell. It leapt up onto the windowsill and flew into the night.

As Gwena watched it go, she suddenly knew that everything was going to be ok. She saw it in those strange metallic eyes. It didn't feel like the bird was telling her—it was as if the Sendsong was simply reflecting a truth that was inside Gwena's soul. A truth she hadn't known was there. It revealed a terrifying strength and an iron will. The image frightened her, making her feel like a stranger in her own skin. But it also gave her courage.

Gwena shook from her daze and shut the window securely before sitting on Bastian's bed and turning the envelope over in her hands. It was thicker than a regular letter. When she opened it, there were three separate sealed envelopes inside. One of them had her name written on the front in fine calligraphy, another was addressed to Bastian, and the third to Lady Everitt Wendrian.

Gwena recognized Felix's handwriting immediately and eagerly opened the letter that was addressed to her.

Gwena,

I need your help. I am no longer in Westdock. But be assured that I am safe and well. I apologize, but that is the only thing I can tell you about my current circumstances. I need you to get the included letter to Bastian, I am worried that he might be in danger. I couldn't risk sending it to him directly, but it's of the utmost importance that it reaches him. Also included is a letter for Lady Everitt Wendrian. It is just as important that this letter reaches her, unopened. She will be at the flower market on Moonday morning accompanied by Malinda, her handmaiden. Malinda must not see you. Tell Lady Everitt you are a friend of

Lilliana's and that this letter is from her daughter.
Give it to her and then leave as quickly as possible.
For Bastian's birthday I gave him two train tickets
to the Heartland. Take those tickets and leave with
him. There's nothing left for you in Westdock,
Gwena. You deserve a better life. Whether you know
it or not, Bastian loves you. He will hate me for
telling you that, but it's about time someone did.
And I know that you feel the same way. I've seen
the way you two look at each other. Step on that
train with him and never look back.

I hope to see you two again before long. Until then,
take care and look after one another.

Your infuriating friend,
Felix

P.S. I'm sorry for not returning the suit. I swear
that I had every intention of doing so. When I see
you again, I will make it up to you, promise.

Fresh tears welled in Gwena's eyes. She was so glad to hear from Felix. His words were like a warm embrace from a friend. She wished she could leave on that train with Bastian more than anything. The fact that she couldn't dashed her spirit with despair. It broke her heart to think of how destroyed Felix would be if something happened to Bastian. At least it sounded like Felix was safe, and by the sounds of it, Lady Lilliana was too. What was he up to? she wondered. How Felix managed to get his hands on a Sendsong baffled her. If he had access to one, why wasn't he sending these letters directly to their recipients? And how had he managed to leave Westdock with the duchess without anyone knowing? She would deliver the letter to Lady

Everitt, at any rate. It felt good to have something to give her purpose. She wondered what Felix had meant when he said Bastian could be in danger. Was he going to warn him about Lord Bardviss coming after him, or something more sinister? Gwena looked at the envelope that was addressed to Bastian and ran her hand lovingly over his name. Even if Bastian miraculously survived Lord Bardviss's galleons, there was no way that she could get this letter to him. She opened it decidedly.

Bastian,

First of all, happy belated birthday! I am sorry that I wasn't there to celebrate with you. I can only hope that you found the special lady you were looking for to be your Sweet Sixteen. You will never guess where I'm headed. I can't wait to tell you, but now is not the time. I've been hired for a job too good to pass up, which will keep me from Westdock for an unknown period of time. I'm sorry that I won't be able to travel with you. I look forward to our next adventure together. But I have an alternative that I think you're going to like. Take Gwena instead. I already told her that you love her, so there's no turning back now. I'm being looked after financially, so all of our savings is yours. Between what we had and what we acquired the other night, you and Gwena should have enough to have some fun before settling down together. Use it to change your stars like you've always wanted. You deserve it, buddy. Once all of this is over, I'll come find you. I'll see you again before you know it.

Your friend and brother,

F

Gwena put down the letter. It confirmed why Bastian was being chased by Lord Bardviss but ignited a flurry of other questions. If Felix knew that Bastian was a prime suspect, and he knew what had actually happened to the duchess, why wasn't he doing anything about it?

Wait.

Gwena's train of thought came to a halt. Did Felix say *savings*?

She read the letter again. It clearly said that Felix and Bastian had savings. She'd completely forgotten about the loot that Bastian had mentioned.

Surely, he wouldn't have taken all of it to the market that day. Which could only mean one thing…it has to be here.

Gwena jumped off the bed and began to search the room. She looked under the beds, in the privy behind the toilet, amid the clothes and in and behind the desk and bedside table. She imagined that it would be in a small spice leaf cigar box or something similar, but there was nothing. She stood on the chair and studied the thatching in the roof, hoping to find some evidence of a hiding place.

"If I were to hide something in this room, where would it be?" she asked herself.

However, twenty minutes later she had still found nothing. Feeling exasperated, she collapsed backwards onto Bastian's bed and something beneath it bounced. She froze for an instant, then rolled off the bed and pushed it aside.

Underneath there was nothing but the wooden floorboards. She studied them until she found one that was loose. She hunted the room for an object that she could use as leverage. Finding a metal spoon, she wedged it between the cracks and pried the board free. Gwena smiled in triumph. Underneath the floor was a pile of coin and trinkets that exceeded her expectations, and sitting on top were the first-class train tickets. She laughed with joy and relief. In the past, if she had come across this she would have scolded the boys. Now, she could have kissed them.

"Thank you, Watchers," she whispered.

She picked up the train tickets and looked at them. They were printed in beautiful cobalt blue and embossed with gold ink. The idea of getting on the train alone terrified her, but it also filled her with hope. Hope that the Stars had something more in store for her. She knew that she wouldn't get this opportunity again, and with the boys or not, she needed to take it.

SPITTING DAGGERS
CHAPTER TWELVE

Bastian felt as though he'd only had his eyes closed for a minute before he was woken by Cricket shaking him. "Rise and shine, landlubber."

"What time is it?" Bastian groaned, his brain pounding against his skull.

"The sun be risin' and so must we," Cricket said cheerily.

Bastian wrapped himself in his hammock. "Tell it to go back to sleep, I'm sure it's up too early."

"Ha! Tell 'er yerself," Cricket laughed and turned Bastian's hammock upside down.

Bastian fell to the floor and a wave of nausea washed over him.

Cricket kicked an empty bucket towards him. "Get it over with then. We got work ta do," he said unsympathetically.

Bastian grabbed the bucket like a lifeline and emptied the contents of his stomach. Between the constant rocking of the sea and his brutal hangover, he felt like death churned in a washer, pulped, and then warmed over.

"I won't be any use to you. Can't I stay here?" he asked, hugging the bucket.

"As cute a couple as ye an' that bucket make, there be no slackin' fer self-inflicted ailments," Cricket said, helping Bastian to his feet and handing him a flask. "Drink that an' ye will be right as rain in no time."

Bastian took the flask and muttered under his breath about how his misery was hardly self-inflicted. He took a sip of the dark liquid and then sprayed it across the room. "Rum?! What are you trying to do to me?" he asked accusingly.

"Get ya through another day! Trust me, mate, the 'air o' the dog be yer only 'ope. This be no time ta be gettin' sober. Let yer poor stomach be eased down from the poundin' it received. No need ta drop 'er ta the depths right before breakfast," Cricket said with an amused smile and handed Bastian a mop. "I'll see ya up there. Don't ferget ta empty yer girlfriend over deck. If yer not there in two, I'll be back ta drag ya by yer undergarments."

Bastian watched Cricket go and then moved into the corner of the room and leaned against the wall for support. He held his nose and knocked back another three large gulps of the rum. It took every inch of his willpower to keep it from coming back up. He slid down the wall to the floor and put his head in his hands, then noticed that there was something on his hands. He held them up to the firebeetle lantern next to him. The large black beetles crawled inside their glass home, dimly lighting the room with their glowing bellies. Bastian's hands were covered with a fine gold dust that glittered in the light. It reminded him of when he played in the red powdered dirt at the back of the temple as a child. There was something in it that sparkled in the sunlight. But Bastian hadn't had his hands anywhere near anything like that lately. He smelt his fingers and rubbed them together, but he couldn't detect anything. He wiped his hands on his shirt, but the dust wouldn't come off. He rubbed his eyes and looked again. Whatever it was, it was still there. He smelled the flask that Cricket had given him and then tucked it in his coat pocket. "Damn pirates," he muttered.

Whatever Cricket was playing at, he didn't appreciate it. As soon as his stomach felt settled enough for him to move, he made his way on deck with the mop and bucket in hand.

Cold air hit him like a sledgehammer. His handsome suit jacket wasn't made to keep out winter. The morning breeze bit all the way to his bones, but he welcomed it, for it also breathed life into him again. The deck was still dark and covered in a blanket of snow. Bastian wondered how they were supposed to mop the decks when they were buried. The sun was just beginning to warm the horizon with its glow. The ocean was so still it looked like glass. He walked to the port railing and emptied his bucket over the edge, watching its contents fall to the water below. Bastian tensed. A gigantic shadow was passing underneath them below the water's surface, a shadow at least as big as the ship. An instant later the shadow was gone, and Bastian wondered if it had been there at all. Probably just a trick of the light, or another one of the morning's hallucinations. He put down the bucket and rubbed his eyes, and then he rubbed his hands together to warm them.

Cricket had been right. Now that the alcohol was taking effect, he did feel better. He knew that he was only postponing his hangover, but without the pirate's rum he would've been completely useless. He searched out Cricket and found him near the bow.

"Change o' plans," Cricket said, and traded him a shovel for his mop. Bastian joined him in shoveling the snow overboard as they watched the sun rise from the ocean, transforming from liquid gold into a brilliant fan of pinks and oranges that reflected in the glassy water around them. As soon as its light reached the deck, the remaining snow glistened brilliantly. Too brilliantly, like there was gold beneath its surface. It reminded Bastian of the way his hands had glittered earlier.

"Are you seeing this?" he asked, Cricket.

"Seein' what?"

"The shimmer that's on *everything*," he said in wonderment, looking at the spectacle around him.

Cricket eyed him with concern. "No," he said bluntly.

"What did you put in my drink?" Bastian asked accusingly.

"What are ye talkin' about? I already sacrificed me own fine brown sugar rum fer yer sorry arse. If I 'ad somethin' ta spike it with, don't think that I'd go wastin' it on yer bag o' bones."

"If it's only rum, then why am I seeing things?"

Bastian looked down at his hands again, now wisping a fine gold mist as if steam was rising off them.

Cricket stopped mopping and studied him. "That be a good question, why are ye seein' thin's?" he asked.

"I don't know. It's as if my hands are…smoking," Bastian said quietly. Voicing it made him realize how insane it sounded.

"Smokin'?" Cricket repeated with a raised eyebrow.

Bastian nodded anxiously.

Cricket stepped close to him and lowered his voice. "Ye better not be holdin' out on me, mate, whatever yer on, ye 'ave got ta give me some!" he said with a smirk.

Bastian put his mop down and sat on the barrel that was beside him. "I didn't take anything, at least not that I'm aware of. Could it be a side effect from that black stuff you put in my drink last night?" he asked.

"Black Powder? Stars no, if it 'ad that kind o' effect, there'd be nothin' left fer the firearms," Cricket jested. "Wait, weren't ye seein' thin's yesterday?" he asked.

Bastian recalled the glowing light from the chest. "Yes…," he admitted. He tried to think of what he'd consumed before coming onto the ship that might've done this to him. He rubbed his eyes with his palms. "Maybe I just need a good sleep," he said.

"Come on, ye can sleep when yer dead," Cricket said, pulling him up. "Are ya stable on yer feet?"

"As much as can be expected, I guess," Bastian shrugged.

"Good. Is yer stomach holdin' itself together?"

"For the moment."

"Yer vision isn't swimmin', er goin' black?"

"No."

"An' ye can hold yer shovel?"

"Yes."

Cricket clapped him on the shoulder. "Then ye'll be fine an' 'ave no reason not ta be cleanin' the deck. Come on then, the breakfast bell will ring soon enough. Back ta work," he said.

Bastian sighed and got back to it. Where his shovel had cleared the deck, it sparkled. Even the air glittered with fine particles of suspended gold dust. He marveled at what he was seeing, but he was careful not to mention it again.

2

After breakfast Cricket showed Bastian where the crew's chores were posted. Bastian found his duties listed under Dodger. He was scheduled to shadow Cricket for the first half of the day and then to assist the master gunner in the armory for the second. He was pleased to see that the rest of his chores were inside. He knew that he needed to find some warmer clothes if he didn't want the weather to be the end of him. He had enough contenders in that department already.

Cricket's first task was to clean and feed the firebeetle lanterns. Bastian's only experience with firebeetle lanterns was seeing them used for town gatherings and at the Wendrians' castle. He recalled one year at the harvest festival when he and Felix had run around opening all of the lanterns. They released the glowing insects inside, filling the night with black armored beetles with transparent wings and glowing orb-like bodies as big as plums. Their light pulsated from their torsos like small stars. Felix had caught one and squished it between his hands, which then glowed until the next morning, giving them away. The sisters of the Order banned them both from eating dinner for the next three nights as punishment. The next time Bastian and Felix came across a lantern, it was locked and protected from tampering. Their fun with firebeetles was over after that. Now Bastian just appreciated their strangeness and knew them for the gold glowing light they delivered.

Cricket showed Bastian the utility closet where the supplies were kept. He took a brown satchel from a shelf and tossed it to him. Bastian caught it and looked inside. There were two glass bottles, one filled with clear syrupy liquid and the other with a strange blue plant. There were also several thin metal disks and a cleaning rag.

"Blue Vine an' Simple Syrup. That diet makes the beetles glow their brightest," Cricket said.

"What are the metal plates for?" Bastian asked.

"Patience, ye'll find out soon enough."

Cricket led him to their first lantern. It was a clever contraption. The lantern had two identical metal bell-shaped chambers on either end of a long glass hexagon. The main housing looked similar to an ordinary lantern, except that it housed firebeetles instead of an enchanted flame.

"Pass me a divider," Cricket requested.

Bastian shuffled through the bag until he found one of the thin metal disks and handed it to Cricket. The pirate slid the disk into a narrow slot at the base of the upper chamber, blocking the flies from entering it. Then he twisted the top off and handed it to Bastian. After flipping a latch on the side of the lantern, Cricket rotated it upside down. He took the top back from Bastian and held it upside down like a cup and poured some of the simple syrup into it and added a generous piece of Blue Vine. Next, he screwed the lid back into place on what was now the bottom of the lantern and took out the metal divider to allow the firebeetles access to the food. They glowed anxiously as they ran to their meal. Once they were all feeding happily, Cricket slid the divider back into place, trapping them in the bottom chamber. He unscrewed the top of the lantern and wiped out the inside of the glass with the rag before replacing the lid and taking out the divider so that the firebeetles had full access to their clean home.

"We turn the lanterns once a week, supplyin' them with fresh food an' drink," Cricket explained.

"Why don't you use Everfire?" Bastian asked. He was curious as to why anyone would choose a light source that needed so much maintenance.

"Because ye can't extinguish Everfire, an' there be moments when it pays ta turn the ship dark in a hurry. Besides, the cap'n prefers the dim light o' the firebeetles, an' I must admit that I do as well," Cricket said.

"How do you make the firebeetles go dark?" Bastian inquired.

"Dream gas, puts them ta sleep instantly."

He pointed to a thin copper pipe that ran along the wall connecting all the lanterns. Bastian studied the piping, curious. It made sense. If Everfire wasn't in a box that could close, then it needed a specially woven bag to block out its light. It would take time to cover every lantern. Normally there was no reason to turn a room dark in a hurry. But on a pirate ship, having that option would definitely have its advantages.

"Yer turn, mate," Cricket said at the next lantern.

He handed Bastian the supplies. Bastian slipped in the divider and started to unscrew the top when something made him pause. The firebeetles were steaming gold mist, just as his hands had done earlier. There were thin wisps of gold dust that rose from them like water evaporating off cobblestones on a hot day. He refrained from mentioning it to Cricket. Instead he clenched his jaw and focused on the task at hand. Put in the food and simple syrup, turn the lantern, replace the lid, trap beetles with meal, clean lantern, remove the divider. He breathed a sigh of relief. The phantom shimmers were making him feel like he was hallucinating. It reminded him of the time that he and Felix had found some Prophet mushrooms in the forest and ate them right before their astrology class. Bastian could've sworn that the pictures of the constellations were coming to life on the pages in front of him. It made it incredibly hard to concentrate, and he found himself wishing that they'd waited to eat them after hours. His current predicament was even more disconcerting, because he didn't know what was causing the visions. If he'd known and was certain they would pass, he might have actually enjoyed the experience, for it was oddly mesmerizing and eerily beautiful.

"Quick learner, eh?" Cricket said, bringing Bastian back to the present. "Do two more, then I'll step ahead and feed the buggers while ye come behind ta clean the glass. That way we can make short work o' it."

"Sounds good," Bastian agreed, rubbing his eyes with the palms of his hands.

He managed to get through the next two lanterns without any hiccups, doing his best to ignore the glimmer that haunted his vision. Then he followed behind Cricket with the cleaning rag as they walked the length of the ship, maintaining the lanterns in one room after another. The first level of the Black Mary had the mess hall, the galley, the sleeping quarters, and the washroom/laundry. At the stern was a set of stairs leading to the captain's quarters.

"Be sure never ta walk those stairs unless ye 'ave been invited," Cricket warned him.

"Have you ever been up there?" Bastian asked.

"Not I, few 'ave besides Snibs. Though trust me when I tell ya that it not be a place ye care ta go. It tends ta be bad news when yer summoned ta the cap'n's doors. Come, the best be yet ta come," Cricket said, leading Bastian down a ladderway to the next floor.

The second level was the gun deck. The walls were lined with cannons on either side and the space was well stocked with barrels of cannonballs and black powder. In the center was a barred holding cell and towards the bow was a large separate room.

"The armory," Cricket informed him.

There were sounds of banging and swearing coming from behind the door.

"This be where ye'll be spendin' yer afternoon. Boom the master gunner tends ta pass most o' 'is time in there. Don't be afraid ta give it a loud knock when ye come ta call…" Cricket paused as if trying to decide how to phrase something. "Boom be…a wee bit strange. 'E be nice enough…just don't look 'im in the eye fer too long," he said.

Bastian cocked his head questioningly. He wanted to ask Cricket to elaborate, but the pirate was already leading them down a metal spiral staircase to the next level. The third floor was awake with noises of flowing water and animal chatter.

"Welcome ta the Green Room," Cricket said, holding out his arms theatrically.

Bastian was awestruck. They stood in a green space that was abundant with plant life. It looked like a soilless vegetable garden. There were four rows of large glass water tanks filled with live fish, and on top of the tanks were garden beds filled with loose stone. The beds were crowded with flourishing fresh herbs and vegetables. Tomato plants and grapevines grew upside down from the ceiling. Natural light flooded in through windows that made up the back wall of the ship and the portholes that lined either side.

The deck was split into two parts divided by a thick glass wall. The other side had goats, ducks, and sheep grazing happily on a floor covered in lush green grass.

Bastian walked over to the garden beds to look at the red fish that swam contentedly in the tanks below them.

"Are these red gills?" he asked.

"Aye."

"But they're a freshwater fish!" Bastian said in surprise.

"Plants don't take well ta salt water."

Cricket showed him a large steam-powered desalination tank in the corner that turned the sea into fresh water.

"She uses Everfire ta create 'er steam, only needs occasional maintenance," he explained and walked Bastian through the rest of the system.

The fresh water was used in the fish tanks and throughout the ship. The fish's wastewater was pumped into the rocky garden beds, flooding the plants with nutrients. The plants in turn filtered the water before it was drained back down to the fish. Bastian was amazed by how well the plants were growing. Everything there was huge and fragrant.

"Whole thin' be Tink's creation, 'e be the ship's tinker. True brilliance if ye ask me. Be the best produce I 'ave ever tasted. An' it be fresh year-round. The fish be fine fer eatin' too, but I prefer the creatures o' the sea," Cricket said.

Bastian was highly impressed by the simple genius of it. They had created their own ecosystem aboard the ship. They would never have to worry about scurvy or lack of nutrients, no matter how long they were at sea.

"You could explore the unchartered waters with this setup, maybe even cross the Desert Ocean!" Bastian said enthusiastically.

"What do ye know about the Desert Ocean?" Cricket asked warily.

His dark expression took Bastian by surprise.

"Same tales as anyone, I suppose," Bastian said hesitantly.

"Let me tell ya somethin' about the Desert Ocean. Those troubled waters *are* the nine realms o' darkness. An' if they're not, then they be far worse," Cricket said ominously and then walked over to greet the sheep. Bastian couldn't tell if Cricket was messing with him or not. He had always been intrigued by the stories of the uncharted waters. The Desert Ocean was massive and had no known landmasses except for the few small dreg islands that floated around the ocean haphazardly. The largest ones didn't exceed an acre and they rarely had any life on them. Ships would run out of supplies long before they crossed the sea and be forced to turn back. Many who sought to explore it had never returned. No one even knew how big it truly was or what was in its waters. Recorded history shows just one man to have crossed it: Boone Jacobs. He was part of the crew of the Shadow Rider, a great galleon that had left the east coast of Equillian intending to cross the sea. A year and a half later the ship drifted up to Westdock. The sails were ragged and the galleon was battered, reduced to an ember of its former glory. Boone was the only survivor on the ship. He was found tied to the mast muttering about sirens and sea monsters. He was plagued by night terrors, and no one could get a word of sense out of him. He died a week after he was brought to shore. The only thing of use found in the ship's logs was that there was no land discovered outside of the moving dregs. It was one of Equillian's greatest mysteries and had in-spired dozens of legends. Bastian wanted to probe Cricket more on the topic. If the Black Mary had explored the Desert Ocean, then he was eager to hear about it, but he got the impression that Cricket wasn't interested in sharing that information. He decid-ed to tuck his questions away for an opportune moment. Maybe once the pirate had a few drinks in him he would feel differently.

Bastian walked to the other side of the deck to join Cricket with the animals. The grass that covered the floor of their pen was impressive. Bastian tried to imagine how the pirates man-aged to make real grass grow so successfully aboard the ship.

"Evergrass rug. One o' the alchemists' creations," Cricket said before Bastian could ask the question.

"*Enchanted grass*," Bastian whispered in awe.

He knelt down and ran his hand through it. It felt as real as any grass he'd ever known. He had always been intrigued by enchanted objects. But he'd never had an opportunity to experience them beyond Everfire. After the ban they had become valuable collectables for the wealthy and out of reach for everyone else.

It suddenly came to his attention that the gold dust he had been seeing was *in* the grass. Not just on top of it, like everything else. But in it. He put his head down next to the rug. The grass blades were like little snow globes filled with the strange stuff. He picked a blade of grass and gold mist seeped out of it, cascading down his fingers like smoke. The part of the blade still in the rug was also leaking gold dust, except that it was rising up and forming into the shape of the missing piece. In a matter of moments the gold dust solidified, and it was as if the blade of grass had never been picked at all.

"Yup, the bloody stuff regenerates. The rug uses the animals' own waste fer nutrients ta provide 'em. Still not sure 'ow I feel about this one, considerin' that whatever goes inta the livestock ends up goin' inta us once we eat 'em," Cricket said.

"If all they're eating is grass and produce scraps, then we have nothing to worry about," Bastian said absently. He was still staring at the grass, mesmerized.

"Ha! I couldn't care less about their waste. It's 'em creatures consumin' the enchantment that I find off-puttin'. Stars know what the alchemists use in that stuff ta create their witchcraft."

"Good point. Well, if one of us loses a limb and it grows back, we'll know what to blame for it," Bastian jested.

"Ha! True. If it 'as that kind o' effect, then I'll start eatin' the grass meself!" Cricket laughed. "Fascinatin' stuff though, isn't it?" he added, as he watched the animals grazing contentedly.

Bastian nodded in appreciation. But he had the feeling that Cricket wasn't seeing the same thing he was.

The pirate grabbed a bucket that was hanging on the wall and began throwing feed to the animals. "The goats be milked every mornin' an' evenin' fer milk an' cheese. The sheep get sheared when the weather turns, ta be used fer tradin'. An' the poultry provide eggs an' make a nice roast. Compostable scraps come 'ere ta add ta their feed, an' o' course they be needin' daily top-ups on their water," Cricket explained, "and the produce gets picked when it be ready. I think that be everythin'," he said, scratching the back of his head.

Cricket showed Bastian the last level, which was in the hull of the ship. It was used mainly as storage. There were bags of grain and flour, barrels of fruit, wine, rum, ale, and anything else that had substantial weight to it. After they had finished cleaning the firebeetle lanterns, they made their way towards the main cabin.

The mess hall was alive with activity as men found their places for lunch. Bastian's buzz from the rum that morning had only just begun to wear off when Cricket put a Black Jack in front of him brimming with grog. The alcoholic mixture appeared to be all there was on offer to drink. When Bastian asked for some plain water, Cricket and the surrounding men laughed at him. Staying inebriated certainly rescued him from his plight that morning, but he was feeling hesitant about the idea of being continually lubricated. Especially while he was dealing with the strange gold phantom. Not to mention that it dulled his senses in a place with untrustworthy company and that constant intake of the stuff would create a dependency he wasn't fond of. But

Cricket informed him that the alcohol sterilized the water and kept them from getting sick.

"Oi, Cricket, ya still 'aven't properly introduced me ta yer shadow."

Bastian looked up from his meal to see Stork, the red-headed pirate from his initiation, approaching their table.

"Where be me manners? Dodger, ye remember Stork from last night. 'E be our navigator and best helmsman, knows how ta get anywhere on Equillian by followin' the stars," Cricket said through a half-masticated mouthful.

Stork shook Bastian's hand and then sat across from them at their table. "So tell me, Dodger, do ye like throwin' dice?" he asked.

"Don't ye pull 'im inta that nonsense, lad 'asn't even been 'ere a day an' yer already lookin' ta empty 'is pockets," Cricket said. "Stork runs the gamblin' circuit on board," he explained.

Stork waved Cricket's words away. "Cricket only be bitter 'cause I collected a pretty bounty from 'is pockets bettin' on ye an' that chest. Don't worry, matey, ye will 'ave a chance ta win it back tammarow. That bein' if yer game enough ta try?" he baited.

Cricket shook his head with an amused grin. "I not be fool enough ta throw yer dice, Stork. I'll cut me losses while I still can, an' save what little I 'ave left, thank ya kindly."

"Suit yerself then, but don't be discouragin' Dodger 'ere. Our thief might be a natural in the game o' chance. If 'e can dodge death, per'aps 'e can charm Lady Luck," Stork said, then he leaned in close to Bastian. "I knew ye would open that chest. 'Ad a feelin' about ya. But tell me true, 'ow did ye do it?" he asked.

Bastian glanced at Cricket, recalling their conversation regarding the chest. He still wasn't sure how he'd managed to open it, but he wasn't about to admit that.

"Trick of the trade," he said with a wink.

Stork gave a good-humored smirk and put his arm around Bastian. "I like this landlubber, might make a good pirate out o' 'im yet."

"This son o' a strumpet botherin' ya?" a man asked, coming up from behind them.

Bastian turned to see the large burly sailor who'd first discovered him on the ship the day before.

"Ye do realize that ye be insultin' yer own mother when ye say that, right?" Stork asked the man.

"It not be insultin' when it be true. Our mother never be ashamed o' 'er perfession. An' ye shouldn't be neither, brother," he said accusingly to Stork.

Stork rolled his eyes and moved aside for the pirate to have his introduction. The large sailor held out his hand towards Bastian. "Don't think that we 'ave been properly introduced either. Name's Rhino," he said.

Bastian shook the pirate's hand.

"These be the twins, Rhino an' Stork. They were born within two minutes o' each other," Cricket said.

"I'm the oldest," Stork announced proudly.

Bastian didn't believe it. The two couldn't have looked more different from each other. Rhino was stout where Stork was lanky. Rhino had thick black hair and a bearded face with an olive complexion, and Stork was fair-skinned with dark red hair and a clean-shaven, freckled face.

"Surely you're having me on?" Bastian asked.

Cricket grinned, and all three pirates erupted in hearty laughter.

"That be the best part o' it mate, truly we're not," Stork said in good humor. "The fact that we shared a womb together be certain. Now, whether we 'ave the same father er not, that be another thin' entirely," he added, and he and Rhino clinked their Black Jacks.

"Ta Mum!" they said in unison.

Bastian laughed, joining in the men's mirth until he felt the burn of a stare in the back of his head. He turned around to see a short, stout pirate with a bald head glaring at him from across the room. The man's features were so disproportionate, it was unsettling.

"That be Spitz. Don't mind 'im, 'e 'ates everythin' that takes air," Cricket said.

The rest of the group stopped their conversation to catch a glimpse of Spitz.

"'E only be spiteful cause ye opened the chest. 'E made that cursed thin' 'is own personal vendetta. Even stuck black powder in the key'ole. When 'e failed ta open it, 'e swore that it couldn't be done," Rhino told Bastian.

"Ye see, ye 'ave made a liar out o' 'im," Stork explained.

"Spitz made a liar out o' 'imself!" Cricket interjected, "'E 'as no one else ta blame fer 'is misery," he said scornfully.

Then he locked eyes with Spitz and raised the back of his pointer finger towards him and spun it in a little circle to indicate that Spitz should go shick himself. Spitz scowled and looked in the other direction. Cricket and company returned to their grog. "The man's a brute who likes ta stir trouble. Don't take 'is bait an' ye won't 'ave anythin' ta worry about," Cricket advised.

"Thanks for the tip," Bastian said.

It appeared that he'd already created an enemy. He didn't like the look of Spitz, or the way that he stared at him. But he would heed Cricket's warning and hope that the pirate found something else to occupy his time. His new friends distracted his fears with a different route of conversation as they finished their meal together. And Bastian found himself enjoying their company. He knew that it would be unwise to truly trust any of them. Pirates had a reputation for stabbing people in the back. But he couldn't help liking them all the same. And even though he wished that he was back with Gwena and Felix, he was beginning to have a sunnier outlook on his surroundings.

3

Bastian knocked cautiously on the door at the back of the armory. The sound of an explosion came from inside and the smell of black powder wafted towards him. He remembered what Cricket had told him and tried knocking again with a heavy hand. Seconds later a short, thick-bodied sailor appeared from behind the door. He was wearing a leather apron covered in black soot, and his face was just as dirty. There was a pair of goggles on his head almost hidden in fiery dark-red hair that stuck up all around them. Thick red chops ran down both sides of his face. The master gunner looked excited to see him. He took off a pair of heavy gloves and held out his hand eagerly. "Ye must be Dodger, the stowaway?" he asked.

Bastian took his hand. "So they tell me," he replied warmly.

"Boom be me name, explosives be me game. Oi be the master gunner aboard this 'ere ship," he said proudly.

The master gunner had a slightly insane air to him. Bastian couldn't quite put his finger on why that was. Maybe because his eyes had an unusual amount of light behind them.

"Come, oi'll show ya around," Boom said and led Bastian into the back room, shutting the door behind them.

"Oi be glade ta 'ave a 'elpin' 'and. Been tellin' the cap'n oi be needin' it fer weeks now. Back in the day oi 'ad 'alf a dozen powder monkeys at me disposal. Now, it just be me an' me lonesome. The other gunners all 'ave other duties ta attend ta, which keeps 'em preoccupied except fer at wartime. The Black Mary be understaffed, she 'tis. But that don't slow us down. We 'ave the finest, most capable crew, each man be worth three sailors at least," he said proudly.

In the center of the room was a table laden with glass beakers and vials of colorful liquids and powders. Around the table, the floor was littered with barrels that had protruding metal spikes, like strange man-made porcupines.

"What are those?" Bastian asked, pointing to the spiky contraptions.

"Sea mines," Boom said nonchalantly. He must have seen the concerned look on Bastian's face because he started to chuckle. "They're not armed, mind ya."

Bastian relaxed a little and directed his curiosity to the table.

"Those be me own personal experiments," Boom said, walking over to join him at the table. "Oi'm always tryin' ta come up with somethin' new ta outsmart our opponents, ya see? Never could stop bein' curious about thin's that go boom!" he said with an explosive gesture. "Guess that's why they call me what they do," he chuckled.

He led Bastian to a set of doors that were behind the table. "This 'ere be where we keep the proper stuff," he whispered secretively and threw the doors open. The storage space was stacked to the ceiling with an array of pistols, daggers, muskets, cutlasses, blunderbusses, and flintlock rifles amid other weapons of various sizes. It had tools and supplies for cleaning and all the ammunition one could hope for.

"Wow," Bastian said with appreciation. He had never seen a deadlier arsenal.

Boom was delighted by Bastian's reaction. "Sometimes oi make me own fireworks ta set alight fer special occasions. Would ye like ta see a demonstration?" he asked, with a sparkle in his eye.

Before Bastian could respond, Boom was back at the table lighting a small round object at his feet. A second later there was a loud *bang!* Sparks shot in every direction and then the whole thing combusted into a cloud of dense yellow smoke. Bastian jumped back and put his arm up to shield himself. When he put his arm down, he couldn't see two inches in front of his face. Boom fanned the air with his hands to disperse the smoke. "Painted Smoke Blinders. Ain't it grand?" Boom asked with a wild grin.

Bastian stood stunned with terror. The mad pirate had just lit a firework while trapped in a room stocked to the teeth with explosives. Fearing what Boom might light up next and hoping desperately to distract the pirate from his pyromania, he quickly interjected, "What can I do to help you?"

"Oh right, straight on track, oi like that! Oi need ye ta help me sift the black powder ta dry it out. Then we need ta roll the barrels ta mix the bits that be separated," he said. "Now let me see 'ere."

He opened a cupboard in the wall and pulled out a large round metal sieve. After looking it over and finding it satisfactory, he handed it to Bastian. "Oi keep tryin' ta get Tink ta fix me up a steam machine that can do the siftin' fer me, but the old salt keeps pretendin' 'e 'as more important thin's ta be doin'. Bah! Oi says, what could be more important than that? If the powder don't work, we'll all be in a right bit o' trouble, won't we?" Boom asked rhetorically. He shook his head. "Ain't nothin' more important on a ship than 'er firepower!… Well, that might not be entirely true, each man plays 'is part. But oi say that it certainly be at the top o' the list! If we can't instill fear inta the 'earts o' our enemies, then we don't deserve ta be callin' ourselves pirates now, do we?" he asked Bastian expectantly.

Bastian shook his head when he realized that it was expected of him, and Boom smiled at him approvingly.

He walked Bastian out of the room to the main section of the gun deck where there was an ample supply of barrels. Boom rolled one over and used a dagger to pop the stopper out of the hole in the top. Then he rolled an empty barrel beside it. He looked them both over while scratching his head. Then he put up a finger as if to indicate a light bulb going off somewhere in the chaos of his mind and ran back inside the armory. A moment later he hurried back with a large metal funnel.

"Best thin' ta do, be ta place the funnel inta the 'ole o' the empty barrel and place the sieve over the top. Then pick up the barrel that be full an' pour 'er over the sieve. I need ya ta transfer all o' the powder from one barrel ta the next. We 'ave an awful lot ta get through before we be done. Any questions?" he asked.

Bastian looked at the dozens of barrels stacked around the floor. He had a feeling that he wouldn't be able to make a dent before nightfall. "Are you hoping to get all of these done today?" he asked.

Boom looked at him blankly for a moment, then burst into deep hearty laughter. "Oh Stars no! Ye'd be 'ere all night! Six barrels a day, oi say. Any more might be bad fer yer health… seriously," he said with a somber expression.

"Got it," Bastian answered uneasily and accepted the funnel from Boom's offering hand. The master gunner smiled at him encouragingly. "Ye be a fine lad, soon we shall make a rogue o' the sea out o' ya!" he said, clapping Bastian on the shoulder.

Then he turned on his heels and disappeared back into the armory, shutting the door behind him.

Bastian exhaled in relief now that he was alone and nothing was exploding around him. He sat down on one of the barrels and ran his hair through his hands. He had a pounding headache. At least nothing down here was glinting besides the fire-beetles. He took a deep breath before taking off his jacket and setting to work.

4

Bastian transferred the last of the sixth barrel through the sieve. Black residue billowed around him, going into his eyes and up his nose. The barrels were heavy, and he found that if he tried to pour them too fast, they spilt across the floor, making twice as much work. He was beginning to see the gold dust again. It glittered on everything around him, convincing Bastian that surely the black powder was to blame. He concluded that the barrels he was sleeping behind the day before were probably full of the stuff and he must've been breathing it in. Perhaps it was a kind of allergic reaction? he wondered. But his head, at least, was feeling better. The work had kept him distracted and he was gradually recovering from his hangover.

By the time he'd finished, he was covered in black soot from head to toe and looked much like the master gunner. He dusted himself off as best he could and knocked on the door to the armory. Boom's face appeared from behind it a moment later, as vibrant as ever. "Yer done already are ya?" he asked, as if it had only been a couple of minutes instead of the three and a half hours that Bastian had been working.

"All done," Bastian returned as enthusiastically as he could muster.

"That be great! If ye could just do one more wee favor fer me before ye go, then?" Boom asked.

Bastian clenched his jaw. "What can I help you with?" he asked, with a tight smile.

"Oi need ya ta oil the cannons 'ere on the gun deck. Not all o' them mind ya! Just the ones that be on the port side. We can tackle the rest tomarra'," he said.

"Sure, no problem," Bastian replied, not seeing much of an alternative. He was disappointed that he couldn't leave to find a bath and some fresh clothes, but at least oiling cannons wasn't a hard or life-threatening task.

Boom fetched a container of oil and an old rag and gave them both to him, then he smiled cheerily and disappeared back into the armory.

Bastian looked down the long row of cannons on the port side. He sighed and put down his jacket again before setting to his new task. Once he fell into a rhythm, he found the monotony of the work refreshing. It gave his thoughts room to breathe. He turned his predicament over in his mind and tried to find an escape route. The first and most manageable problem on hand was the weight in his coat pockets. He still held the rest of his plunder from the Wendrians' castle, and he knew that keeping it there was a liability. It was only a matter of time before it would be discovered and taken. Or worse, his life taken for it.

He couldn't wear his jacket forever, and he didn't want to. With work like today's, Gwena's gift would quickly be ruined.

Finding himself alone created an opportunity that he was eager to take advantage of.

He looked around for a potential hiding place. The firebeetle lanterns glowed faintly, casting the cannon's long shadows across the floorboards as the ship rocked steadily from side to side. There were some scattered piles of rope and stacks of cannonballs, but nowhere with any sort of security. He walked up and down the deck's length looking for anywhere with potential, scanning every nook and cranny he could find. He was looking around the last cannon on the stern side when the ship shifted abruptly, causing the cannon to roll backwards towards him.

Bastian stumbled out of the way and fell to the floor. "Bloody Shick," he muttered, cursing the Star Stirrer for pulling his mischief. He turned his head to push himself up onto his feet and noticed a hole where the wheel of the cannon had been. It looked like an abandoned mouse's home. He crawled over to inspect it, sticking his hand inside and feeling out its interior. It was roughly the size of his fist and as empty as a beggar's pockets, a perfect fit for his purpose.

"I take it back, Shick. You've done me a service, thank you," he muttered to the spirit.

He looked around to confirm that he was alone, then recovered his jacket and took out each of his treasures and placed them gently into the hole, one by one. Seeing some straw and a discarded bit of wood, he laid them on top of his valuables as an extra layer of protection in case his hiding spot was discovered. Once he was satisfied that everything was well concealed, he carefully pushed the cannon back over the opening and secured the wheel lock.

He finished oiling the cannons on the port side and then put the oil and cloth neatly outside the armory door before heading to the upper deck, leaving before Boom had the chance to assign him to another task.

5

"What in the Stars 'appened ta ya? Ye look like one o' Boom's experiments," Cricket said when he saw Bastian.

Bastian looked down at his black clothes.

"Please tell me that jacket o' yers at least wasn't ruined?" Cricket asked.

Bastian held it up for view. It wasn't spotless, but he had managed to keep the worst from it.

"Thank the Stars fer that. That jacket will be mine one day, mark me words. Every man 'as 'is price."

Bastian laughed and shook his head. "I wouldn't be so certain, this jacket has way too much sentimental value to be replaced with trinkets. You know, my insides are probably just as black as I am after the amount of powder I've sifted," he said.

"Ha-ha, now yer initiation be complete, saturated in black from yer guts ta the skin on yer nose. Congratulations, mate, now yer a true pirate," Cricket laughed, slapping Bastian on the shoulder.

"You wouldn't happen to have a spare pair of clothes, would you? And I am awfully keen on a wash, if the Black Mary has a place for such a thing?" Bastian asked.

"O' course, matey, we be pirates, not savages! Though I don't blame ya fer askin' the question, the way some folks smell around 'ere. Come, follow me," Cricket said.

Cricket led Bastian to the washroom, where there was a single bath covered in dark stains with a pull shower overhead.

"We call 'er Betsy. She ain't warm er pretty, but she gets the job done."

He showed Bastian how to use it and recommended that he only use the water when he needed it. Then he left to find him some new clothes.

Bastian eyed the bath warily. "Hiya, Betsy. Please be kind."

He undressed and climbed into the tub and then pulled on the triangular handle above him. Freezing cold water flooded down. Bastian gasped in surprise and retreated to the opposite end of the tub. He could see why most of the men chose to be dirty. He quickly found the bar of soap and washed himself as well and as fast as he could, his hands fumbling with stiffness from the cold. Then he held his breath and pulled on the handle again. The freezing water came bucketing down once more, and the water turned black around his feet as it washed the powder from him. He could've used another two rinses, but he decided that he would rather be silty.

To his relief, Cricket was there with a fresh pair of clothes the second he was finished. Bastian climbed out of the tub eagerly and took the small hand towel Cricket offered him. After drying himself off as best he could, he put on the new clothes. It was a pair of brown fisherman's pants with a cream cotton shirt and a dark warm wool jacket.

"These be me own personal threads. Ye can wear them until next port an' then I be needin' them back. Er ye can keep them in exchange fer yer jacket," Cricket offered with a sly smile.

Bastian laughed. "I owe you one, mate. I will return them as soon as I can get my own. I can't thank you enough," he said gratefully.

He welcomed the change. As smart as he had felt in his fine jacket, it wasn't nearly as practical or as warm as Cricket's coat. He had to admit to himself that in that moment the trade was tempting.

He transferred over the contents of his pockets: his slingshot and lock-picking kit, his smoke pouch and Everfire box, his pocket watch, his coin purse, and his pencil and sketchbook. His belongings didn't fit nearly as well in the two pockets of Cricket's coat as they had in the various pockets that lined his own. Cricket showed him to the crew's wooden lockers where he could safely store his personal items. The pirate helped Bastian to choose one that wasn't occupied and even tracked down a lock to secure it.

"These locks might keep us out, but they can't keep yer 'ands out, can they?" Cricket asked.

Bastian shrugged. "I'm not going to lie, they're one of the easiest things to pick. But I'm not entirely stupid. I imagine that stealing from pirates would be nothing short of suicide," he said.

Cricket grinned. "Yer smarter than ya look then," he said in jest.

"Better than looking smarter than I am," Bastian returned in good humor.

A moment later the dinner bell rang, and they followed its call.

The mess hall was filled with men and their boisterous voices. Bastian and Cricket joined Stork and Rhino at the table and dug into Doc's hearty stew. The day's work and the previous night's festivities started to catch up with Bastian, and he was feeling exhausted. The voices of the men around him sounded distant, as if they were underwater. The gold shimmer started creeping into the edges of his field of vision, like the phantoms of a bad migraine. Then suddenly, all at once, it increased in scope and intensity, flooding the room around him. Everything glimmered brightly and gold dust began wafting from his arms as if he was burning off the strange stuff. He rubbed his eyes and looked down at his hands. They were glowing, and powdered gold flakes were billowing up from his palms. He closed his hands into fists and buried his head in his arms.

"Are ye alright, mate?" Cricket asked.

"I need sleep," Bastian said and hurriedly excused himself from the table.

He fumbled his way down the hall towards the sleeping quarters and into his hammock's embrace. He curled up into a ball and closed his eyes, praying to the Stars that a good night's sleep would set him right. He retreated into thoughts of Gwena and played over the memory of their last moments together before he fell into a deep and troubled sleep.

6

The next day Bastian felt rotten. He opened his eyes cautiously and looked around the room. Everything was back to normal. He sighed in relief. He looked at his palms and was relieved to see that they finally looked like his own two hands again. Thank the Stars for that, he thought. He'd gotten at least nine hours of sleep, yet for some reason, he felt the worse for it. For the last two and a half days he'd been fueled by nothing but adrenaline, love, and alcohol. Now that the excitement had stopped, he was left feeling at the bottom of the barrel, and he faced his reality with a whole new sobriety. It was Moonday. The train would come and go from Westdock in a matter of hours. He'd hoped to have reached another port by now, but since leaving Westdock, the Black Mary had seen nothing but the open sea. Now hope was gone, and despair filled Bastian in its place. He prayed to the Stars that Gwena and Felix would make the train. If only he knew they were safe, his mind would ease a little. He was forced to face the cold truth of his predicament and admit that it might be months before he could see either of them again—if he was lucky enough to escape the Black Mary. And even if he could make it off the ship, he wouldn't know where they were or how to find them. The Heartland was a huge city, and looking for them there would be like trying to find a drop in the ocean.

At breakfast Bastian welcomed his grog. He sat at the middle table next to Cricket and the twins, nursing it absently.

"How're ye goin' after last night, mate?" Cricket asked him.

"Yeah, what was all that about?" Stork asked with a mouth full of oatmeal.

Bastian shrugged. "I wasn't feeling well, just needed an early night I guess."

"Ye feelin' better now then?" Rhino asked.

"Mildly."

"It can take a while ta get yer sea legs. I still remember me first week aboard, I was emptyin' me guts fer the first three days," Cricket said.

"True! I remember that, poor soul, ye were only a wee lad then. An' that's not the only ailment the rockin' gives ya, it can make ya feel tired constantly before yer used ta it," Stork added.

"Aye, yer adjustin' far better than most. Especially consider-in' the circumstances," Rhino weighed in.

"Give it a week, an' ye'll be feelin' yerself again," Cricket said.

"Thanks," Bastian said. But as much as he appreciated their words of encouragement, none of it touched on the real cause of his torment.

Bastian welcomed his list of chores that day, grateful for the distraction from his misery. After breakfast, he shadowed Cricket and Stork on the top deck while they checked the ropes and mended the sails. The snow had melted, and the sky was a bright blue dotted with wispy white clouds that moved with the wind. Bastian found the weather much more tolerable with Cricket's wool jacket. As the pirates checked the rigging on the main mast, Bastian looked at the carvings that covered its sur-face. The pictures of sea creatures and legends of the deep were incredibly detailed. He ran his hand along the wood. His own experience in whittling gave him a deep appreciation for the skilled craftmanship.

"Someone must 'ave been really bored, eh?" Cricket jested beside him.

"It's amazing! I've never seen a carved mast before. Surely there's a story behind it?" Bastian asked.

"Man was called Whittler. Fer reasons I'm sure ye can imag-ine. Died before our time."

"Whittler carved the masts ta record the 'istory o' the Black Mary," Stork said, coming up beside them.

"Surely not! Every sea creature in folklore is included here," Bastian said.

Stork and Cricket exchanged a humored glance.

"Folklore, ye say? What creatures are ye referrin' ta exactly?" Cricket asked.

"All of them! Mermaids, selkies, and the rest."

"When we get ta Port Trinity, we be takin' Dodger ta Sirens Cove," Stork said to Cricket.

"Aye. Yer in fer a real treat, Dodger. Not only do mermaids exist, but they'll spoil every other woman for ya," Cricket grinned.

"Ye should be grateful that ya got picked up by the Black Mary. Ye 'aven't yet lived if ye think that the best parts o' this world be fiction," Stork said.

Bastian was dumbfounded. Could mermaids really exist? Sure, sailors told tales, but he had never believed them. He wasn't even sure if he could believe them now. Nevertheless, he looked at the stories depicted in the carvings with a fresh eye. There were pictures of mermaids, sirens, selkies, and sea serpents. The images told dark tales of deathly stormy seas, stolen treasure, and giant monsters of the deep. One particular scene stood out to him. It was a series of images depicting the Black Mary in a heated battle with a colossal sea creature that had a huge head and a tangle of arms. The carvings made it look like the Black Mary defeated the monster, but then Bastian kept seeing parts of the animal reappear in other images. Sometimes it was a single long suckered limb, and sometimes just the top of its head or its glaring monstrous eyes.

If these depictions had any truth to them, then the Black Mary had seen wonders and horrors beyond belief. And the fact that it was still afloat was nothing short of a miracle.

"What's the story behind this one?" Bastian asked, pointing to the picture of the battle.

"Ah, that be the Kraken. It be told that years back the crew o' the Black Mary killed 'er, but that she was only a babe, the daughter o' the real queen o' the deep. An' 'er mother 'as been followin' us ever since, waitin' fer 'er opportunity at revenge," Stork said ominously.

"Now that one I'm not so sure I believe," Cricket interjected. "Sure, the Black Mary could 'ave killed a Kraken. I 'ave seen enough in me time ta believe it. But that 'er mother follows us still be nothin' but a tall tale. I been with the Black Mary nearly all me life, an' I 'ave never seen the slightest evidence o' the beast."

"Ask Bullseye about it if ye like. 'E will tell ya o' the vast shadow that 'aunts our trail. 'E swears that 'e 'as seen it over a dozen times," Stork said.

"A shadow? A shadow could mean anythin'! Ye need nothin' but fear an' a little imagination ta give form ta shadows. I've 'eard tell that Whittler was so affected by the battle with the Kraken that 'e became plagued with night terrors and started ta see the beast everywhere the ship turned. The Kraken's mother, 'a! 'Elp me fix the last sail before I kraken ya both!" Cricket jested, cracking a piece of rope towards Stork's leg. Stork dodged the blow and the two laughed together as they headed towards the next mast.

Bastian lagged behind, transfixed on the carvings. He recalled the shadow that he'd seen passing underneath the ship the day before, and a shiver ran up his spine.

After Bastian finished helping Cricket and Stork mend the last sail, he went below to the gun deck to sift more black powder and oil the remaining cannons.

As the day progressed, Bastian's misery only got worse and soon he was clouded with depression. He sifted the powder absent-mindedly, while his thoughts looped in circles. He envisioned Gwena back in harm's way with her father and Felix captured by the castle's guards. The thing that haunted him most was that there wasn't a single thing he could do about it. He wanted someone to blame. What were the Stars playing at? The three of them had been so close to having everything they'd always wanted, only to have it taken away. Could the Watchers really be that cruel? Didn't the three of them deserve happiness?

At supper, Bastian joined Cricket, Stork, and Rhino in the mess hall. The meal was a delicious duck roast, which mildly warmed his spirits.

"Are ye alright, Dodger? Ye seem a bit downhearted, matey," Cricket asked, concerned. Bastian shrugged and then drained his Black Jack eagerly. "What do you have to do to get a proper drink around here, instead of this watered-down piss?" he asked.

"Watered-down piss? Just yesterday ye were askin' fer plain water, an' now there be too much in yer grog fer ya? 'Ave ya already fergotten the punishment that yer stomach only just recovered from?" Cricket asked, amused.

"No gulpers tonight, mate, unless yer lookin' ta get reprimanded," Rhino said.

"That's a real shame, cause I know a wicked Westdock drinking game that I would like to teach you lads," Bastian said with a malicious grin. His emotions were in turmoil and he needed something to numb the pain.

"What be ailin' ya, lad? Sounds like ye be lookin' ta get hung," Rhino asked. He and Cricket exchanged worried glances.

"Leave the lad be, we all know that this life takes adjustin' ta. Dodger be a grown man, if 'e wants ta wash 'is worries, then let 'im," Stork said, putting his arm around Bastian. Then he lowered his voice conspiratorially, "I did tuck away the rest o' the bottle from yer initiation the other night. It be strong enough ta put 'air on yer chest, but if we mix it with our grog, then they still aren't really gulpers, are they?" he said with a wink.

Bastian grinned. "You're a good man, Stork. Tell me that you'll share it with me?"

"O' course, mate, I can't let a man drink alone."

Bastian turned to Cricket and Rhino. "Come on, lads, join us? We can't play the game with only two. I guarantee you won't be disappointed."

Cricket sighed. "Go on then, I always 'ave been a sucker fer punishment," he said with a smirk.

"If ya can't beat 'em, then join 'em," Rhino said.

"Brilliant! Well then, what are we waiting for?" Bastian asked, rubbing his hands together with anticipation.

Stork left to fetch the bottle of liquor. Bastian's drinking game was one that he and Felix had made up to exploit young aristocrats in the upper-class taverns. They could play the game for hours and remain mostly sober, while the young nobles around them drank to excess and openly divulged the secrets of the well-to-do families. Felix would tuck the information away to use for blackmailing them later. The wealthy are saturated with dark deeds they're eager to keep covered. To them, a reputation is worth far more than a bulging bag of coin—and their eagerness to hide their own dirt is equally matched by their eagerness to spill the secrets of their fellows. Besides being useful in that manner, the game was also loads of fun.

Stork returned and began filling their glasses under the table, while Bastian explained the rules of the drinking game.

"The game is straightforward enough, it's called Old Mother Shicker. It's modeled around a classic Westdock verse called

Old Mother Dicker, a simple rhyme, but if you aren't careful, then it can easily tie your tongue into knots. It goes like this:

Old Mother Dicker had a rough-cut punt,

A rough-cut punt had she.

Not a punt cut rough,

But a rough-cut punt

With a pole at the stern and a flag at the front.

It might sound like a children's nursery rhyme, but don't be fooled, it only takes a simple slip to quickly lose its innocence. The game moves in clockwise order and is played in three simple steps:

1. Each player takes a turn saying a line from the verse.
2. If a player messes up the verse, then they have to take a drink and start the rhyme again from the beginning.
3. The person whose turn falls on the last line has to run through the whole verse alone.

If that player manages to make it through the whole thing without making a mistake, then they pour their glass into a pot in the center and the person to their left starts the verse again. However, if they mess it up, then they have to drink the pot in the center and start the verse again themselves. Any questions?"

The pirates looked at one another:

"Sounds like fun!"

"I'm game"

"Let's give it a go then," they said.

Bastian taught them the verse and then they ran through a practice round. Once they were ready to begin, he started the game off with "Old Mother Dicker had a rough-cut punt."

He was followed by Stork and then Rhino. The next line fell on Cricket before returning to Bastian for the final phrase.

They made it through two rounds of the verse before Stork slipped up by saying *Old Mother Shicker* instead of *Old Mother Dicker*. "Bloody Shick!" he swore to the Star Stirrer as the others laughed and cheered around him. He took a hearty drink and started the verse again. Rhino slipped up next by combining *cut* and *punt*, and then he botched the verse a second time and had to drink again.

The more the men drank, the more easily their tongues became tied and the more fun the game became. Soon all three pirates were well lubricated and thoroughly enjoying themselves. Bastian wanted to be sharing their mirth, but he just couldn't shake the dispiriting cloud that hung over him. He was so familiar with the poem that he could have said the words flawlessly with a mouth full of cotton, which was completely counterproductive for drowning his sorrows. He waited until the pot in the center was half full, and then he made his tongue slip on purpose. He started the verse again and was pleased that no one made a mistake before the last line came back around. He began reciting the whole verse and then intentionally stumbled, mocking frustration as he eagerly drained the pot in the center. But he still felt sober. The amount of alcohol that he'd consumed and the rate that he drank it should have knocked him on his ass. Especially considering that Stork's spirit must've been at least a hundred proof, given the way it leapt up in flame for his induction.

All Bastian wanted was to be intoxicated, lost in the happy haze of inebriation, but it never came. Instead, he found himself becoming more somber and bitter by the minute.

He was feeling desperate and longed for something to give him an escape from his agony.

"Why don't we teach the dodger o' death a real man's game?"

Bastian looked up to see who had spoken. It was Spitz, the pirate with the unsettling features who had been giving him the death stare the day before.

"An' what would that be, Spitz?" Cricket asked, frustrated by the interruption.

"Spittin' Daggers," Spitz declared, staring intently at Bastian.

Everyone at the table stopped what they were doing and looked at him.

"Don't be stupid, ye know full well that game be banned by the cap'n 'imself," Cricket said.

"An' fer good reason," Rhino added.

Spitz put his hands on their table and leaned in towards them. "Yes it 'as, but ye lot don't seem ta 'ave much regard fer the cap'n's rules," he said, nodding towards their drinks.

He grabbed the center pot from their game and drained it. "That's some fine grog ye got there," he said with a cruel grin.

"What do ye want, Spitz?" Cricket asked in a low and steady tone.

"If the Dodger plays a round o' Spittin' Daggers with me, then I'll ferget what I seen 'ere. Otherwise, ye lot can expect ta be kept onboard at the next port. Where are we 'eaded again?" he asked.

"Jaxland," Stork said solemnly.

"That's right, the island o' rogues. I'm sure ye won't be missin' much."

Bastian's company looked at one other with weighty expressions.

Jaxland? Bastian thought. Where was that? He knew the geography of Equillian like the back of his hand. He'd spent years pouring over maps of the world, fueling his dreams to see other places. According to every map that he'd seen, there was no port this far from the mainland in any direction, unless you were travelling skyward towards the Windswept Isles in *Sky View*. Wherever it was, the looks on the pirate's faces told Bastian that Jaxland was a port they didn't want to miss.

"Come now, lads, enough with the long faces, this night is supposed to be about fun! The more games the merrier. Sure, I'll play with you, Spitz," he said cheerily, half hoping that he *would* find trouble.

"No!" Cricket, Stork, and Rhino all said in unison while Spitz smirked.

"Shick, now I really am curious. What's the premise?" Bastian asked eagerly.

"'Tis stupid, that be what 'tis," Cricket said, glaring at Spitz.

"Nothin' but throwin' insults at one another," Rhino said.

"That's the game? Throwing insults at one another?" Bastian asked with a snort.

It couldn't be more perfect, he thought. His internal turmoil was making him crave combat—a friendly round of verbal sparring could be his perfect remedy.

"What are you guys so worried about? If Spitz wants to trade pleasantries, then I'm happy to oblige. I mean, come on, finding insults for him is so easy, it's practically unfair. Look at the man, his face looks like a deformed potato. Not to mention that he shares his name with a tiny dog," Bastian said in jolly jest.

Spitz gave a satisfied grin and Cricket put his face in his hands.

"Well, ya 'ave done it now. Stars 'elp ya, Dodger."

"Done what?" Bastian asked.

But Rhino stood from his seat, towering over Spitz before anyone could answer him. "Ta the nine realms o' darkness with ye an' yer connivin' ways, Spitz. Dodger doesn't 'ave a clue o' 'ow the game works. Even if ye were ta play, 'e already be half-seas over. Ye know bloody well that gives ya an unfair advantage," he said.

Spitz spat on the floor at Rhino's feet. "Rules be rules. Privy ta the game er no, Dodger 'as cast the first stone an' the game be laid," he said, with obvious pleasure.

"Can someone please fill me in on what is happening here? What did I do?" Bastian asked again.

"By throwin' the first insult ye 'ave just accepted 'is challenge. It's exactly what Spitz wanted, ya fool! Now ye will 'ave ta play till the thin' be done," Cricket explained.

"Will you look at that, I must have a natural instinct for the game!" Bastian said delighted, while his company shook their heads at him.

"Stand up," Spitz ordered.

"Right-o," Bastian said in good spirits and stood from his chair.

He stumbled slightly as he tried to find his feet and realized that the alcohol had taken effect after all.

"It was nice knowin' ya, Dodger," Stork said, holding his Black Jack up to him.

And then the pirate started taking bets from the sailors around him. Stork never seemed to miss an opportunity to capitalize on a situation. He reminded Bastian of Felix in that way.

The tables were pushed back to form a clearing and Spitz went to one end of the space as Bastian was led to the other by a man whose skin was completely covered in tattoos. The rest of the crew sat at the surrounding tables, eager to watch the spectacle.

Bastian was trying to figure out why Cricket and the twins were so worried about a game. Was Spitz particularly good at insults? he wondered, when suddenly, a man put a dagger in his hand.

"What's this for?" he asked.

Bastian looked down at the razor-sharp blade that he held and terror washed over him. He had never wielded a weapon outside of his slingshot and his tongue. Even when faced with a fistfight, he dodged the blows without ever throwing a punch. He prayed to the Stars that he hadn't just walked into a knife fight. His ignorance in the use of such an object wasn't even his primary concern. What worried him the most was that he was feeling particularly reckless. That, combined with the alcohol he'd just consumed, canceled out any good judgment he might have had. His current life predicament made him feel completely powerless, like a caged animal. He wanted to scream and do something stupid. And now someone had handed him a dagger?

He took a deep breath.

He looked up and saw Spitz tucking his own dagger behind him in the belt of his pants. Bastian followed his lead and did the same with his own. The tattooed sailor who had armed him stood beside him on a bench ready to make an announcement. "After every insult a player makes, 'e must take a drink. First person ta draw their dagger loses," the man declared.

Bastian relaxed a little. If the dagger wasn't part of the game, and it was the first player to draw his dagger who was the loser, then what did he have to worry about? Of course, if Spitz stabbed him, then he would be the real loser regardless. He just hoped that Spitz's intention was to win the game and not to fill him with holes. Spitz paced the floor across from him as he cast the first insult.

"Ye know why a thief could never be a true pirate, Dodger?" the pirate began. "Because 'e be too lily-livered ta face the men 'e be takin' from," he said and took a drink from his Black Jack.

Bastian grinned. He highly enjoyed banter. It was the only sparring that he was any good at. Especially with men like Spitz, who had inflated egos. Back in Westdock, Felix had to shut Bastian up when they went out, because he was so prone to offend someone after only a couple of drinks. It had gotten him thrown out of several establishments on more than one occasion.

"You know why you could never be anything *but* a pirate, Spitz? Because you couldn't face a man or woman without them cringing," Bastian returned merrily.

The surrounding men laughed and Spitz sneered. Bastian took a long, hard drink. His Black Jack was filled with grog instead of Stork's potent spirit, but he welcomed it all the same.

"At least I inspire fear in me enemies. Ye couldn't frighten a babe if ya tried," Spitz said.

Bastian snorted. "You know, I'm sure you're right. Though I can't say that I *have* tried or would ever want to. On the contrary, you only have to look at a child and they burst into tears. Your face is probably the essence of their nightmares. You must be so proud that you scare little children," he said mockingly.

"Better ta scare little children then ta be scared by them. Ye be so cowardly, that if a babe said *boo*, ye would run away like a little girl," the pirate returned.

Bastian could tell that he was ruffling Spitz's feathers. The pirate had clearly underestimated Bastian's experience in insolence.

"The only girls running are the ones that you try to engage in conversation. You don't even have the charm to make up for your appearance. Tell me, Spitz, do they make you pay extra at the brothels?" he asked, spurring laughter from the onlookers.

Spitz's face turned red, but it didn't slow him down.

"Women don't need charm er good looks when ye know what ta do with 'em. But that be somethin' I expect ye ta know nothin' about. Yer cowardice be a clear reflection o' what ye be lackin' between yer legs," the pirate said angrily.

"OOOhhh!" shouted the men around them.

"It wouldn't matter how big your equipment is, Spitz, or how well you know how to use it, you'd need to be Shick himself to make up for your features," Bastian returned, taking another swig of his grog.

By the expression Spitz wore, Bastian imagined that any moment steam would burst from his ears.

"Yer filled with nothin' but 'ot air, boy. It will only take the prick o' a pin ta shrink ya down. If that tongue o' yers gets plucked out, ye'll 'ave nothin' left," Spitz said, spraying saliva with his rage.

Bastian laughed at Spitz's wrath, which only infuriated the pirate more. Bastian knew that he was playing with fire, but he didn't care. He was craving the conflict and had no inhibitions left to stop him.

"It's an insult, not the weather, Spitz. Now I see your name has a double meaning, a warning sign to anyone who meets you. Hey, me name be Spitz, the spittin' an' yippy dog," he said loudly, mimicking Spitz's accent.

The room erupted in laughter and Spitz's face contorted unpleasantly. Then his temper appeared to cool and he smirked wickedly, making him look like a poster child for night terrors.

"It be no wonder that yer mother threw ya away after takin' one look at ya," he started cooly. "Even as a babe she knew that ye were nothin' but a snivellin' runt that weren't worth the keepin'. I seen the mark ya bear. Yer a discarded bastard. Child o' the

Stars, they call ya. But yer bein' 'ere be a clear sign that even the Stars 'ave seen fit ta abandon ya."

Bastian's jaw clenched. Spitz could insult his courage and his manhood all he wanted, but mention of his mother shot straight to the heart. He never knew why he was dropped off at the steps of the Star Temple, or why his parents had abandoned him. The Order erased all records of your previous life once you were delivered to them. Bastian found his hand wrapped around the hilt of his dagger before he even registered what he was doing. A cool anger raged inside of him. It gave him an odd sort of clarity and his mind quickly calculated that he wouldn't be able to beat Spitz in a knife fight, but if he threw his dagger, then he might be able to end him before it started. Bastian knew then that he was capable of killing a man, and it terrified him. His conscience watched helplessly from a distant place as he moved to draw the blade. But it seemed that the Stars hadn't abandoned him yet, for he was saved from himself by a stone grip obstructing his wrist.

"Enough," its owner's voice hissed behind him.

Bastian turned to see Snibs, the quartermaster. Snibs took the dagger from Bastian's hand and addressed the crew, "Enough! Whose idea be it ta play Spittin' Daggers against the cap'n's orders?" he asked the men.

The room fell silent.

"Spitz, this be yer final warnin'. If I catch ye doin' anythin' unsavory again, Stars 'elp me, I will abandon ye on a dreg island in the Desert Ocean. Yer banned from leavin' the ship at next port!" Then Snibs turned to Bastian. "Dodger, yer comin' with me."

EQUILLIAN EXPRESS
CHAPTER THIRTEEN

Gwena woke to the first morning light creeping in through Bastian and Felix's window. She had a slight headache from the drinks she'd had the night before. To make matters worse, she'd hardly slept—all night she'd been electric with anxiety, staying up late figuring out what she needed to do before her journey. Besides packing her own things, she'd sorted most of Bastian's and Felix's belongings into two piles, one to be discarded and one to be given away. After that, she'd gotten to work sewing the coin from the boy's stash into the hem of her dress. She knew better than to travel alone with a bulging bag of coin. But once she'd finished all that, thoughts of Bastian in danger and the daunting reality of her departure had haunted her for the rest of the night. Now it was Moonday and the train was due to leave before noon on the hour of The Plunger: The reckless spirit who delights in games of chance and risk taking. Her voice whispers jump when you're standing near a cliff's edge, but she's also a guiding hand when needing courage to take a leap of faith.

How appropriate, Gwena thought.

The flower market would open in a couple of hours. Gwena would make sure to be there early so that she didn't miss Lady Everitt. She got up and inspected the wounds on her back. They were already starting to heal and most of the pain had subsided. She dressed, trying to distract herself from the journey ahead by focusing on the tasks in front of her. She off-loaded the discard pile into the butcher's rubbish bin out back, gagging at the sweet smell of rotting meat. Then she looked over the items to give away. The boys' books could fill a small library. Most were Felix's, and they ranged vastly in content, from physics and chemistry to the latest social etiquette, how-to books as well as philosophy, music, and poetry, to name a few. Gwena tucked Bastian's copy of *The Words of the Watchers* into her bag and gathered the rest of the books with the boys' clothes. She pulled out Bastian's suit pants and a pang of grief tightened her throat. She sat down on Bastian's bed, composed herself, then lovingly folded his pants and put them in her bag. "I'm not giving up on you yet, Bastian William Sanders. You better not dare give up either," she whispered. Then she sat down at Felix's desk and pulled out a fresh piece of parchment.

> *Dear Bastian and/or Felix,*
> *I can only hope that this letter finds you. I have taken*
> *your savings and left for the Heartland. I plan to check the*
> *Heartland's central posting house every Phenday. Please send*
> *word there when you can. I hope to see you both before long.*
>
> *Love,*
> *Gwena*

Gwena folded the letter carefully, sealing it in an envelope from Felix's desk. She stowed it away and then put the rest of Felix's stationery and writing materials in the giveaway pile. She added the boy's collection of pocket watches, except for one small silver one that she kept for herself, their bedding, and a few other odds and ends. Then she bundled it all together and made another journey out the window.

Gwena dropped her donations off at the local orphanage on her way towards the flower market. There was a gentle curtain of fog hanging in the air around the harbor. As Gwena walked along the boardwalk, the rising sun burned it off into little wisps around her feet. She turned the corner and walked up the stone path towards the plaza. The Moonday market was much less crowded than the Starday market. Most commoners were back at work, which meant that the patrons who frequented the flower market were mainly aristocrats or shop owners looking to decorate their businesses. Gwena put up the hood of her travelling cloak and scanned the stalls filled with colorful plants and flowers. She couldn't see Lady Everitt, so she occupied herself looking at a display of blue dew-drop roses and frost lilies. She tried to think of how she was going to separate Lady Everitt from her handmaiden when she had an idea. There was a cart filled with colorful bouquets of forget-me-nots and ivory-lace posies behind her. It was staffed by an older gentleman with white hair and a well-groomed white mustache that turned up at the ends.

"Hello there," she greeted him.

"Good morning, miss. Staying warm I hope?" he asked with a friendly smile.

"Yes, thank you. I have a special request that I'm hoping you can help me with."

"Of course, what can I do for you?"

"Lady Everitt Wendrian will be here soon with her handmaiden. It's Malinda's birthday, but she's so busy with her work at the castle that she won't have a chance to celebrate. I'm a friend of her sweetheart—he asked me to purchase one of your finest bouquets and request that you give it to her and sing her Jolly Birthday for a few extra cwips, if you're willing?"

"I would be happy to! I'm the lead tenor in the Seafoam Choir and every girl deserves flowers and a round of Jolly Birthday on her naming day!" he said charmingly.

"Brilliant! You're a star," Gwena said.

She picked out his largest bouquet and tipped him generously. Then she moved around the corner to wait for her opportunity. Not five minutes had passed when she saw Lady Wendrian come into the market. She was a beautiful woman. Tall and lean with dark chestnut skin and stark white hair braided elegantly to one side. She was walking gracefully next to her handmaiden, lost in conversation. Gwena waited for them to approach the flower cart. As soon as they walked by, the charming old gentleman jumped out in front of Malinda with the bouquet in hand and burst into song.

Jolly, Jolly Birthday
Jolly Birthday, Jolly Birthday!
Jolly, Jolly, Birthday
Jolly Birthday to you!!

On this day, your name day…

Malinda stood stunned as the man sang to her. Gwena grabbed Lady Everitt's hand pulling her to the side and speaking close to her ear,

"I have news of your daughter."

Lady Everitt followed Gwena around the corner without hesitation. They stood between two large potted ferns and Gwena produced the letter that Felix had instructed her to deliver.

"Take this, it's from Lilliana."

"Where is she? Is she all right?" Lady Everitt asked with desperation.

Gwena hesitated. She wanted to be able to answer her questions, but she didn't have the answers. She recalled Felix's words about leaving quickly and looked at Lady Everett apologetically.

"I don't know, I'm sorry," she said. Then she pushed the letter into Lady Everitt's hands and hurried out of the market.

As Gwena walked back to Tucker Street, she couldn't get Lady Everitt's desperation out of her head. First there was her husband's disappearance and now to also lose Lilliana. She couldn't imagine what the woman must be going through. Gwena reached the loft and climbed up through the window. She looked at the bare room and sighed. Then she shouldered her quiver travelling bag and made her way down to the butcher's.

Gwena walked into the butcher's shop. It was a small store with various types and sizes of sausages and salami hanging from the ceiling. Below that was a glass display case, its shelves filled with prime cuts. There was a robust woman chopping meat behind the counter. She had blond curly hair tied tightly in a bun and was wearing a white apron stained with blood.

"Excuse me," Gwena said politely.

The woman, hands on her hips, looked Gwena up and down before speaking curtly, "Yes miss? How might I help ya?"

"I'm a friend of Bastian and Felix's. Are you the owner?"

The woman's expression instantly warmed. "Ah, come on in lass! A friend of them boys is a friend of mine. They're lovely chaps, they are. My husband and I are the owners. What can I do for ya then?"

"Bastian and Felix have taken a job with a merchant ship and had to leave immediately. They don't know when or if they'll be returning, so they sent me to clear their room and to settle any debts."

"Oh, isn't that a shame! I mean it's great that they got a job worth takin', but I'll be sad to see them go."

"They're very sorry for the short notice. They said that they'd be happy to pay for two extra weeks for the inconvenience."

"Aren't they sweet? No, no, there be no need for that. We have an apprentice who'll be happy to move in there. Fillin' the space won't be a problem. I'll miss them, though. Those boys always put a smile on my face. I don't think they owe much, always paid their rent on time. Let me see here." The woman disappeared into the back and then returned a moment later with a paper in hand. "Here 'tis," she said, scanning the document. "They just paid last week, so five cwips should cover the rest."

Gwena reached into her pouch and counted out the coins. "I also have a favor to ask," she said while handing over the payment.

"What's that?"

"I have a letter for Bastian and Felix. It's very important that it gets to them if they do return. Could I leave it with you? I would be happy to pay you for your trouble."

"Oh no, it's no trouble at all. Give the letter here, I'll look after it."

"Thanks so much! I really appreciate it," Gwena said and handed the woman the envelope. The butcher took it and then offered Gwena a spiced mince pie.

"Take this before ya go, on the house. Ya need some fat on those bones."

Gwena took it gratefully, "Thank you! I still haven't had breakfast. Well, I best be off, I have a train to catch!"

Gwena walked towards the train station with her bag across her back and her cloak wrapped tightly around her. As the marble pillars and the thick wood beams of the station came into view, butterflies began dancing in her stomach. The stationhouse was a beautiful building. The expense of riding the train limited the passengers to aristocrats, which meant that there was rarely more than a handful of people there. A shame, Gwena thought, for it was too magnificent not to be enjoyed by everyone. Inside, there were murals on the high ceilings that depicted the harbor and fishermen bringing in their catch and a tile mosaic of Equillian inlaid in the floor. The morning light streamed in through three high-sitting large round windows. All the other patrons there were richly dressed nobles. The women wore thick woolen dresses with warm fur travelling cloaks, and the men wore fine woolen suits with heavy woolen coats, their heads adorned with either a fedora or the more formal top hat, as was the common fashion. Gwena sat down on one of the benches and watched the giant clock that was set in the wall over the platform. It was half an hour until the train's departure. She double-checked her long quiver travelling bag to make sure she had everything and then pulled out her embroidery to pass the time. Fifteen minutes before The Plunger constellation was due to rotate under the Guiding Star, the peacock-blue steam engine hummed into the station and a conductor dressed in a smart purple uniform started taking tickets. Gwena took a deep breath and collected her things. She made her way to the platform and stood at the end of the line of passengers waiting to board the train.

"Gwena."

Her whole body froze at the sound of her father's voice behind her. She slowly turned to face him. He looked ragged, wearing the same clothes she had last seen him in. His beard was untrimmed, his hair was disheveled, and there were heavy shadows under his eyes. Gwena's heart sank. His expression was desperate, and she could tell that he was drunk.

"Papa," she said in a devastated whisper.

"Gwena, you don't have to do this. Come home. What happened the other night…it was a mistake. I never should've hurt you…I love you, Gwena. Things will be different, I promise."

Tears leapt into Gwena's eyes. She hated seeing her father like this. "I can't, I'm sorry, Papa," she said apologetically.

Her father's eyes began to water. She had never seen him cry, not even after her mother had passed.

"I need you, Gwena. Please don't go, please? I don't know what I will do without you," he pleaded.

The conductor cleared his throat behind her. "The train will depart shortly, miss. Are you coming or staying?" he asked.

Gwena hesitated for a moment, looking at her father. She desperately wanted to run into his arms and tell him that she loved him and that everything was going to be ok. She wanted to believe that if she did, things would be different between them, better. But in her heart, she knew that no matter how much she wished it, her father wasn't going to change.

"I'm coming," Gwena said, turning to the conductor and handing him her ticket.

"Gwena, you come back here, I forbid you to get on that train!" her father said angrily.

Gwena faced him. "I'm not a child anymore, Papa. This is my life, and I am going to make the most of it," she said, and she boarded the train.

Gwena wiped her tears, trembling as she walked past the other passengers settling into their seats. The train was richly clad with elegant trimmings and a red velvet carpet. She made her way towards the back of the train, walking through the fine dining car and past a swanky cocktail lounge with a grand piano. Next, she reached the first-class sleeping car and walked its length until she found the cabin that matched her ticket, number 48. She stepped inside and closed the door behind her, leaning against it for support. She shut her eyes and took several deep, shaky breaths. When she finally looked around, she saw the compartment was surprisingly spacious and luxuriously decorated with fine furniture and rich velvet curtains. To one side, two plush blue armchairs sat next to a large window with a small round table between them, and to the back of the cabin was a double bed. The quarters were fit for royalty. A smile parted Gwena's lips like a ray of sunshine breaking through clouds of sorrow. She walked over to the window and looked outside. The train was leaving the station and gradually picking up speed. A moment later she had a clear view over the trees straight to the ocean beyond. As they followed the curve of the coastline, Westdock receded behind them. The sight of her hometown disappearing from view filled her with terror and excitement all at once. She sat down and suddenly felt a great weight lifted from her. Her future was a blind spot, a blank page with an unwritten destiny, and this time, she held the pen.

SPICED KAH
CHAPTER FOURTEEN

Bastian followed Snibs down the ship's corridor in silence. He had a bad feeling that this night would be his last.

I'm sorry, Gwen, sorry I couldn't take you out of Westdock, sorry I couldn't fulfill my promise to return to you and give you the life of happiness that you deserve. And I'm sorry that it's all because of my own insolence and stupidity, he apologized to Gwena in his thoughts.

Bastian swore to himself that if he joined the Stars that night, he would dedicate himself to watching over her. They reached Snibs's quarters at the back end of the ship and the quartermaster opened the door for him. "Get in," he commanded.

Bastian did as he was told. It was a small room, but it was luxuriously decorated. Having private quarters was testament enough to Snibs's position, but its lavish appearance spoke even more highly of his standing.

"Have a seat," Snibs said, gesturing to a chair in the corner.

Bastian sat down. Across from him was Snibs's bed, neatly made with a rich satin blanket. Everything in his quarters was meticulously clean and organized, from the several pairs of boots neatly lined beneath his bed to the stacks of papers and books perfectly aligned on his small writing desk. It surprised Bastian. He never would've guessed it from looking at the man. Snibs might've been handsome once, but his chosen profession had clearly ruined any good looks he had. His skin was sun-weathered to a thick leather and pockmarked with burns and scars. His left eye was covered with a dark patch outlined in gold thread. His rough appearance and authoritative nature inspired unease. Bastian couldn't help but feel nervous around him. He could think of at least twelve unpleasant things he would rather do than be stuck in a room alone with the man. Snibs sat on his bed across from him, studying Bastian.

"What's yer story, Dodger?" he asked.

Bastian hesitated. "What do you mean, sir? I don't understand the question."

He was as drunk as could be from the back-to-back drinking games and extremely nervous about his current predicament. Snibs had woken him from his suicidal stupor, and he found himself greatly regretting his decision to attempt to drown his sorrows. If the quartermaster hadn't shown up when he had, Bastian was sure that he'd either be a murderer or dead by now.

"By Shick, yer a wreck, lad. 'Ere, drink this," Snibs said, offering a mug filled with a hot dark red liquid.

Bastian took the cup gratefully. "Thank you," he said in earnest and took a shaky drink. "Is this spiced Kah?" he asked in surprise. Kah was a sort of hot spiced alcoholic tea that had a bittersweet flavor and was signature to Westdock. It had a real kick to it that would keep you up for hours and was often drunk with breakfast or to help cure a hangover.

"Aye, I 'ave a real taste fer it. Finest thin' in Westdock if ya ask me. I always make sure ta pick up a bachelor's barrel when we come ta port," Snibs said.

"Always? But surely, the Black Mary has never come to port in Westdock before? I'm sure I would have recognized it," Bastian said while taking another drink.

"Ye should never be so sure o' anythin', nothin' be truly certain. An' believin' that it be only prevents ya from findin' the whole truth. The Black Mary 'as many forms. No port 'as ever seen 'er the same way twice," Snibs said and poured a mug of Kah for himself.

Bastian found Snibs's hospitality confusing. Wasn't he supposed to be getting a reprimand? Instead Snibs was giving him expensive Kah from his own stores.

"I don't deserve this, my behavior in there was completely inappropriate. I'm sorry, I don't know what came over me," Bastian said suddenly.

"I'm glad that we can both agree on that," Snibs said with a compassionate smile that made Bastian begin to warm to him.

"Spitz must really despise ya. 'E be smarter than 'e looks. If ye 'ad drawn that dagger, then ye would 'ave received punishment far worse than losin' a game. A sailor that pulls a weapon on 'is fellows gets a dozen lashes from the cat-o'-nine-tails. An' if ye 'ad managed ta stab the man, then ye would 'ave been killed by one o' 'alf a dozen unpleasant ways o' me choosin'. Ye see, on the Black Mary, if ye can't be trusted, then yer put down like a mad dog," Snibs explained matter-of-factly.

Bastian felt a lump in his throat. Of course, he should have known that the game would have such consequences. It had been banned by the captain himself. How could he have been so stupid? No wonder Cricket and the twins reacted like they did. Bastian guiltily drank his Kah in silence.

"Now, that bein' said, I know that Spitz's grudge against ya be no fault o' yer own. An' I can clearly see that ye be 'urtin'. Bein' isolated on a ship in the middle o' the ocean ain't easy. We all 'ave our moments. It takes time ta adjust. Though usually those moments come about three weeks inta sea, rather than three days. What be troublin' ya, landlubber?" Snibs asked.

As much as Bastian was relieved that he wasn't being punished, he hardly had the desire to share his feelings with Snibs.

"As you said, I'm having trouble adjusting to the whole situation. I've never been out at sea for more than a day…and I've been seeing things," Bastian said. That at least was true.

Snibs took a drink from his mug while he studied Bastian. "What do ye mean seein' thin's?" he asked.

"A strange shimmer on everything, sometimes rising up like smoke. I don't know what's wrong with me," he said uneasily.

"I'll 'ave Doc take a look at ya, me guess be that yer sleep deprived an' nothin' more. But it never 'urts ta check all the same."

"Thanks," Bastian said in earnest. He would welcome a doctor's opinion.

"So, tell me, what was it that ye be seekin' refuge from in Westdock?" Snibs asked.

"If you don't mind, I would rather explain that to the captain."

Snibs snorted with laughter. "Don't get ahead o' yerself, matey, the captain doesn't 'ave the time fer such thin's. Just because ya opened a chest, doesn't make ya important. Ye earned yerself a chance ta prove yerself, nothin' more."

"But I did prove myself, that's what the chest was, wasn't it?" Bastian asked.

"The chest kept ya from becomin' fish food. Now ye 'ave opened it, we don't 'ave any more chests that need openin', do we? So, how much use are ya now?" Snibs asked him.

"You're right, I'm no use at all. My skills are about as useless on a ship as a rake in the middle of the ocean. So, drop me off when we reach Port Trinity. You can be rid of me, and we can both go our separate ways and carry on with our lives," Bastian said.

All of Snibs's warmth disappeared. He crossed his arms and regarded Bastian with a hard stare.

"Where do ya think ya are, lad? This be the Black Mary, not a charity house!"

"I'm not asking for charity! I opened your chest and gave you my gold. And I've been working for my keep like the rest. That's something isn't it?" Bastian asked in earnest.

Snibs sunk his dagger into the desk next to Bastian threateningly.

"Ya need ta learn yer place, boy. I don't know if yer incredibly naïve er just stupid. I'm goin' ta ask ya one more time, an' this time I want an answer. What were ya seekin' refuge from?" Snibs asked again evenly.

Bastian tensed, suddenly acutely aware that he was trapped in a small room with no way out. If Snibs wanted to end his life right there and then, he could do it easily, and no one would even bat an eyelid.

Bastian swallowed. "I was accused of kidnapping the duchess," he said.

Snibs stared into his eyes, searching them for any sign of deception, and then he laughed. "Why, pray tell, would anyone believe that ye be capable o' such a thin'?" he asked.

"Because I was seen outside of her quarters right before she went missing."

Snibs raised an eyebrow. "An' did ya do it?"

"What? Kidnap the duchess? No! I was only interested in her jewels. I can't even imagine why anyone would want to. I'd rather pluck my eyelashes than spend time with a spoiled noble."

Snibs smirked, "We 'ave that in common." He stood up and refilled his mug. "What be the punishment waitin' fer ya there?" he asked.

"I don't know, locked up in the castle's dungeons until they find out what really happened to her, I suppose. Or worse, maybe. Lord Bardviss does seem to hate me," Bastian said, running his hands over his face.

"So, the Black Mary saved ya from bein' locked away in a dark an' miserable cell, er worse?"

"I guess so…."

"We 'ave a code on the Black Mary. If someone saves yer life, then ye be indebted ta them. If ya betray the code, then yer life be forfeit. An unreliable sailor be nothin' but a liability. —So, ya want off o' this ship?" Snibs asked.

"You have to understand, I have plans, life plans. Volunteering on a ship is one thing, being trapped on one is quite another," Bastian protested.

"Oh, I'm sorry that us savin' yer arse 'as been such an inconvenience. Were ya not the one who jumped onta our ship, askin' fer our 'elp? Or am I mistaken?" Snibs asked without sympathy.

Bastian looked at his boots silently.

"Ye 'ave two choices, landlubber. Either ye can accept the fate ye 'ave been given, an' show us one good reason why we should waste any more o' Doc's good cookin' on yer sorry bones. Er ye can walk the plank and swim back ta that invitin' cell waitin' fer ya back at Westdock. What's it goin' ta be?"

"I'd like to stay, if you'll have me," Bastian said meekly.

"Then yer in luck, because an opportunity ta repay yer debt an' prove yerself 'as presented itself. The captain 'as a little task fer ya," Snibs said, and he poured Bastian another mug of Kah.

KITE FISH
CHAPTER FIFTEEN

Felix listened to the pitter-patter on the ship as they passed through a gentle rainstorm. It was late in the afternoon on the second day of their journey, and Felix was on his twenty-second game of solitaire. Lilliana was in her private quarters doing Stars knows whatever it was that she did, and Roy was running the control station.

"Sport, come take a look at this," Roy called out to him.

Felix pulled himself from his game and walked onto the flight deck. Roy was sitting at the control desk staring intently out the window. Felix followed Roy's gaze to the rain outside. The visibility was ghastly. They were flying blind through a dense rain cloud. Then suddenly, a flash of silver flashed passed the window.

"Did you see that?" Roy asked.

Felix walked up to the glass to have a closer look and squinted. There was a shimmer of silver light that darted through the clouds. A moment later there was another and another. "What is it?" he asked.

"Kite fish," Roy said.

"Fish?"

Suddenly a large school of the silver creatures passed in front of them.

"Whoa!" Felix said, stepping back in surprise.

Each fish was about a foot in length, its silver scales tiny and reflective like a mirror. They looked like trout dipped in quicksilver with fins that fanned out on either side like wings. Because they were reflective, they blended perfectly with their surroundings, making them almost impossible to see until they caught the light.

"What are they doing up here?" Felix asked, stepping back up to the glass.

"They come up from the ocean when it rains to get the cloud beetles. It's their main food source," Roy explained.

"But how?"

"Elevator gas. They produce it in their guts. The fish have two bladder-like organs that they fill up with the stuff when they want to rise, and then they let it out again when they want to go down. Pretty neat, isn't it?"

"Incredible!" Felix said, laughing in delight as he watched the kite fish weave in and out of the clouds.

"Want to go fishing?" Roy asked.

"Shick yes!" Felix returned with child-like enthusiasm.

"Ha-ha, come on then," Roy said, motioning for Felix to follow him.

The pilot opened one of the storage compartments in the common room. He passed Felix a raincoat and a fishing hat and then shouldered a large canvas bag before ascending the ladder to the upper deck.

Felix pulled on the coat and hat and followed after him.

Outside was beautiful. The wind was still, and the clouds were thick and grey with a curtain of mist falling all around them. The sun haloed the clouds like a solar eclipse, its light reflecting off the water and casting rainbows around the ship.

The school of silver fish were dancing in and out of the billow around them, turning upside down and swirling around the airship. Felix beamed with delight. He'd never seen anything so wonderful.

Roy led Felix to the stern and put down his bag. He pulled out a bucket, a tackle box, and two canvas contraptions with a handful of long thin rods.

Roy unfolded the canvas and began inserting the rods into thin sleeves along the edges.

"What's that?" Felix asked.

"It's called a fishing kite. Developed by a man named Charles Wain. I'll put this one together for you," he said.

Felix watched with curiosity as Roy finished assembling the strange kite. It was painted like a grey cloud and had at least a dozen fishing lines dangling beneath it. Roy attached beetle-like lures to the ends of the lines and then tossed the kite off the back of the airship into the wind. The wind swept it up on a thirty-five-degree angle behind them, the lures swaying like a flying swarm of beetles. Roy handed the kite's line to Felix. "Ever flown a kite before?" he asked.

"Once or twice."

"Then you'll get the hang of it in no time. It's exactly the same," Roy said and began putting together the other one for himself.

Once both kites were in the air, Roy showed Felix how to weave the kites back and forth to make the bugs look alive. To

Felix's delight, it wasn't long before two kite fish wriggled at the end of his lines.

"Nicely done champ, you're a natural!" Roy said.

"This is brilliant!" Felix beamed.

Roy showed him how to pull his catch in, and then they sent out their kites again. An hour later, the bucket was brimming with fish. "That should do us for tea," Roy said.

They pulled their kites in and disassembled them. Roy showed Felix how to gut and clean the Kite Fish, and they took them below for supper.

Roy cooked their catch to perfection with butter and some of Westdock's signature spices. Their flesh was sweet and flaky. It was arguably the best fish Felix had ever had. He and Roy were jovial that evening, they joked over dinner while Lilliana ate in silence. The Sendsong still hadn't returned with a reply from Lord Bardviss, and Felix could see that was weighing heavily on her. After their meal Lilliana retired to her quarters while Roy cleaned up. Felix walked to her cabin and knocked lightly on the door.

"Who is it?" Lilliana asked.

"May I have a word?"

"Come in, if you must."

Felix opened her door and stepped inside. The place was a mess, with clothes and books scattered across her bed and on the floor. It surprised him, considering her status, but then he reminded himself that she was used to having servants clean up after her.

"What is it?" she asked impatiently.

"I was just wondering if you wanted to join Roy and me for a round of poker?" he asked, doing his best not to step on anything.

"No. I have a lot of work to get through," she said.

"What are you working on anyway?" he asked. In the last two days she had hardly left her room. He picked up one of her books and read the title out loud: "*Legal Pitfalls of Co- Ownership.*"

Lilliana sighed, "If you must know, I'm studying up on law because my father and my uncle jointly owned the family estate in Sky View. When my uncle passed, my father gained full ownership, and then he disappeared. Now the whole thing is a right mess, and my cousin Arianna hasn't answered any of my letters concerning the issue. I have no desire to take her home away from her, but if she was only willing to buy us out, then my mother wouldn't be so desperate for Lord Bardviss's financial security. When we reach Sky View, I need to talk to her about it, but I want to know all of the legalities regarding the situation before I do."

"Wow, you were right, you really do have complicated problems. Not life threatening like the troubles of us commoners, but certainly more of a headache," Felix said.

Lilliana smiled, "To say the least."

"Well, if you change your mind and decide that you want a break from this riveting content, you know where to find us. I promise I'll go easy on you, and Roy is rubbish at cards, so you're guaranteed to turn a profit," he said with a grin.

Lilliana laughed. "I don't need you to go easy on me, I could kick your derriere at cards any day."

"Oh really? I'll take that as a challenge. But you better have some coin to back up those fancy words, my lady. We aren't playing for peanuts."

"I may come out in a bit," she laughed.

"Until then, happy studying," Felix said, and he left her room.

Felix and Roy played cards for several hours, but Lilliana never joined them. Felix found himself feeling disappointed. Ever since seeing the newspaper article, Lilliana had been cooped up in her room. Even though Felix would never admit it, he was beginning to miss her spunk and verbal sparring.

2

It was the third and final day of the airship's journey to Sky View when the Sendsong finally returned. Felix was enjoying midafternoon tea when he heard the beating of its great wings. He dropped his unfinished scone and ran towards the deck. A moment later Roy and Lilliana were behind him. The magnificent white bird was waiting patiently, perched on the railing of the ship. All three of them walked over to it and waited with anticipation. The bird sang a short and pleasant melody and then its letter compartment popped open. Roy invited Felix to collect its contents. Felix took out a letter and four bulging bags. The second that the compartment was empty, it snapped shut and the Sendsong took off.

Felix opened one of the bags. It was filled with coin and every one of them was a ducket. He gave a low whistle. This was far more than he'd expected. A single ducket was worth five times the wagon coins that he'd requested, and there were four purses full instead of two. "Maybe we were wrong. By the looks of it, Lord Bardviss values you very highly, my lady."

Lilliana smiled and breathed a sigh of relief.

"Let's get below deck where we can look this over more comfortably," Roy said.

They all agreed and headed back inside. Felix dropped the bags on the table and sat down. He turned the letter over in his hands, admiring Lord Bardviss's family crest in the black wax seal. Once everyone was seated around the table, he handed it to Lilliana. She opened the letter and read it aloud.

> *Dear Debt Collectors,*
> *I don't know who hired you or what their intentions are, and I don't care. Whatever they are paying you, I'll double it. I have included four purses of duckets for your service. If that's not enough, then name your price. All I ask is for you to ensure that Lady Lilliana does not return. I hope that amount is sufficient for your trouble? What you do with her is entirely up to you. I hear that you can make good coin from the slavers for highborn.*
> *Sincerely,*
> *L. H. B.*

Lilliana's voice began to trail off feebly towards the end. Felix was completely stunned. He knew that Henry Bardviss was an ass, but not that he was a royal vindictive scheming serpent of an ass. All three of them sat shocked into silence.

"What now?" Lilliana asked in a whisper, her gaze averted to her feet.

"Um, leave it with me. I didn't anticipate this. I just need a bit of time to think it over and I'll come up with a plan," Felix said reassuringly.

"It appears that Lord Bardviss's ill intent spans deeper than we realized. I think we should continue to your cousin's and ask for her help," Roy said.

"What about Mother and Natasha? My family is down there with that serpent! I thought that by leaving I was protecting them, but instead I've left them open to the wolves! Oh,

Stars, I'm going to be sick," she said, and all the color drained from her face.

"You can't blame yourself for this. We still don't know his intentions. There's no reason to jump to conclusions until we have more information," Roy said.

Felix nodded. "He's right, for all we know you could've just dodged a bullet. If he has no regard for your life, then he might have been planning to end it the second you two were hitched. At least you've bought you and your family some time. Whatever Lord Bardviss is planning won't take place overnight. He's made his move and now we know where he stands and can plan accordingly," he said.

Lilliana nodded without looking either of them in the eye. "Please, excuse me," she said, quietly pushing herself from the table and hurrying to her chamber.

Roy watched her with concern and ran his hand through his peppered hair. "I better talk to her," he said and followed after.

"Well, Shick," Felix said to the empty room. He picked up the letter and read over it carefully, trying to figure out what it all meant. Then he dropped the note on the table and stared at the bulging bags of coin in front of him. On one hand, it was the best outcome he could have asked for. According to his agreement with Lilliana, all this wealth belonged to him. It was enough for him to start a new life just about anywhere. Negotiations with Lord Bardviss were over, and he hadn't even had to promise Lilliana's return, which meant that according to their verbal contract, his work was done. He could take his spoils and jump on the next airship back to Westdock.

But for some reason that course of action didn't sit well with him. If he went back to Westdock now, what would he do? If things went well, then Bastian would be leaving on the train with Gwena for the Heartland today. Without them in West-dock, was it even worth going back? If he followed after them, he would only be a third wheel with those two now. This was Bastian's chance to win Gwena's heart and Felix knew that he would. Those two belonged together. He didn't need to get in the way of that. He could take his spoils and set himself up nicely on some quiet corner of Equillian, find a nice wife, and have the family he'd always dreamed of. Or he could stay and maybe do something good for once. He had to admit that it would be incredibly satisfying to bring justice to that noble douchebag. And who knows, maybe by helping the Wendrians he could inspire them to notice their common people. What is going on with me? he wondered. Am I finally growing a conscience? Or is it that I enjoy being needed by the aristocrats and tasting their life of privilege? And hey, if I can promote some good along the way, well, why not?

They would be at Sky View tomorrow. Seeing the Windswept Isles was the opportunity of a lifetime. Having his contract with Lilliana fulfilled meant that he was a free man. It made him much more comfortable with his current predicament. He could stay to see how things played out and leave whenever he wanted to. Felix smiled with a renewed sense of purpose. His small life was now plump with possibility, and he liked it. Who knows, maybe the Stars have a plan for me to amount to something after all, he thought.

3

Felix lay awake in his bed listening to Roy snoring lightly on the other side of the room. He wished that he could be resting as soundly, but for the life of him he couldn't get to sleep. He kept mulling over Lord Bardviss's letter, trying to come up with his next move. And he was worried about Lilliana—she'd skipped dinner that night. She was carrying such a burden: protecting her family, Westdock, and the world from Lord Bardviss, securing her family's future, and finding her father. All things that Felix knew nothing about. He'd always felt like he'd gotten the short stick by not having a family and not being highborn, but he'd never known how much responsibility came with those things. He realized now that he'd been taking his complete freedom for granted, and he was beginning to think that maybe Lilliana wasn't so privileged after all. Felix stared at the ceiling for several more minutes before resigning himself to a sleepless night. Deciding he may as well get one last view of the stars before their journey ended, he silently rolled out of bed and grabbed his blanket.

Felix reached the top of the ladderway to the main deck and was surprised to see that it was already occupied. Lilliana was sitting against the Everfire column looking up at the stars. Her long dark red curls cascaded around her shoulders and she had her knees tucked up to her chest. Felix hesitated, not wanting to disturb her.

"There's enough space for both of us," she said without turning.

"Fair enough," he said and hoisted himself on deck. "Couldn't sleep either?" he asked, taking a seat beside her.

"Not a wink," she said, her gaze still averted to the stars.

Felix could see that she'd been crying. He noted how delicate and graceful she looked in that moment. With her guard down, she was even more beautiful. He suddenly realized that she was only wearing a dressing gown and a thin robe. "You must be freezing!" he said.

She shrugged absently. Felix took off his blanket and threw it around her shoulders. She accepted it without thanks, but he could tell that she was grateful.

"You know, things aren't as bad as they seem. If your letter reached your mother as intended, then even a forged letter in your hand won't convince her that you've run away. With a little luck, all you'll have to do is wait for Lord Bardviss to condemn himself," he said.

Lilliana frowned. "So, I presume you're returning to West-dock then, now that you have your spoils?" she asked.

Felix studied her. "Isn't that what you want? I thought you'd be eager to be rid of me."

Lilliana didn't answer.

"I was thinking that I might stay for a while. I've never seen Sky View. I hear it's a nice place," he said.

"You know that you don't have to do that. You've fulfilled our agreement."

"I know."

He followed her gaze to the sky. It was foggy with stars despite the light pollution from the large shaft of Everfire. They were silent for a time while they both stared at the cosmos.

"I don't think I could ever tire of watching the stars," he said.

Lilliana looked at him for the first time since he'd come on deck. Her eyes were dry now and Felix could see that her fighting spirit had returned. "Are you a believer?" she asked.

"A believer in what? You mean that the spirits of our ancestors live in the stars and guide our fates?" he asked.

"Yes," she said.

Felix held back his left ear to reveal the tattoo of the seven-pointed star that marked him as a child of the Order. "Was kinda ingrained into me," he said.

"You're a Starchild?" she asked in surprise.

"Was. I think that my brother and I are the only ones in history to have ever been kicked out. Pretty sure we made them reconsider the permanence of a tattoo," Felix smirked.

Lilliana laughed. "Why does that not surprise me?" she asked.

Felix mirrored her grin. "I don't know, why does that not surprise you?" he asked in return, humored by how much it amused her.

"I don't know," she said laughing.

Stars, was she gorgeous! It was almost unfair. As much as she infuriated him, he couldn't stop thinking about kissing her.

"Why do they tattoo you? Isn't that child abuse or something?" she asked.

"Probably. I'm sure that the only reason they apply a local anesthetic is to prevent noise complaints from the neighbors. The screams of small children might dampen their reputation," Felix jested, and Lilliana laughed.

"No, that isn't fair, the Order was better to us than we deserved. Having this mark means that I will always be welcomed into any temple on Equillian. They will house, feed, and clothe me no matter how old I am. Once a Star Child, you are forever in their care. Even most commoners with parents don't have that kind of security. As much as I respect the Order, though, their way of life never suited me. Don't get me wrong. I'm grateful for their upbringing. I feel very fortunate to have been raised as a Star Child. But I have no desire to return there."

"I've always been intrigued by the Night-Watchers, but it was never part of my education. My father told me that study of

the Stars was as useless as theatre and poetry. He always empha-
sized history and arithmetic and had me memorize battle tactics
from the old wars. He would say, 'A great duchess must learn
from history. Nothing happens that hasn't happened before,
and everything that has happened before, will happen again. By
studying the failures and victories of our forefathers, we can prepare ourselves for anything that the future has in store,'" Lilliana
said, mimicking her father's deep voice.

Felix smiled. "Learning history certainly has its benefits. But
I have to say, he's completely wrong about theatre and poetry.
It's the arts that teach us about humanity and what it means to
be human. Battle tactics might be useful in times of war, but it's
empathy that can prevent conflicts from happening altogether."

Lilliana smiled at him and Felix looked to the sky.

"And no one knows history better than the Stars. The
Watchers are the keepers of the past, present and future," he said.
"They see everything and they see it all at once. That's why people look to them for guidance—their vantage allows them to see
and know what we cannot."

"Will you teach me some of the constellations?" Lilliana
asked.

"Of course."

"I only know the Guiding Star and the Time Keeper constellations. Same as everyone else, I suppose. There's Shick now
marking the midnight hour," she said, pointing out the constellation of the short fat man, dancing naked with a cup of wine
in hand.

"Ah, Shick the Star Stirrer. The mischievous spirit who med-
dles with destinies, steals maiden's hearts, and misplaces keys.
One of my personal favorites," Felix said, and Lilliana smirked.
"Another of mine is Lady Luck, you can see her up to your left."

Felix took Lilliana's hand and guided it towards the sky.

"If you look just there, you can see her long legs taking an easy stride with her cloudy star dress billowing behind her," he said, using Lilliana's finger to trace the constellation.

"But my absolute favorite, is her daughter, Serendipity. The beautiful maiden who brings unlikely moments of happenstance to pass. Everyone knows her as the time keeper of the seventh hour, but what most don't know is that Serendipity favors underdogs and star-crossed lovers, bringing them luck when it's least expected, even against the most unfavorable odds."

"I like that. And who's that one?" Lilliana asked, pointing to a cluster of stars behind the billowing dress of Lady Luck.

"Ah, that's the Luck Chaser. His story is a bit of a tragedy. He's in love with Lady Luck and chases her ceaselessly in hopes that he might win her heart. But what he doesn't realize is that if he just stopped and stayed in the one place, then she would come to him," Felix said, pointing out the way the stars connected to make the constellation. He turned to Lilliana and caught her studying him.

"What?" he asked.

"I was wrong about you. I'm sorry that I judged you so unfairly," she said.

"I suppose it wasn't that unfair, really. I mean, admittedly, I am a selfish bastard."

Lilliana laughed and then she regarded him with a serious expression. "You do pull off a good nobleman, but you know, the things about you that give away that you're not are the best parts. I'm sorry for taking you away from Westdock and the life you love. I can't say that I regret it, because I'm so grateful to have you here, but that was completely unfair of me…I will be honored if you choose to stay," she said earnestly.

Felix smiled. He opened his mouth to utter another well-timed witty remark, but Lilliana stopped him with a kiss.

He froze in surprise for a split second and then cradled the sides of her face gently with his hands and kissed her back. When she'd kissed him in the castle days before, it had been rough and contrived. Now her lips met his with a soft and sensual finesse that threw him off guard. They kissed passionately for several minutes before stopping for breath. Then Lilliana pulled away from him, straightened her ruffled hair with her fingers, and looked out at the view as if nothing had happened. Felix was stunned. He'd never kissed a girl like that before, or been kissed like that before, for that matter. Kissing had always been the means to an end and never lasted long. It had never been much of a pleasure for him in and of itself until that moment. Damn, Lilliana was a good kisser.

"If you tell anyone about that, I will kill you," she said pointedly.

Felix smiled, "Do you have your pistol on you my lady?"

"No, why?"

"Because as long as we're pretending that this never happened, I'd like to do it again," he said, leaning in to kiss her gently. She kissed him back, sinking her lips into his. He pulled her into his embrace and they kissed each other eagerly. Then Lilliana pulled herself away. "This has gone far enough. I never intended this to be an invitation to my bed," she said, clearly in conflict with her own desires.

"I would never presume that it was. But if you kiss me like that, then you can't blame me for wanting more," he said. "Where did you learn to kiss like that anyway?"

"That's none of your business."

"Well, you're certainly teaching me a few things. That thing you do with your tongue I find particularly intoxicating. Can you show me again?" he asked, leaning towards her.

"No!" Lilliana said pushing him away in good humor.

Felix smirked. "Can't blame a man for trying."

"Actually, I can. You really need a lesson in etiquette," she laughed.

"Etiquette? That rubbish belongs with your class, my lady. Living without it is one of the many freedoms that belong to us commoners. And believe me, it makes things a lot more fun. Particularly in the bedroom," he said with a roguish grin.

"Speaking of the bedroom, I'm going to bed. It's freezing out here," Lilliana said, and she stood to leave.

"Are you sure I can't come with you? I could help to warm you up," he offered.

"No, but thank you…this has been…nice," she said, smiling despite herself.

"What has? I thought that nothing happened?" Felix jested.

"Yes, and don't you forget it."

"Don't worry, I could never forget this," he said grinning widely.

Lilliana blushed and then headed into the cabin. Felix watched her go and then he looked to the sky. "Stars, am I in trouble! This is your doing, Shick, you bastard," he said to the Star Stirrer and then he retreated inside.

Felix reached his bed and realized that Lilliana still had his blanket. "Shick," he muttered. He made his way to her quarters and knocked quietly on the door. A moment later she cracked it open.

"I'm sorry to bother you, I just need my blank…" he began, but before he could finish his sentence, Lilliana pulled him inside her room and shut the door.

FIRE!

CHAPTER SIXTEEN

Bastian left Snibs's quarters an hour after he'd entered them. He was relieved to be away from the man's unsettling company. But the dimly lit hallway towards the mess offered minimal relief from the misery he felt. All his hopes of escaping the ship had been extinguished. He would be lucky if he survived the next month, let alone ever saw Gwena and Felix again. There was music floating towards him from the mess hall, a haunting tune about a woman who lost her lover to the sea. As Bastian approached the room he could see the men immersed in the melody, waving their Black Jacks to and fro in time to the music that Dagger played on his fiddle. Some sang along, and others murmured in quiet chitchat off to the side. Bastian toyed with the idea of joining them, but he didn't feel up to showing his face after his earlier display and he was eager to avoid running into Spitz. But even Spitz's death wish for him seemed so small and trifling now compared with what was in store for him. He didn't care anymore—he knew he was doomed regardless. He found his lack of concern slightly liberating, as if somehow by letting go of his attachment to life, fear had nothing with which to control him. Instead of joining the men, he slipped past them as quietly as a mouse and made his way up to the top deck.

The cold, cloudless night embraced him with its icy chill. He pulled his hands into his sleeves and hugged his chest. The waves crashed gently against the Black Mary in a soothing lullaby, and for a moment he contemplated jumping in. Something was rather comforting about the idea of letting the ocean wash all his troubles away as it carried him silently to the bottom. But just because he didn't fear death in that moment, didn't mean he was eager to meet it. He was too curious about the world to leave it by choice, and any glimmer of hope that he might see Gwena again was enough to keep him fighting until the bitter end. He looked to the stars, as bright as torches, and could see several constellations staring back at him. The Phoenix, the Hanged Man, the Fool, and the Star Fisher. The sisters of the Order used to say that the constellations present in times of need were the ones to look to for guidance. Hmm, that's about right, Bastian thought. The Fool stepped blindly into the unknown, and the Hanged Man had death hanging over him. At least the Phoenix was a good sign, resurrection and rebirth from the ashes of one thing to the beginning of another. The Star Fisher fished for shooting stars, and when he caught one, he used it to grant a single wish that he thought was most deserving. "Well, Star Fisher, I don't know if my wish is the most deserving, but if you get a catch, I could really use one right about now," Bastian said to the constellation. The stars twinkled back at him silently. He always felt better when looking up at the small beaming points of light, if for nothing else than to put into perspective just how small his problems were in the grand scheme of things. He pulled out his spice leaf pouch. There was a single sheet of thyme tree paper left. Bastian chuckled at the irony of it before rolling a puff-stick and lighting it up with his Everfire box. At least there is one, he thought, and he savored its sweet salvation.

Bastian's moment of bliss was interrupted by a tune being slurred drunkenly above him. He looked up and tracked the voice to the crow's-nest high on the mast overhead. Sitting in it was a man wearing a leather trench coat. He was waving a cutlass in the air with his left hand as if it were a baton that he was using to conduct his melody. In his right hand he held a bottle that he drank from. The pirate stopped singing and turned his bottle upside down, clearly disappointed that it was empty. He looked down towards Bastian, who dove behind one of the barrels to avoid being spotted.

"Ye alright there, mate?" the pirate called down to him.

Bastian backtracked into view. "Fine," he said, waving awkwardly. "Idiot," he muttered at himself.

The pirate sheathed his sword and tucked his bottle into his belt before making a descent towards him. Bastian hesitated, not feeling up for a conversation. But he wavered too long, and suddenly the pirate was standing in front of him. The man was taller than he was, with a lean muscular build and long black hair that was tied back. Bastian immediately recognized his features. The man was a sea-gypsy. One of the vagabonds that resided in groups of small ships along the Spotted Isles.

His brown eyes were cloudy from too much drink and he reeked of rum.

"Good evenin'," the man said, attempting a charming smile.

Bastian smiled back uneasily. The pirate was even more in-toxicated than he was.

"Would ye be so kind as ta watch me post while I relieve myself?" the sailor asked, swaying from side to side.

"You mean up there? You want me to hold your watch as lookout in the crow's-nest?" Bastian asked.

"Aye, 'elp a brother in need. That's a good lad," the pirate said, patting him on the shoulder and then heading off in the other direction.

"Hey! I never said that I would do it," Bastian called after him.

The pirate turned on his heels and came back around. "Well, will ya er not?" he asked.

Bastian hesitated. "It's a long way up there, and by the time I'm up you will most likely be finished with your business, and I'm not sure I feel comfortable taking another man's post without permission from the captain," he said, more because he didn't want to do it than because he was worried of being reprimanded.

The pirate looked him over. "What be yer name, lad?" he asked.

"Dodger."

"Well, Dodger, I need ta empty me britches an' wet me parched throat, troubles o' the flesh, I'm sure ye can understand. Now sposin' somethin' were ta come inta our mists right when I be away, do ya think the cap'n would be more upset at ya fer helpin' a brother in need, er fer leavin' the Black Mary exposed without a watch?" he posed.

Bastain sighed, "Alright, I'll watch your post. But don't take too long. I'm not dressed for this weather."

"O' course, matey, I can't thank ya enough. Name's Falgo by the way," the pirate said, shaking Bastian's hand. Then he whistled the rest of his tune as he went. Bastian watched him go before heading to the ropes that led up the main mast. He swore under his breath and warmed his hands as best he could before ascending towards the perch.

The view from the crow's-nest was breathtaking. The stars encircled him, reflecting their light in the gentle waves below. He could see every constellation in the winter's sky. As cold as it was, Bastian was glad for the excuse to stay outside a little longer. He found himself wondering if Gwena might be looking up at the same stars in that moment. It was the one view they could share no matter how far they got from each other. Bastian wondered if Gwena and Felix had made the train. If they had, they'd both be on their way to the Heartland now. The thought gave him a pang of regret. The golden ticket to everything he'd ever wanted had been in his hands, and now the opportunity had passed him by. At least if Felix and Gwena had gone, then they could look after each other. And who knew, if the Stars were merciful, then maybe, one day, he could join them.

Bastian was pulled from his thoughts by a faint glow on the horizon. He squinted to get a better view and then noticed a spyglass tucked in the ropes above him. He grabbed it and pointed it towards the light. As he adjusted the focus, a ship came into view, a ship he would have recognized anywhere. It had the figurehead of a woman dressed for battle holding a spear, and it belonged to Lord Bardviss, a war galleon from his own personal fleet. So, they had finally caught up to them. Bastian had begun to wonder if they were still coming. It seemed like such an insane waste of resources to send a warship just for Bastian. But then, most nobles he'd met had more coin then sense. He was a little surprised to be found, considering the direction the Black Mary was headed. Ships never had any reason to come this far west. The wind started to pick up, filling the galleons full sails. With only half of the Black Mary's sails down, the enemy ship was gaining on them. As the ship came closer, Bastian's throat went dry. Another ship of equal size was close on the tail of the first one, and they were both rapidly approaching. Not only was the first galleon bigger and better gunned than the Black Mary, now there were two.

Bastian instinctively grabbed hold of the bell rope and pulled on it heavily, sounding the alarm. In less than a minute, men poured onto the deck and Snibs stood at the base of the main mast bellow him. "What do ya see, Fal…Dodger?" he called up in surprise. "What in the Stars name are ye doin' in the crow's-nest?" Snibs demanded.

"Never mind that, there are two galleons tight on our tail!" Bastian yelled down.

He dropped the spyglass to Snibs, who caught it and held it to his eye.

"If these ships 'ave anythin' ta do with that bastard lord that ye set on us, then ye better pray ta the Stars that they be easy ta take, landlubber!" he said.

Then he hurried off and began barking orders to the crew. Bastian's chest tightened. Every time he thought things couldn't get any worse, Shick had to prove him wrong.

Bastian spotted the captain coming onto the deck outside his quarters. His long naval jacket billowed around his feet in the wind, and his intense gaze scanned the deck and the oncoming ships. He didn't show even the slightest hint of concern. It was the first time that Bastian had seen the captain since the incident with the chest. He recalled Snibs's words about the captain being too busy to see him. He wondered what it was that he was too busy with. Snibs appeared to do most of the heavy lifting. Even now, at the brink of battle, the quartermaster was the one ordering the crew. It seemed to Bastian that the captain didn't do anything at all. But the man's face told a different story. It was stressed with worry lines and there were dark circles under his eyes, telling tales of sleepless nights. And his hard edge certainly didn't speak of a life of leisure. The man was a mystery. There was something about him that Bastian found alluring, like a bolted lock to a keeping room door. He was itching to know what might be on the other side.

Bastian's thoughts were interrupted by Cricket crawling into the crow's-nest beside him, holding a long flintlock rifle.

"What are you doing up here?" Bastian asked in surprise.

"I should be askin' ye that question! I'm a sharpshooter, this be me post in times o' war. What bloody business do ye 'ave up 'ere?" Cricket asked, just as surprised.

"None whatsoever," Bastian laughed, and Cricket laughed with him, clapping him on the shoulder. Bastian couldn't have been gladder to see him.

"We clearly 'ave much ta catch up on. I thought I 'ad seen the last o' ya after that stunt ye pulled back there," Cricket said.

"Yeah, about that…I feel like a proper fool…" Bastian said, running his hands through his hair uncomfortably.

"Don't sweat it, mate, by survivin' Snibs ye 'ave passed the worst. On the bright side, the way that ya stood up ta Spitz 'as earned ya a real badge o' respect with the crew. An' 'avin' respect from these men be worth their weight in gold."

Bastian let out a sigh of relief. "It's nice to know that there's some sort of silver lining to my idiocy, I could really use that right now. Not that it will matter much considering the circumstances," Bastian said.

Cricket laughed, and then he drew a small spyglass from his pocket, lashed it to the top of his rifle with a leather tie, and looked through it at the approaching ships. He handled his rifle with complete ease, which made Bastian realize how deceptive Cricket's young and innocent- looking face was.

"So, you're a sharpshooter?" he asked.

"Aye."

"Remind me not to get on your bad side."

"Believe me when I tell ya that ye really don't want ta," Cricket said with a sly grin.

And Bastian believed it. He knew that it would be naïve to think that Cricket hadn't killed before.

"What should I be doing in all of this?" Bastian asked.

"Is there anythin' ye can do?"

Bastian was at a loss. His only experience on a ship was as a fisherman's hand, and when it came to conflicts, his expertise lay in escaping the fight altogether.

"I'm pretty good with a slingshot," he jested.

"Ha!" Cricket laughed. "Don't think that annoyin' the enemy will 'elp much. The best thin' ye can do, then, be ta stay out o' the way. May 'as well stay 'ere, ye can't get a better view than this."

The sound of several loud shots split the air, and seconds later a spray of water flew up beside them from a cannonball that narrowly missed the ship.

"Stars, they're firing on us!" Bastian said.

Cricket laughed. "Yer in fer a long night if that rattled ya."

The nest shook and Bastian looked down to see Falgo approaching their perch. The drunken gypsy-pirate whose watch Bastian was covering climbed up beside them and sat down with a fresh bottle in hand.

"Lads," he said, nodding in greeting, "what did I miss?"

Then he pulled out the cork of his bottle with his teeth and had a long, hard drink. Bastian stared at him in disbelief. "What did you miss? You do realize that we're under attack?"

"Aye, ye did a fine job, matey," Falgo commended, clapping Bastian on the shoulder. "Would ya care fer some rum, lads?" the pirate offered.

"I won't say no ta that," Cricket said and took a swig from the bottle. "What do ya think, Dodger, 'ave ya been watered enough yet?" he asked and handed the bottle to him.

Bastian was well and truly watered, but considering the circumstances he was hardly eager to sober up. He took a drink of the potent rum before handing the bottle back to Falgo.

The galleons were almost upon them now and Bastian was sure that their next volley would be in range. He looked down and saw Snibs standing on the railing of the bow, holding onto the ship's line. He addressed the crew in a thunderous voice, "A pair o' twins be creepin' up our backside, lads, shall we teach the wenches some manners?"

"Aye!" the crew yelled back enthusiastically, and Bastian watched in fascination as they all manned their positions like a well-oiled machine. Not a single man showed any sign of fear or uncertainty of the oncoming battle. Bastian appeared to be the only one who was even remotely concerned about the attacking ships. In fact, the pirates looked like they were enjoying themselves and eager for the fight.

Men were lugging barrels covered with spikey protuberances to the top of the poop deck and Bastian realized that they were the sea mines from Boom's collection in the armory. Boom was directing them where to go, his chest puffed out with pride. "Be careful now! One wrong step an' it won't be our enemies in pieces," he warned cheerily.

The sailors cursed as they threw the first two mines off opposite sides of the stern. They were joined by a long thick rope that sank under the water slacking between them. Boom counted seconds with a raised hand and after five had passed, the men grabbed four spikey barrels with large yellow *X*'s painted on them and threw them into the ocean. Boom signaled another five counts before the men threw the remaining three mines overboard. The barrels floated and bobbed in the water, evenly dispersed between the Black Mary and the attacking galleons.

"I saw those in the armory. How do they work?" Bastian asked Cricket.

"Watertight barrels filled with black powder. Each o' those soft lead spikes be hollow and house cylinders storin' sulfuric acid surrounded by potassium perchlorate and sugar. When the enemy ship hits one o' them nasties, the spike is crushed, breakin' the glass cylinder inside. The ingredients combine an' create a flame that ignites the black powder in the center and…" Cricket made an exploding gesture with his hand.

Bastian raised his eyebrows and looked out at the floating barrels in the darkness.

As soon as they were a safe distance from the sea mines, Snibs cried, "Drop the anchor, port broadside!"

A moment later the Black Mary was wrenched backwards and quickly turned to the side. Suddenly the left flank of the ship was facing the oncoming enemy,

"Ready the cannons, chain shots port side, round shots starboard!"

"Chain shots port side, round shots starboard!" the crew echoed down the line to the gunners.

Bastian watched as the gun crews on the port side loaded the cannons with two steel balls connected by a four-foot chain.

It was clear that the enemy ship had been hoping to surprise them under the cover of darkness, but luckily, with Bastian's warning they didn't have that advantage. The leading galleon passed between the first two barrels that bobbed amid the waves. The hull caught on the rope and pulled it forward. The ship hit the next four barrels which were marked with *X*'s and the mines combusted into a dense cloud of yellow smoke, instantly blinding them. The men on their deck began yelling in panic as they realized their predicament, but it was too late.

The ship had too much momentum to stop, and as it continued forward the rope lost its final slack and the two barrels on either end were pulled into both sides of the hull. They exploded on impact with a deafening sound, causing chaos to erupt on the enemy's deck.

A second later, they hit the final wave of sea mines and all three erupted into the front of the enemy's hull, crippling it. Smoke was still heavy in the air and the Black Mary's cannons were armed and ready.

"Fire the first round!" Snibs ordered.

The order was passed down the line and chain shots erupted out of half the cannons on the port side. They whipped through the air, hitting the enemy sails head on. The chains tore through the front mast and brought it crashing down.

"Second round, fire!" Snibs called, and the other half of the cannons were lit. Chain shots tore through the remaining rigging and within minutes of the fight, the leading galleon had been decimated. With its main mast down and remaining sails tattered and few, it was paralyzed.

The second galleon came up beside it and positioned itself for an attack. Sound erupted from its cannons and iron shots tore through the railing on the deck of the Black Mary. Pirates dove out of the way, narrowly missing being hit. Splintered wood rained down on them.

"Starboard broadside!" Snibs commanded and with the anchor down, the Black Mary made a sharp turn in place and made ready for a counterattack.

"Fire!"

Shots exploded from both levels of the Black Mary's cannons on her right side and they showered the galleon. The wind had changed, now pushing the pirate ship from behind.

"Turn 'er 'ead on an' reload! Prepare the sails fer speed, we'll ride this gale ta their decks!" Snibs bellowed.

The crew made haste to drop the sails, scaling the lines with ease while the gunners below readied the cannons. As soon as all the sails were in place, the Black Mary was turned to face its enemy. The galleon fired another round, but with its target shifted, the shots fell short of their mark. The cannonballs splashed into the ocean, spraying water onto the deck of the Black Mary.

"Full speed! Prepare ta ram 'er in the sweet spot, lads, an' make ready the 'ook and lines!" Snibs ordered. Bastian looked down and saw Stork at the helm steering with expert skill and precision.

"Better 'old on," Cricket advised.

Bastian gripped the sides of the crow's nest, his knuckles turning white as the ship's full sails sped them towards the galleons.

Dark clouds filled the sky and Bastian could see the promise of a storm on the horizon. He closed his eyes tightly and braced himself as they collided with the enemy ship. The boards made an ear-splitting crack as they gave way beneath the force of the Black Mary. "Don't let 'er escape! Release the 'ooks!" Snibs ordered. The pirates swung long ropes with grappling hooks towards the galleon. The hooks caught on the galleon's railing and the men pulled the lines taught, preventing any chance of the enemy's escape. Bastian watched in amazement at the skill with which the crew maneuvered the Black Mary. The pirates had positioned the ship between the two galleons at such an angle that none of the enemy's cannons could reach them. Some of Lord Bardviss's men were repositioning the ship's guns in an effort to defend themselves, while others aimed their rifles towards the Black Mary.

Cricket stood and aimed his own rifle at the galleon's deck. "Take cover," he said to Bastian. Bastian ducked low in the nest and covered his head, while Falgo drank casually beside him.

"Take 'em down, lads!" Snibs cried.

The enemy started firing, and Cricket and the other sharpshooters fired a return round. Bastian saw several of their adversaries fall and knew that one of them had been from Cricket's shot. He wondered if he would recognize any of the men on Lord Bardviss's ships. Westdock's population wasn't huge, and it was more than likely he'd encountered a few at least, even if it was only brushing past them on the streets to plunder their pockets. He tried not to think about it as Cricket's rifle brought another man down. Bullseye was in the crow's-nest on the adjacent mast and was firing two rifles, one in each hand. Every shot the pirates fired hit their target, mowing the enemy down. But they weren't the only ones taking casualties. Bastian could see several pirates on the deck below who had been hit. A couple of them lay unmoving, their limbs at odd angles. Bastian felt sick. He couldn't help but think that in any moment, that could be him.

"Place the gangplanks! Prepare ta board 'er, lads! Take anythin' worth 'avin' an' nothin' that's not. We be takin' worthy recruits fer the men lost. Ye all know the routine, lads, two men left ta the lifeboats ta keep ar reputation intact, an' the rest can be sent as an offerin' ta Davy Jones," Snibs declared.

The crew erupted in cheers and pushed the gangplanks across the gap to the adjacent ship while dodging the enemies' shots. "Shall we show these scallywags who they be messin' with?" Snibs asked the men.

"Aye!" the crew called back enthusiastically.

"Raise the colors!" Snibs commanded.

The Black Mary's flag was raised, and the pirates poured across the planks with weapons drawn. The enemy was preparing to meet their attackers when they spotted the Black Mary's sign above the sails. The ship's Jolly Roger was a cutlass and a skeleton key crisscrossed in front of a white skull. The men on both galleons stopped short and a look of horror struck them. They pointed at the flag, and Bastian could see the morale drain from their faces. Even he had heard of the Black Mary's mark—countless rumors circulated Westdock's port of the pirate ship that couldn't be stopped. It was surreal to see the signature flag waving in front of him.

Lord Bardviss's men dropped their weapons and held their hands up in surrender as the pirates approached. Their white flags were raised, and the fight was done.

"So that's it?" Bastian asked in disbelief.

He couldn't believe that the fight was over so soon. The Black Mary had taken down the two galleons like it was child's play.

"Aye, the spoils will be plundered an' it will be done," Cricket said.

Bastian let out a sigh of relief and leaned back against the metal bars of the crow's-nest.

"Good show, lads!" Falgo yelled down to the crew, holding up his bottle respectfully.

And then he froze, staring intently at the sea behind the first galleon. Bastian followed Falgo's gaze. There was something in the water. He couldn't see anything in the darkness, but suddenly the hairs on the back of his neck stood on end.

"By Davy Jones," Cricket whispered, and his face drained of color.

Falgo drew his sword, and the drunken pirate was suddenly focused and steady. Then Bastian saw it. A gigantic mountain of water was rising up from the ocean. Men from both galleons began to shout in panic. For a moment Bastian thought that it was a colossal tidal wave, then two monstrous eyes opened from the middle of the bulge. They shimmered in the moonlight, neon green and yellow with a black slit down the center of each one, and they locked onto Bastian.

Bastian stared back, petrified. The creature was filled with swirling gold particles, and as it rose from the water it began to steam billowing gold dust.

"The Kraken!" a man cried from below.

"By Shick, the stories be true," Cricket muttered, staring at the creature.

Bastian recalled Stork's tale and the illustrations that covered the mast. But the carvings did no justice to the beast that appeared before them now. It was far more terrifying than anything he had ever seen or imagined. He could see its skin in detail now—it was constantly changing color between shades of green-blue and grey as if it were the ocean's surface itself. All three ships turned their weapons on the creature. The galleon that was nearest fired its cannons, and the shots disappeared into the monster like they were striking water. The gigantic head sank back into the sea, and for a moment Bastian thought that they had scared it off. Three seconds passed and then the monster erupted from the ocean with a vast spray of water between the two galleons and turned its eyes on the Black Mary. Cricket didn't miss a beat.

He reloaded his rifle and pointed it at the Kraken's eye, firing his first round. Bullseye emptied his own rifles and both pirates hit their mark. The creature gave a blood-curdling, high-pitched scream. It writhed upwards, lifting two gargantuan suckered limbs out of the water and brought them down heavily, one on each galleon, nearly splitting the ships in two. What was left of them started taking on water and rapidly sinking. Men began crowding the lifeboats and the rest jumped overboard, making a desperate attempt to flee the monster. The Kraken raised three more of its arms out of the water and stretched them towards the Black Mary. One grabbed a pirate and dragged him into the oceans depths as he screamed. The pirates scattered to take cover. Bastian was stunned with terror. He sat in the crow's-nest, transfixed by the scene around him.

"Stand yer ground! The creature be nothin' but flesh and blood, fire with everythin' we 'ave!" the captain cried, taking control for the first time since the fight began.

His words restored the men's spirits. They collected themselves and joined the fight with a new vigor. Falgo handed his bottle to Bastian and grabbed a rope from above them. "See ya on the other side, lads," he said, and he swung himself towards the Kraken with his sword in hand. He met one of the creature's arms as it was pulling back for a strike and sliced it clean in two. The piece that was cut off wriggled wildly as it fell into the water with a giant splash. The men cheered.

Dark clouds completely covered the sky now, and the wind picked up. The ship began to sway this way and that. The pirates shot their pistols and rifles at the creature, but they had no effect.

"Aim at the eyes!" the captain shouted, and the cannons were repositioned.

"Ready, fire!"

The shots discharged. The cannonballs hit the Kraken straight in the eye and it recoiled in pain, only to turn on them once again with vengeance. Thunder erupted from the clouds. Streaks of lightning were striking the water in the distance and it began to rain.

"Give 'im all ya got!" the captain bellowed.

Bastian felt helpless. He wanted to assist the crew, but there was nothing he could do. He held fast to the mast for dear life as the storm worsened. The Kraken grabbed the railing with two thick suckered limbs and used another to pluck a pirate from the deck. The man flailed in the creature's grasp and yelled to the Stars to save him. Men hacked at the large appendages that held fast to the ship, and the monster emitted another blood-curdling scream. Bastian held his hands to his ears. The rain was falling heavily now, and he was completely drenched. Cricket swore beside him as the rain deemed his weapon useless. Bastian spotted Falgo on the deck. The pirate had been transformed. He acted with precision and purpose, wielding his cutlass towards the monster's grip. With a single blow, he sliced off one of the limbs that gripped the ship. The Kraken tore off a chunk of the railing in outrage. Water gushed onboard as the waves crashed around them. Falgo grabbed hold of a rope hanging from the middle mast and swung himself at the beast. He sliced through the tentacle squeezing the flailing man and saved the pirate who hung from its clutches. Enraged, the monster grabbed hold of the ship with every limb it had left, promising to rip the Black Mary to shreds and send her to a watery grave.

"Step aside, lads!"

The men turned to see Boom in a straddle stance at the front of the stern with his red hair on end and that strange glimmer in his eyes. He wore a metal contraption that looked like a small cannon on his shoulder attached to a metal tank on his back.

"Go back ta the depths, ya foul beast!" he yelled at the creature and then bright yellow liquid jet-streamed out from his device. The concoction soaked the Kraken and then ignited into flame.

"That's *Sea Fire*," Cricket muttered, awestruck.

The monster screamed in torment as it was consumed by flame. It let go of the ship and thrashed about, but the fire only burned hotter the more it struggled, needing more than water to be extinguished. The Kraken struck the ship and the sails caught alight. Then, in a dire attempt to save itself, the creature dove headfirst into the water. Its beaked mouth opened from underneath its head for a final scream, revealing row upon row of jagged teeth in a circular pit at the center of its flailing stubs and remaining appendages. Boom threw a clay pot with a lit fuse directly into the gaping cavern. The creature's mouth closed around the clay pot and the Kraken disappeared beneath the waves. For a second everyone was quiet, staring in disbelief, then *boom!* a great explosion came from beneath them. The Black Mary jolted violently, forcing Bastian's head into the mast, and everything went black.

CASIO

CHAPTER SEVENTEEN

asio sat in his deep leather armchair thumbing through his great-granduncle's first journal. It had been a while since he'd picked up the old books that he'd inherited from his uncle, Rupert Finley. The pages were well-worn from the hours he'd spent riffling through them over the years. It didn't take him long to find the entry that he was looking for. It had been carefully underlined by a much younger version of himself.

I saw Jeffrey today. He told me that he doesn't want the glasses that I've made for him. I only just finished the custom lenses that his parents commissioned me to make to filter out the spectrum that has been plaguing his vision for the last three weeks. When I asked him why, he told me that he likes seeing the phantom. He said that it allows him to do things that he couldn't do before, that he can make anything he imagines just by looking at it. I asked if he could show me a demonstration and Jeffrey immediately changed one of my crystals into a perfect sculpture of a dragon, simply by looking at it... I don't even know where to begin with this. Naturally, I was taken aback, admittedly I was even a little frightened. What Jeffrey did was impossible. He said that he discovered the ability a week after he'd first seen me, but that he'd been too scared to show anyone, and that he thought it had something to do with the gold dust.

If what he says is true, then it means that the "dust" that Jeffrey is seeing is not a phantom at all, but something that is actually there. I always knew there were things in our world that could not be seen by the human eye, but this baffles me entirely. I asked Jeffrey if he has told his parents, and he said that he hasn't. I recommended that we keep it our secret and warned him about using his ability where anyone could see it. I have grown fond of the young man. He reminds me of my own son and this power of his scares me, primarily because if anyone were to discover it, it would put him in grave danger. I've spent the remaining hours of the day searching through my research books and I haven't found anything even hinting at something like this. I have expected for some time that Jeffrey's eyes have extra cone and rod receptors, which is what's allowing him to see a spectrum that is generally invisible. Even if this is the case, there is still so much unanswered. I am still unsure as to why or how his eyes have developed in this way. And why it has only started now that he's come of age. The biggest mystery of all is the spectrum itself. It seems to be something that has never been formerly detected by any means. My head is full of questions. Tomorrow I plan to pay *a visit to the Hall of Scientific Study to consult the books in their library. I won't be able to ask anyone about it outright, but I am hoping that I can learn something from recorded history…*

There was a knock at the door. Casio closed the journal and locked it away in its high cupboard, and then made his way to the door. He cracked it open, carefully obscuring the right half of his face.

"Sorry ta disturb ya, Cap'n."

"What is it, Snibs?"

"The repairs are under way. We 'ave managed ta patch 'er well enough ta keep 'er afloat until we reach Jaxland."

"An' the boy?" Casio asked.

"Doc 'as just confirmed that the Dodger is goin' ta live. I told 'im about the visions that 'e 'as been seein', Doc said that 'e will 'ave a look, but that it's most likely nothin' but stress.'"

"Good. Bring 'im ta me quarters. I want ta speak with 'im when 'e wakes."

"Consider it done," Snibs said and he left to fulfill his orders.

Casio closed the door and walked to his dressing room table. He sat down in front of its tall looking glass and studied his reflection. His left eye was still the same blue that he'd inherited from his mother, but the iris of his right eye was now entirely gold. It had started as a gold ring around his pupil that over time had spread outward until there was nothing else left. Casio picked up a small jewelry box from the table and opened it. Inside was a thin green circular lens. He picked it up delicately on one finger and placed it into his gold eye. With a couple of blinks the lens set in place, and his gold iris became a deep green.

He closed his left eye and instantly the world was an emerald hue, and everything around him glittered with fine gold dust.

Fate deals the cards that set the game
and every player takes their place.
No soul can know what each hand holds,
only time reveals such mysteries.
Each player lays their cards in turn,
believing that they control their destiny,
blind to the web that connects us all.
Every deed is not a single song,
but alas, a single note in life's symphony.

-The Words of the Watchers: Article 42

ACKNOWLEDGMENTS

Writing this book has been like raising a child. It started off small, its soul an intriguing mystery. Then it grew and took form, its voice realized, its personality revealed. It ripened into maturity and eventually declared its independence, showing me that it's now a part of this world as its own entity, without me. And like raising a child, raising this book has taken a village. It has taken me seven years to create the world of Equillian and to write this first book, and I never could have done it without my village. So, thank you. Thank you first and foremost to my husband, Ben. Without his encouragement, above and beyond support, and unwavering belief in me this book never would have been written. Thank you to my first readers, my A-team. Ben, Terrel, Kalind, Laura, Marty, Nola, and Dad. I couldn't have had anyone better, you guys are all-stars, this book would not be nearly as good without you, and I can't tell you how grateful I am for your time, input, and support. Especially you, Nola Ruth, who went above and beyond to find and show me the rough edges and the missing pieces that I couldn't see. Thank you, Lynne Lampe, my editor extraordinaire. My grammar would be an absolute mess without you. Your contribution to this book and your friendship along the way has been priceless. Thank you, Carlos Quevedo, for my amazing and beautiful cover art. It has encouraged and inspired me throughout my writing process, and I am so proud and truly honored to have your work representing my book. Thank you, Daniel Landerman, for helping me on the journey to finding my cover art. Your work has always inspired me and continues to do so, I'm so grateful to have your encouragement and support. Thank you, Eric Praschan, my friend and mentor. You have been such a huge support, inspiration, and guide throughout this journey, and I cannot thank you enough. Thank you, Kath Wilham, my formatting artist. Thank you for teaching me how books are supposed to go together and for transforming my story into a beautiful and professional book. Thank you to my fellow Dames, the Dame Good Writers. You gals have been my anchor and helped to keep me happy, inspired, and sane while writing this book. Thank you to my children, Kyler and Arya. They were born while this book was being written and have grown with it. You two are my everything. And it is your love and smiling faces that encourage and inspire me to be the best that I can be and to settle for nothing less. Thank you to my Mom, for instilling in me a deep love for stories. I treasured the countless hours we spent reading books together, staying up late and sitting in the car before school just to turn another page. And thank you Mom also, for introducing me to writing when I was a child, it's because of you that I was writing long before I ever knew that I was a writer. And last but certainly not least, thanks to you, my readers. Without you I couldn't do this, and I don't want to do anything else. I truly hope that you enjoyed this book. I live to bring you good stories, and I endeavor to bring you the best stories that I can for as long as I live.

If you enjoyed this book please take a moment to leave a review. I would love to hear what you think of *Equillian's Key*, and every review is a huge help for making it possible for me to continue writing.

Thank you,

K.L. Harris

AUTHOR BIOGRAPHY

When I was a child, what I wanted to be more than anything was a champion in a fantasy world. I was devastated that I couldn't tame dragons or be hired for quests of valor for a living. As soon as I could, I left home and stepped out into the world seeking adventure. I moved to the opposite side of the globe to study acting for film in Australia. I traveled that country and others, I trained in various martial arts, made movies, learned magic tricks, and earned pocket change pouring beers in dodgy taverns and entertaining children as a pirate. Then one day suddenly it hit me, I no longer wanted to be in a fantasy world, I had fallen in love with the world that I'm in. I've fallen in love with all of its imperfections and the beauty found in its dark places. I love its mystery, I crave to explore every facet of it, to know it intimately, to give it voice. And from that, this book was born.

www.masterofmakebelieve.com